Praise for *The ...*

"An artfully crafted coming-of-age story that will take the reader on an exquisite olfactory adventure."   —*Kirkus Reviews*

"This coming-of-age story delights the senses."   —*Booklist*

"A magical novel . . . Blending fantasy with a realist family drama."
—*Publishers Weekly*

"For lovers of *Chocolat*, *The Scent Keeper* evokes emotion and magic through the senses."   —Jennie Shortridge, author of *Eating Heaven*

"Bauermeister deftly weaves plot and language into a luminous discovery of love—for another person, for a place, and ultimately for oneself."
—Carol Cassella, nationally bestselling author of *Oxygen*

"Bauermeister's heroine, Emmeline, might also be kin to Jane Eyre. . . . This sensual novel is pure pleasure reading."
—Adrianne Harun, bestselling author of
A Man Came Out of a Door in the Mountain

"Some very special books have the power to change the reader. This is a book to be devoured, no, to be inhaled, and held deeply."
—Dave Boling, author of *Guernica*

"One of the most enchanting, unique books I've ever read."
—Anna Quinn, author of *The Night Child* and owner
of the Writers' Workshoppe and Imprint Books

ALSO BY ERICA BAUERMEISTER

FICTION

The School of Essential Ingredients
Joy for Beginners
The Lost Art of Mixing

NONFICTION

500 Great Books by Women: A Reader's Guide
(with Jesse Larsen and Holly Smith)

Let's Hear It for the Girls: 375 Great Books for Readers 2–14
(with Holly Smith)

THE
SCENT
KEEPER

ERICA
BAUERMEISTER

St. Martin's Griffin
New York

For the islands

Published in the United States by St. Martin's Griffin,
an imprint of St. Martin's Publishing Group

THE SCENT KEEPER. Copyright © 2019, 2020 by Erica Bauermeister. All rights reserved. Printed in the United States of America. For information, address St. Martin's Publishing Group, 120 Broadway, New York, NY 10271.

www.stmartins.com

Designed by Devan Norman

The Library of Congress has cataloged the hardcover edition as follows:

Names: Bauermeister, Erica, author.
Title: The scent keeper / Erica Bauermeister.
Description: First edition. | New York : St. Martin's Press, 2019.
Identifiers: LCCN 2018055448 | ISBN 9781250200136 (hardcover) |
    ISBN 9781250200143 (ebook)
Classification: LCC PS3602.A9357 S32 2019 | DDC 813/.6—dc23
LC record available at https://lccn.loc.gov/2018055448

ISBN 978-1-250-62262-4 (trade paperback)

Our books may be purchased in bulk for promotional, educational, or business use. Please contact your local bookseller or the Macmillan Corporate and Premium Sales Department at 1-800-221-7945, extension 5442, or by email at MacmillanSpecialMarkets@macmillan.com.

First St. Martin's Griffin Edition: February 2020

10 9 8 7 6 5 4 3 2 1

PROLOGUE

We are the unwitting carriers of our parents' secrets, the ripples made by stones we never saw thrown. If I close my eyes and breathe, I can still smell the sparkling, brittle moment my father broke my trust, and with it his heart. I can smell the honey of my mother's promises.

Maybe you will smell them, too, and more as well. The simmering heat of a boy too scared to let go of anger. The bright numbness of a girl who lost everything in an instant of heroism. The scents of rain, and salt, and just a hint of pipe smoke. Things that happened before you found your way to me.

I can feel you, my little fish, swimming in the tidal motion of my blood, my breath. We humans are almost entirely made of water, except for the stones of our secrets. May mine become solid places to land your feet as you cross the wide river of your life. May they be stones to build a home, not take you under. This is my gift to you.

Let me tell you a story.

Let me tell you everything.

PART ONE

The Island

THE BEGINNING

Back before there was time, I lived with my father on an island, tucked away in an endless archipelago that reached up out of the cold salt water, hungry for air. Growing up in the midst of the rain and moss and ancient thick-barked trees, it was easy to forget that the vast majority of our island was underwater—descending down two, three, five hundred bone-chilling feet. Forever really, for you could never hold your breath long enough to get to the bottom.

Those islands were a place to run away, although I didn't understand that at the time. I had nothing to run from and every reason to stay. My father was everything. I've heard people say that someone is their "whole world," their eyes filled with stars. But my father *was* my world, in a way so literal it can still grab my thoughts, pick them up, and toss them around like driftwood in a storm.

Our cabin was set in a clearing at the center of the island. We were not the first to live there—those islands have a long history of runaways. Almost a century ago there were French fur trappers, with accents that lilted and danced. Loggers with mountainous shoulders, and fishermen who chased silver-backed salmon. Later came the draft dodgers, hiding from war. Hippies, dodging rules. The islands took them all in—the storms and the long, dark winters spat most out again. The beauty there was raw; it could kill as easily as it could astonish.

Our cabin had been built by the truest of runaways. He set up in a place where no one could find him and built his home from trees he felled himself. He spent forty years on the island, clearing space for a garden and planting an orchard. One autumn, however, he simply disappeared. Drowned, it was said. After that the cabin was empty for years until we arrived and found the apple trees, opened the door. Raised the population of the island to two.

I don't remember arriving on the island myself; I was too young. I only remember living there. I remember the paths that wandered through those watchful trees, the odor of the dirt beneath our feet, as dark and complicated as fairy tales. I remember our one-room cabin, the big chair by the woodstove, and our collection of stories and science books. I remember the smell of wood smoke and pine pitch in my father's beard as he read to me at night, and the ghostly aroma of the runaway's pipe tobacco, an olfactory reminder that had sunk into the walls and never quite disappeared. I remember the way the rain seemed to talk to the roof as I fell asleep, and how the fire would snap and tell it to be quiet.

Most of all, I remember the drawers.

My father had begun building them when we moved into the cabin, and when he was done they lined our walls from floor to ceiling. The drawers were small things, their polished wooden fronts no bigger than my child-sized hands. They surrounded us like the forest and islands outside our door.

Each drawer contained a single small bottle, and inside each bottle was a piece of paper, rolled around itself like a secret. The glass stoppers of the bottles were sealed with different colored waxes—red in the top rows, green for those below. My father almost never opened the bottles.

"We need to keep them safe," he said.

But I could hear the papers whispering inside the drawers.

Come find me.

"Please?" I'd ask, again and again.

Finally, he agreed. He took out a leather book filled with numbers and carefully added one to the list. Then he turned to the wall of drawers, pondering his choice.

"Up there," I said, pointing up high to where the red-wax bottles lived. Stories always begin at the top of a page.

My father had built a ladder that slid along the wall, and I watched him climb it almost to the ceiling, reaching into a drawer and drawing out its bottle. When he was back on the ground, he carefully broke the seal. I could hear glass scritching against glass as he pulled out the stopper, then the rustle of the paper as he unrolled it into a plain, white square. He leaned in close, inhaling, then wrote another number in the book.

I meant to stay still, but I leaned forward, too. My father looked up and smiled, holding out the paper.

"Here," he said. "Breathe in, but not too much. Let the smell introduce itself."

I did as he said. I kept my chest tight and my breath shallow. I could feel the tendrils of a fragrance tickling the inside of my nose, slipping into the curls of my black hair. I could smell campfires made from a wood I didn't recognize; dirt more parched than any I had ever known; moisture, ready to burst from clouds in a sky I'd never seen. It smelled like waiting.

"Now, breathe in deeply," my father said.

I inhaled, and fell into the fragrance like Alice down the rabbit hole.

Later, after the bottle had been stoppered and sealed and put back in its drawer, I turned to my father. I could still smell the last of the fragrance lingering in the air.

"Tell me its story," I asked him. "Please."

"All right, little lark," he said. He sat in the big chair and I nestled in next to him. The fire crackled in the woodstove; the world outside was still.

"Once upon a time, Emmeline . . ." he began, and his voice rolled around the rhyme of it as if the words were made of chocolate.

Once upon a time, Emmeline, there was a beautiful queen who was trapped in a great white castle. None of the big, bold knights could save her. "Bring me a smell that will break the walls," she asked a brave young boy named Jack . . .

I listened, while the scents found their hiding places in the cracks in the floorboards, and the words of the story, and the rest of my life.

THE SCENT HUNTER

After that, I asked every day: "Please can we open another one?"

He'd relent eventually, but never as often as I wanted him to.

"The bottles protect the papers," he said. "If we open them too often, the scents will disappear."

It made no sense to me. Scents were like rain, or birds. They left and came back. They told you their own stories, letting you know when the tide was low or the oatmeal was done cooking or the apple trees were getting ready to bloom. But they never stayed.

Even as a young child, however, I understood that those scent-papers were different, magical somehow. They held entire worlds. I could recognize bits of them—the smell of a fruit, but one more full and sweet than anything I had ever tasted. Or an animal, lazier than any I had ever met. Many of the scents were utterly foreign, however—sharp and fast, smooth and unsettling.

I wanted to dive into those worlds; I wanted to understand what made their smells. Even more than that, I wanted to be Jack the Scent Hunter, the hero of my father's stories, flying through the canopies of dripping jungles and climbing to the tops of mountains, all to catch the fragrance of one tiny flower.

"How did he do it?" I asked my father. "How did Jack find the scents?"

"By following this," he said, tapping the bridge of my nose.

I paused. "How?" I asked.

My father smiled. "You just get out of its way, I suppose."

I didn't understand exactly what he meant, but from then on I tried my utmost to let my nose lead me. I lifted it to every change in the weather, and then checked the smell of the dirt to see how it responded. The salt from the sea was a constant twist in the air, but when I breathed in I noticed how it got stronger when the waves were crashing. I caught a bright green scent, falling through the Douglas firs like a waterfall, and tracked it back to the breeze, the way it moved through the tops of the trees, brushing the needles together.

Every day I was out of my loft at dawn, determined to find every smell I could.

"You're my wake-up call," my father said as I clattered down my ladder. "My lark of the morning."

We spent much of our days outside. We raised chickens for eggs and tended the fruit trees and the vegetable garden. Even so, the majority of our food was gathered from the untamed portions of our island. I cannot remember a time when I was not a part of this process, and by the age of eight, I considered myself an essential, if not quite equal, partner in our survival.

"Foragers feast," my father would say, and we'd set out into the woods, cedar bark baskets in our hands. In the summer, we harvested bright red huckleberries, and salal berries so dark blue they looked like night in your hand. In the fall, we found mushrooms hiding under the trees—I was captivated by the convoluted morels, each one a labyrinth of nooks and crannies.

"Tell me its story?" I asked my father one day. I pushed the curls back from my face and looked up at him. "Please?"

He looked down at me and thought for a moment, considering the morel in my hand.

Once upon a time, Emmeline, he began, *Jack found himself in an enchanted forest where the trees were as tall as the sky. In the forest there was a beautiful sorceress who lived in a mansion made of scents, and when Jack saw her, he fell in love. The sorceress took him to her magnificent house, but once he was inside, he found he could not get out.*

"Oh no," I said, shivering into the danger of it.

"Should I keep going?" he asked.

"Yes, please."

"I won't let you go," said the sorceress, *and she led him into a room filled with a fragrance so mesmerizing he forgot the world outside. Whenever he started to remember, she showed him another room, each more enchanting than the last.*

Jack wandered that mansion for years, until one day he discovered a room he'd never seen before. When he entered, he smelled a scent that took him back to all the things he wished he'd done, and all the things he had wished he could be. Then he saw a key, hanging by a blue ribbon on a hook next to a door.

I waited in anticipation. I loved magic keys.

And so, my father said, *he took the key and opened the door and never went back again.*

I waited, thinking there would be more, but my father just put the mushroom in my basket.

"That's not enough, Papa," I said. Even I knew endings were more complicated than that.

"Oh but it is, little lark," he said, and kissed me on the head. "Now, let's get going. These baskets won't fill themselves."

~

Perhaps the best place to forage was our lagoon, an oval of protected water, ringed by rocks and fed by a narrow channel that churned with the tide.

You could spend your whole day harvesting there. Along the shore were wild onions and sea asparagus and the grassy stalks of sea plantains; under the beach rocks were tiny black crabs no bigger than my thumbnail. The boulders that lined the shores were packed with barnacles and mussels, and the seaweed came in infinite varieties. My favorite was bladderwrack, with its little balloons that popped in your mouth and left the smell of salt behind.

The best work, however, was hunting for clams.

"There!" my father said, pointing to a spout of water that fireworked up from the beach. I raced toward it, trying to get there quick enough to catch the spray and feel it run through my outstretched fingers. But even though I was small and fast, I arrived to find only the smell of salt and a slight indentation in the sand at my feet. I stuck a small stick next to the spot to mark it.

"There's another!" I yelled, and ran down the beach in the other direction.

"Good job," my father said, following the trail of my sticks with a small shovel in his hand. At the end of an hour of running and digging, our basket was full.

Usually, we'd have to save the clams, drying them for the winter, when the dark came and wrapped around us like a heavy blanket. I didn't like winter; the rain turned into a mood of its own, and the food on our plates faded in color until all that was left were dry things—apples, clams, a crackle of seaweed. My father faded, too, and his stories disappeared almost completely.

"Do we have to dry the clams?" I asked, and that day my father smiled his summer smile and agreed to a picnic. We made a fire and cooked the clams, adding some wild onions and sea asparagus for flavor, and ate out of bowls made of abalone shells, with mussel shells for spoons and berries for dessert. Then we sat on the sand as the sky turned the palest of blues, and my father watched the water snarl its way through the narrow channel.

It always made me nervous, that channel. Four times a day the tide changed, and the water started its rush in or out of our lagoon through the winding, rock-filled passage. It was an angry, dangerous thing, eager to chew up anything that came near its mouth.

My father saw the way I was studiously avoiding looking in its direction and lifted his mussel shell spoon in a toast.

"Here's to the channel that keeps us safe," he said.

It did, that much was true. Except for the lagoon, our island was entirely steep sided, its edges a vertical plunge down to the water. Evergreen trees clung to its steep rock walls, their lowest branches sheared off in a perfect horizontal line denoting high tide. The only way to access the island was through the channel. I had seen pictures of castles, towering things, impervious to all below. Our island was a castle, its angry channel our drawbridge.

"It's scary," I said.

"But it keeps out pirates and bears," my father noted.

I had seen pictures of both in my books. I had no desire to confront either.

"Here's to the channel," I said, and raised my spoon.

Every once in a while, we arrived at the lagoon to find the beach wildly scattered in seaweed, all the way to the high-tide mark.

"Mermaid party," my father declared, and it made sense. The sand was decorated with such abandon that only the most fanciful of creatures could have done it.

"Let's see if they left us anything," he'd say. We'd check behind the rocks and search the huckleberry bushes that lined the beach. Sure enough, we'd find treasure. Black plastic boxes with heavy closures that snapped shut tighter than a scent bottle. Inside were the most marvelous presents—rice and flour, chocolate and coffee. Sometimes there were even books or shoes or clothes.

One day, when I was nine or so, we discovered a particularly wonderful treasure trove—two black boxes, one of them containing a new pair of boots and a blue rain slicker, just my size.

"How do the mermaids know what we love?" I asked my father.

"They're magic," he said, and it made sense, for only magic would be able to find a way through our channel.

We hoisted the boxes in our arms and carried them triumphantly back to the cabin. Jack might hunt little flowers, but we had scored big and heavy game. We feasted that night, but carefully, putting most of our plunder in the pantry. We knew the ocean was a fickle thing, its mysteries unpredictable. It could take as much as it gave. The lingering scent of the runaway's pipe tobacco was a never-ending reminder of that.

After dinner, my father and I read books to each other, as we always did. My father loved the science books, and he would teach me about the weather or the stars or the names of the trees around us. We spent hours looking at drawings of peculiar sea creatures, and flowers and animals that seemed to come from another world.

"What's that?" I asked, pointing to a picture of a brown animal with slender legs and a little beard on its long chin.

"A goat," my father said.

"Are goats real?"

He nodded.

"Would the mermaids bring me one?" The goat looked quick and smart and maybe funny. A goat could be a friend, I thought.

My father paused for a moment. "You never know what a mermaid will do," he said finally.

"Can we ask them?" We always took the empty boxes back to the beach. *Be kind to the mermaids*, my father always said, and we'd write a thank-you note and leave it inside the box.

"Try it and see," he said with a shrug. "You never know." The subject appeared to have reached an end. This was how it often was with my father. He could spend hours telling you all about the inner workings of a tree or the weather, but other times, he just stopped talking.

"How about a story?" I asked, taking advantage of his silence to swap the science book for the big, thick collection of fairy tales. Its cover had golden writing and a picture of a princess and a crumpled little man who fascinated me. The fables inside were fantastical, intricate things, filled with girls who slept forever and houses made of candy and lies.

My father had told me that many things in fairy tales weren't real, but my problem was I didn't always know which ones. I knew the woods were real, of course, but for me, living on an island with only my father, the image of two children holding hands was no less extraordinary than the idea of spinning straw into gold. I wondered what it would be like, to hold a hand the size of my own, to know someone else who had more questions than answers. I wondered about a lot of things back then.

"Why don't I have a mother?" I asked my father, staring at the illustration of a woman with long blond hair, a child in her lap.

"Because you have me," he said. He turned the page, and I saw the picture of the wicked lady with the pale skin and dark hair, staring into the mirror. My father hadn't given me a real answer to my question, but he'd offered a reasonable trade-off, I figured—for in fairy tales, where there were mothers there were always witches.

I flipped through the stories, feeling the breeze of the pages, leaving the woman behind. About halfway through the book, there was a gap, strange as a missing tooth. I was drawn to it, every time. I loved to run my finger along the space, feeling the ragged edges tucked into the spine.

"Was there a story here?" I asked my father.

"It wasn't a good one," he said.

I looked up at him, a question in my eyes, but his only answer was a kiss on my forehead.

"That's enough for tonight, Emmeline. It's time for larks to go to bed."

I climbed up into my loft and lay there among my blankets, thinking about mermaids and goats and mothers, missing pages and witches. About fathers who don't tell you everything you want to know. But the day had been long, the boxes heavy, and my father's love was a sure and steady thing in the room below, so I didn't ask any more. Maybe everything would have been different if I had.

THE MACHINE

Even more mysterious than mermaids or goats was my father's machine. Once a season, he would use it to make a new scent-paper. I would wait during the long stretches in between, feeling my excitement growing. At last, my father would open the pantry, take down the machine from the top shelf, and unwind the long length of soft gray fabric that protected it. Inside would be the sleek, silver box, about the size of a half loaf of bread, with a hinged lid that lifted to expose a panel with innumerable tiny holes.

My father would lift the machine up, aim it across the room at the wood-stove, and push the black button on its side. I could hear a whisper of air through those holes, as if the machine itself were breathing, and then a series of clicks. Finally, with a whir and a whoosh, a square of paper came slowly rolling out of a slot at the base of the machine.

"Let me smell," I'd say, darting in before the paper made its journey into the bottle. Every time, I hoped for magic—a new world, something I had never smelled before, like the scent-papers in the top rows. I breathed in, excited for the lush unveiling of an unknown flower, the puzzle of an unfamiliar spice. Perhaps it would be a scent so unexpected I could only take it in as a color or a feeling. Whispering blue. Dancing orange. Anger. Joy.

But every time I was disappointed. There was no fragrance on the new square of paper.

"Why doesn't it have a smell?" I asked my father.

He looked puzzled. "It does" was all he said as he wrote a series of numbers on the back of the paper, then rolled it up and tucked it in a glass bottle. Sealing it tight with melted green wax, he put it in an empty drawer in one of the bottom rows.

It was not a satisfying answer, but I could not imagine my father would keep creating scent-papers that didn't work. So how did this no-smell paper turn into one of those other, fantastical creations? I could feel the red-wax bottles waiting, high up, glittering and unattainable. Did they scatter magic down through the rows, change the others through proximity? That didn't seem likely. Maybe the new ones were like caterpillars, who took their odd squishy selves and disappeared into their cocoons only to emerge as something else. Or maybe it was the simple process of sitting so long that made them grow, like some darkness-loving flower. Anything was possible.

I was ten the year I became determined to have a scent-paper of my own, one I could keep and observe. But my father was sparing and careful with the machine. One paper a season, he reminded me, and he stuck to the schedule, although many nights I would look down from my loft and see him bent over the table as he cleaned and tinkered with the machine's small, shimmering parts. To someone else, his behavior might have seemed obsessive, but when you live on an island—when you gather or grow your food and fuel and water, when the weather can be your friend or enemy, changing by the day—being sparing and careful just seems like common sense.

So I never questioned my father's care with the machine; I only waited with ever-increasing anticipation for the perfect opportunity to make my plea. Autumn started its slow slide toward winter. I could feel the cold coming in the air. I sensed my father drawing into himself, like a squirrel hunkering into its nest. And then one morning I looked outside to see a world articulated by frost.

"Today?" I asked my father, and he understood what I meant. It wouldn't have been hard to figure out. My impatience had been compounded by five days of rain that washed the light from among the trees, holding us in. But that day the sky was clear, the frost writing its message across the veins of fallen leaves and the vertical outlines of grass: *It's time.*

My father took the machine down from its place in the pantry.

"Please," I said. "Will you make one for me this time?"

"This is not a toy, little lark," he said.

"It can be my birthday present."

"Your birthday isn't for quite some time." But I could hear the almost smile in his voice. I was close, I could tell.

"Half birthday, then. I'll be careful with it, I promise."

He looked over at his leather book, the one in which he took his notes. He picked up the machine and did what he always did—aimed it across the room and pushed the button. The paper came out and he put it in a bottle. I watched, my disappointment dark and hard. I had waited so long.

But then he picked up the machine again. I thought he was going to put it away, but instead he pushed the button one more time. The holes breathed in, and with the familiar whirr and whoosh the paper came out. He waved it softly in the air, then handed it to me.

I looked at him, amazed. He smiled all the way to his blue, blue eyes.

"What drawer would you like to put it in?" he said. "We can write your name on it."

I lifted the paper to my nose and inhaled. All I could smell was the smoke of our familiar fire, the fading aroma of our oatmeal from that morning.

But I had my own scent-paper in my hand, and I was ready to be patient. The ones in the red-wax bottles told me what *could* happen, and my body thrummed with anticipation. This paper would not go in a bottle, nor hide in a wall. I would keep it in my jacket pocket, deep down where it was safe and dark. I would protect it, but I would also hold the process in my hand.

My thoughts flew in excited circles. What new world would I get? Was it random, which one came through the paper? Or did the paper choose with you in mind? Who would the paper think I was?

"Emmeline?" my father prompted.

"No drawer," I said.

"Are you sure?" My father's hands shifted nervously as he watched me put the paper away in my jacket pocket. "It'll last longer in a bottle."

"I want to smell it change," I said—and now he seemed sad, but I didn't know the why of that, either. Perhaps it was that you weren't supposed to try to catch magic. The fairy tales were always saying that.

But this was different. This was science, I told myself. I would unravel the mystery, following the principles my father had taught me as we'd walked through the woods.

Assess the situation, Emmeline. Eliminate the variables. Determine the best course of action.

Even at the age of ten, however, I suspected that science wasn't my only reason for keeping the paper.

It was cold that morning, but maybe the bite in the air would wake up the fragrance on my paper a little early. I didn't have any idea how long it might take to make a new world. Did the scents have to travel here from far away? Were they already in the paper, waiting to be released by time?

The frost crackled under my feet as I set off. I told myself I just wanted to see the progress of the Sitka spruce that had fallen years before in a storm. Over time it had become a horizontal birthplace for dozens of slim new saplings, which rose up like exclamation marks along the decomposing trunk. I scrambled my way up onto it, although it was sodden from the day's rain and soaked the knees of my pants. Perhaps, I thought, if I was a little higher, the paper would be able to catch the scents more easily as they traveled.

I stood on the top with my feet in the thick moss, careful to avoid the new saplings, and slipped my hand into my pocket. I could feel the sharp corners of the paper. I knew it might be risky to bring it out into the light, but I told myself that the trees were so dense in this part of the forest that there was barely any light anyway.

I exhaled, pushing out all the air that I had collected from the forest. I, too, would be a clean slate, ready for a new scent. I positioned my hand around the square, protecting it as best I could, and then I drew it out and brought it close to my nose. I breathed in.

Nothing. Only the fragrance of the cabin. I put the paper back in my pocket, disappointed.

And then I stopped. I wasn't *in* the cabin. I was in the forest. I smelled my jacket collar, my hair, the skin of my hands and arms, to see if that was where the scent had come from. There was definitely a residual smell— wood smoke, coffee—but it was faint and so interconnected with me that it was merely notes added to myself. The fragrance on the paper had been different, separate. I pulled it out again. Breathed in deeply, eyes closed.

The forest seemed to disappear. I was in the cabin, every scent of it alive: the dried apples in the pantry, the basket of onions in the corner, the lingering whisper of pipe smoke.

I pulled my face back, and there was the smell of the old Sitka spruce, the damp moss and winter. I put my nose to the paper. Cabin.

The new scent-papers weren't blank at all.

I raced back to the clearing, already pulling the paper from my pocket. But when I entered the cabin, it was empty. My father must have gone on a foraging expedition.

All the better. I could test my theory before I told him. I raised the scent-paper to my nose. There was the cabin, exactly as it had been in the forest. Perfect. I put the paper back in my pocket. I breathed in.

The smell of the actual cabin was no longer what was on the paper, I realized. We'd lost an apple tree the year before and the logs were finally dry enough to use as fuel. The scent of apple wood is a particular one, sweet and round, impossible to mistake. We hadn't been burning it earlier, but it was in the stove now, its fragrance like a song. I breathed in, then exhaled and held up the square to my nose. There was no mistaking it—paper and cabin were no longer the same.

I went over to the lower rows of drawers and opened one at random. Hands trembling, I broke the green-wax seal of the bottle within.

This is for science, I told myself.

I pulled out the scent-paper, making a dark nest with my hands to focus my inhalation. The fragrance was slightly different. I opened another bottle and then another. I breathed in variations in wood smoke, smelled clams both fresh and dry, the scent of freshly gathered apples. Mud from my shoes and the smell of autumn leaves in the rain. The differences had been there all along, but I had been distracted, waiting for an entirely new world—a shift into an unknown realm. What was on those papers was far more mysterious.

Memory.

I melted the green wax as I had seen my father do, resealing the bottles. My work wasn't as good as his, and I hoped that he wouldn't pull them out of their drawers anytime soon.

When he returned I was waiting, sitting in the chair by the woodstove.

"I know what they are," I said triumphantly.

"What are you talking about?"

"The scent-papers."

My father was taking off his hat and coat, so I couldn't see his face.

"They're memories," I said.

My father stopped, his coat half hung up on the rack.

"What makes you think that?" he asked in his curious-scientist voice.

"Well," I began, and he turned to listen, his face neutral, then interested, nodding attentively as I related each step of my process.

"Well done, little lark," he said when I was finished. "I'm proud of you."

I inhaled his words and kept them deep inside. They made me want to stay there where it was warm. But I had another question. I'd been thinking about it ever since I figured out what the scent-papers were.

"Are those Jack's, then?" I pointed toward the fantastical scents in the upper rows of drawers.

My father looked startled, then nodded.

"Yes," he said.

"Will he ever come back for them?" I asked.

My father turned to look at the wall of drawers.

"No," he said. "It's our job to protect them now."

Protect them from what? I wondered. There was only us on the island. I started to ask my father what he meant, but he had already gone back outside, getting more wood for the fire.

THE GIFT

All I could think about from then on was becoming a scent hunter. If the red-wax scent-papers were memories, Jack's memories, then that meant there were extraordinary worlds beyond the boundaries of our island, and scent hunters who explored them in a way no one else could. I didn't know if I'd ever get out there, but I wanted to be ready.

"Teach me to be like Jack," I said to my father. He paused, and for a moment I saw a sad quiet in his eyes, but then he ruffled my hair.

"All right, little lark," he said. "Get your jacket."

We went out into the middle of our clearing. In front of us, the vegetable garden lay dormant, ready for winter; the chickens clucked quietly in their coop nearby. Beyond them, the woods waited, full of possibilities. My father stood still for a moment.

"Okay," he said. "Find me a new egg. But keep your eyes closed."

"In the chicken coop?" I was still looking hopefully out at the trees.

"That's where the eggs are." He smiled.

A chicken coop seemed far too ordinary for a scent hunter, but I closed my eyes and allowed the world to be overtaken by sounds. The clucking of the chickens, the little puffs of their conversations. The sound of a squirrel's tiny claws scrabbling up a tree. A winter wren, its song clear and sweet. Then I heard the latch on the chicken coop lift, and my father ushered me inside.

"Breathe in," he said. "Remember, just a shallow one first."

I let the air into my nose, like the lap of a low tide. I smelled the sharp tang of chicken manure, the memory of summer in the dried grass.

"Now," my father said, "forget your nose. Open the back of your mind. Listen to the story."

I inhaled again, slow and deep, and felt the smells flood my head, so full and three-dimensional I could almost wander among them. I could smell the water in its bowl, not quite fresh, and the busy, ruffled odors of the chickens as they moved about, searching for a place to settle. I waited, pondering what a new egg would smell like. My mind started to wander, letting in the scent of the damp earth outside, the smoke slipping from our chimney. Then I pulled myself back to the task at hand. Jack would pay attention. So would I.

There. In the midst of all the big, musty smells, there was something new. Soft. Small. Its warmth didn't move like the chickens did, but lay still, like a rock soaking up the sun.

Eyes still closed, I made my way carefully across the coop. The smell was clear as a beacon. I put my fingers out, swept them across the dried grass. One of the chickens pushed against my knee and I moved her gently aside. I lowered my hand, searching. There.

I came out of the coop, the egg held aloft, my grin bright and broad. I was a scent hunter. Just like Jack.

"And that's how you do it," my father said, smiling.

I found another egg, more quickly this time, and we cooked them both for breakfast.

"What's my next task?" I asked my father after we had eaten. "That one was too easy."

He cocked his head at me. "Find the first day of spring," he said.

If any quest required patience, that one was it. We had just started winter and spring was an eternity away. I knew how the dark days would come and the rain would settle on our good humor until it was cold and sodden. The storms would arrive and the winds would scream and the trees would throw their branches at our roof. Winter was no time to go searching for scents. Smells in the winter were sad things, moldering by the fire or curled up under the roots of trees. But Jack would do it, I told myself, and so every day I put on my jacket and went hunting.

In the end there were more smells than I ever would have thought. The rain and the fog opened them up to anyone who was paying attention. We didn't really get snow on our island, but each time the cold left and the rain came I could smell life wanting to come back, like a tide shifting in the ground. I could hear the trees whispering, "Is it time yet?"

The days grew shorter and shorter, until finally the world tipped and the balance shifted back in the other direction. A change was coming—I could smell it. It was like the rustling in your dreams before you finally wake up in the morning. That gentle tug on the strings of gravity as the slack tide changes direction and starts to pull you out to sea.

One morning I awoke to a new and familiar fragrance coming in the front door. My father had always told me that my birthday was the first day of spring. Not a specific day of the year, but the feeling—an undercurrent of warmth waking up the earth. The scent of violets. Green in the air, he called it. It didn't matter that sometimes we went backward into winter again; my father told me that happened all the time. There was no problem with celebrating more than once, he said, although I only got to count the first one for my age. Eleven for me, then.

My nose told me my father was not in the cabin, but as I listened I heard his footsteps approaching on the trail. There was another sound mixing in with them, too, but this one was brighter and quicker. I scrambled down the ladder. The sounds came together up the porch stairs, and then I saw my father standing in the door. With him, held loosely on the end of a rope, was a goat, black, with one white hoof. It was beautiful.

"Look what I found," he said, as if discovering a goat was a natural occurrence. We were on a small island surrounded by water. The only new things that arrived came to us by magic, in black plastic boxes. But there was a goat, on a rope held nonchalantly in my father's hand.

"Happy birthday," my father said.

The goat watched me, its yellow eyes bright and amused.

"I'm Emmeline," I said, stepping out onto the porch. The goat raised its white hoof in the air, as if to command us to do her bidding. I knelt to be nearer to her, and she lowered her hoof and leaned forward, butting her nose against my hand until I petted her.

"A real Cleopatra," my father said. The goat looked up at him, her head cocked.

"Who is that?" I asked, gently running my hand down the stiff, short hairs of her neck.

And he told us about the long-ago ruler of a faraway country, who got her way using boats filled with rose petals and baths of musk.

Cleopatra the goat rapidly became Cleo, but both names fit. She was still young enough for a nickname, but she had aspirations of grandeur, my father said. She ruled us from the very beginning.

My father set about making a shed for Cleo—her palace, he called it.

"Your job," he said to me, "is to get her acquainted with the island."

"By myself?"

"You're old enough now. And you won't be by yourself, will you?" He smiled. "There's nothing to hurt you here. Just promise me you won't go to the beach," he added, his voice serious.

"I promise," I said, and I meant it. The idea of having free run of the island with Cleo at my side was better than anything I could imagine. I would happily take whatever restriction was required.

Every day after that, the moment my foraging or gardening or lessons were over, Cleo and I set off. At first I kept her on a rope, but it soon became apparent that she would go wherever I went—or perhaps more accurately, that I would go wherever Cleo did. She always led, but never more than four steps ahead, always looking back to make sure I was with her.

We made a game of tracking every path on the island, some so faint that I had never seen them before. I thought we had discovered them all, but then one day we found a slight indentation in the mass of salal bushes that grew between the trees like a great sea. Normally, getting through their stiff branches was impossible without a machete, but someone had made a path once and the hint of it was visible in that gap in the forward line. Cleo's thick hide didn't care about the sharp edges of the leaves, and her feet were sure between the roots. She threaded her way through and the trail seemed to open behind her. I followed, worried that the bushes might close again and we would never find our way home, but Cleo was determined and I couldn't turn back without her.

After a time, I heard water slapping against rocks in the distance. The waves sounded sharper, not like the gentle lapping of the tide against the sand of our lagoon. Cleo and I pushed through a last gasp of green to find ourselves on a bare, gray landing of wind-smoothed rock, about ten feet wide, the sky huge beyond it. We inched close to its edge and stared out at an endless horizon of islands, and then down to the water far below us.

My eyes had never had such distance to travel. I didn't know what to do with all that space. It felt as if it could reach out and grab me, take me with it. I backed up, one step at a time, until my heels banged into raw, wet wood. I looked behind me and saw a bench tucked into the very edge of the woods, half-crumpled to the ground by rain and time.

The runaway's, I thought.

I leaned down and touched its crumbling surface, wondering what had brought that man to this open place, to sit here and look back to what he'd left. What was out there?

Cleo and I stayed on that bluff for a long time before we took the path back to the cabin. I didn't tell my father what I'd found, worried that he might not let me go back. I didn't know what I thought about that place; I only knew that my father had never showed it to me, and somehow it seemed impossible that he didn't know of its existence. My father knew everything.

After that, Cleo and I started going to the bluff almost every day, and over time, my initial fear gave way to curiosity. I would bring lunch with me, and Cleo and I would share it as we sat closer and closer to the edge, watching the big water. Sometimes we saw a whale or a shining fleet of dolphins, or brown logs in the distance that looked like they were swimming. Sometimes a motorboat passed by, growling like a giant, angry insect. I had known these things only as pictures in my father's science books, or the collection of fairy tales. Out on the bluff, the lines between the kinds of books blurred. I hid from the boats, certain they held pirates.

Once, however, I saw a boy with red hair standing at the back of a fishing boat. He looked young, perhaps my age. Cleo and I came back every day for the next week, but I never saw him again. It made me wonder, though—where was his home?

That evening over dinner, I asked my father, "Why are we here, Papa? Why are there no other people on our island?"

My father put down his fork. "People lie, Emmeline," he said, "but smells never do." He seemed to think that explained everything.

"All people?" I persisted. "What about Jack?"

"Even Jack," my father said, and his face grew so dark I didn't ask any more.

But it was then I knew I wouldn't ever tell my father about the trail to the bluff. He had his secrets, but this one was mine.

Time passed. Another spring approached. I turned twelve, my legs and arms growing like saplings, strong and lean. When we went to the lagoon, I could now catch the clam water as it squirted into the sky, dig deep into the sand and find the waiting shells myself. I could make a fire with a bow drill and a piece of dried moss, use a sharp knife to pry a barnacle from its rocky shelf in the time it took to count to two. My foraging basket was always as full as my father's now, and more and more often I filled it on my own, on my way back from my adventures in the woods with Cleo.

Cleo and I had taken to running along the tops of downed trees, my arms outstretched, her cloven feet sure and steady. But I wanted to be higher still. I started climbing up the standing trees, branch by branch, pretending I was Jack the Scent Hunter. Sometimes, clinging high up in the evergreen branches, surrounded by the gentle clacking of their needles, I would catch a tantalizing whiff of something else—a warm tendril of baking bread, far in the distance. A faint wake of the grumbling black odor left behind by boats. Pieces of a story my father would never tell me. A world I would never see. I would crane myself out into the air, feeling the branches bend beneath my weight. It all left me feeling more restless, and lonelier than before, but when I finally climbed down, there was Cleo waiting for me.

My father had taught me how to trim Cleo's hooves and brush her. I loved the rhythm of my hand moving across her strong back, her teeth nibbling at me as I worked. It was a way to end each day. At night, I would hear her bleating in her shed; my father told me that goats liked to bundle up together, no matter the weather. I would wait until he was asleep and then I'd sneak down my ladder and out to her shed, snuggling next to Cleo until she quieted down. Sometimes I fell asleep and didn't wake up until it was almost light.

Sometimes on those nights, I worried that there were too many secrets piling up between my father and me. But there was something about laying my head against Cleo's flank, the solidity of her warm and compact body, that made me feel full inside. That made me feel as if there were more than two people in the world. So I said nothing.

THE SCENTS

That summer when I was twelve, my father started getting quieter, his stories disappearing even though winter was still a far-off thought. He no longer asked what Cleo and I had found on our explorations, and never said what he had done while I was gone, although I realized one day it had been a long time since I had come home to find a full foraging basket on the table.

But I was happy with Cleo, and I rationalized that my father wouldn't tell me what was going on even if I asked. Then one day I walked in the cabin door and saw him standing in front of the woodstove, its door open, one of the scent-papers in his hand. An empty bottle was on the table, a ring of red wax still clinging to its stopper.

"What are you doing?" I asked.

He shut the stove door and sat down heavily on the bench at the table.

"They're going," he said.

"What?"

"The scents. They're disappearing."

"Let me smell." I thought perhaps it was his nose.

But it wasn't. When my father raised the scent-paper to my face, there was nothing there.

"How long has it been out of the bottle?" I asked, trying to apply the scientific principles he had taught me.

"It doesn't matter," he said. "It won't change. I've been checking them for weeks. The top row is almost gone."

My first reaction was a feeling of betrayal: he'd been opening the bottles without me. Then his words sunk in—the scents were leaving us.

I thought of the bottles in the upper drawers, the worlds they contained. The way some had felt like flying and others like swimming and one like being held in the gentlest arms I could imagine. I'd always thought I could hear them whispering amongst themselves as I fell asleep. When was the last time I had listened? I spent almost every night out in Cleo's shed now. Perhaps the scent-papers had been quiet for a long time. Perhaps they'd wondered where I was. Maybe that was why they'd left.

"What were you going to do?" I asked my father, pointing toward the woodstove.

"Burn it," he said, the scent-paper still in his hand.

The violence of the idea shocked me. "Why?"

"Some of the first fragrances men ever created were made to burn," he said. "*Per fumare*—through the smoke. It was a way to talk to the gods. I wanted to send the scent home."

"But what if we find a way to get it back? Wouldn't Jack want us to try?"

He shook his head. "It's impossible."

I saw the resignation in his face. He had given something up, although I had no idea of its shape or origin. All I knew was that my father was in pain.

"Let's burn it, then," I said.

We walked over to the woodstove, opened its door, and stood, looking at the fire. My father paused and seemed to go inside himself for a moment. Then he dropped the paper in. We watched as the flames caught its edges and curled them into light, then blackness. The smoke that emerged was a blue so clear it surpassed the sky, the water, my father's eyes. And then, the fragrance.

It was big and full, shimmering with a strength its scent-paper had never had. This was no brief window into a world. This was the thing itself. I closed my eyes and the cabin walls vanished. I could smell the sweet spice of just-cut grass, and a sparkling conversation of flowers—lush and creamy, sharp and quick, dusty and soft as memory itself. They came together like bird songs overlapping. There was sunshine, pulling out the fragrances with its warmth. I could feel it on my skin, surrounding me in a way the heat of our woodstove never could. I stood in the middle of it all, inhaling. I had never felt so full of anything before.

I don't know how long it lasted, only that it left a bit at a time until there was just the rain outside and the faint smell of tobacco again.

"Oh," my father said, and his eyes were filled with tears. He reached toward the fire as if to pull the paper out, but it was well and truly gone.

My father changed after that. He'd always been fascinated by the bottles, but the loss of that scent-paper shifted something in him. The pressure in the cabin grew until I could smell it, heavy and hot. I watched his eyes, flicking to the upper drawers no matter what we were doing. When we went out collecting food, he would return to the cabin earlier and earlier, leaving half our potential harvest on the beach. One afternoon, something finally seemed to break, and he took down another red-wax bottle, unsealed it.

"Okay," he said, and opened the door of the woodstove.

The act of burning a scent relaxed him for a few days, but then the whole process started again. Each time it speeded up, the lull afterward disappearing more quickly, the tension rising faster. Before I knew it, the top row was gone. I was worried about what would happen when he got through those upper, transcendent bottles and found himself left with only old versions of our life.

"Why don't we make new scent-papers?" I asked him. "We could take the machine outside. Cleo and I have found things. We could show you."

I was willing to give him all my secrets, even the bluff overlooking the world. But my father shook his head.

"What if we made a new scent-paper of one of them?" I said, pointing to the third row from the top. "Start over?"

He looked at me, hope springing into his eyes, and for that moment I was Jack the Scent Hunter, brave and smart and full of ideas. I was Emmeline, the daughter he loved more than anything else.

"Okay," he said. "Let's try."

He took down one of the bottles and held it for a moment. Then he snapped open its red-wax seal with the practiced motion I knew so well, and pulled out the paper inside. The scent was undetectable, as we knew it would be, but we had a plan now. Together we walked over to the stove.

"You hold it," my father said, handing me the paper. It lay in the palm of my hand, light and full of silent mystery. It had one chance left to express itself, unless we could catch it again.

My father got down the machine. He opened the lid, exposed the holes.

"Now," he said, and I threw the paper in the fire. As the smoke curled off its edges and the heat traveled into its core, the fragrance emerged—a bursting, juicy sweetness of flowers, a rich and humid warmth. My father depressed the button on the machine, and waited anxiously as the new paper came out of the slot. He shook it, like always, held it at arm's length until the smoke had cleared. He opened windows, let in the fresh air. The cabin came back to itself. Finally he brought the paper to his nose and breathed in.

I watched, hope turning sour as his face fell.

"No," he said, handing the paper to me. I inhaled, began my dive into the flowery fragrance, but then, mingled in, came the smell of tobacco. Cedar smoke. Last night's dinner. My own sweat.

"It's not right," my father said.

I started to ask him what was wrong with a scent that had me in it, but I realized that even if he had an answer, I wasn't sure I wanted to hear it.

After that, the machine stayed on the shelf.

THE BEACH

My father put the empty bottles back in their drawers, where they sat waiting—for what, I had no idea. I spent as much time outside as possible. I wanted to be away from the claustrophobia of the cabin.

The one place I didn't go was the lagoon. I'd promised my father back when Cleo had first arrived, and promises were broken at great risk—that was the cautionary rule of every fairy tale, I knew.

But as week followed week, I began to question that pact. My father was falling into himself. He hardly left the cabin, and I had to remind him that the garden and the chickens needed tending. Autumn was upon us—we needed to gather and dry the fish, clams, and seaweed that would get us through the winter. Those things were at the beach, but my father showed no inclination to go himself.

"Foragers feast, Papa," I said one morning, holding out a basket.

He said nothing. Then, slowly, he shook his head. He wouldn't leave the bottles. I could see that now.

That was when I decided—if he wasn't going to take care of us, I would. I pulled the basket close and set out, whistling for Cleo, who came immediately to my side. When I got to the fork in the path, out of sight from the cabin, I headed toward the lagoon.

It was a fine day, the scent of the dirt and trees around me just starting to mellow after a summer of rampant growth. The berries were plentiful, and I could have gathered them, but my sights were set on the beach. I ignored the nervous buzzing in my ears, the way my nose seemed to be working overtime. We needed food, I told myself. I was going to its main source. There was nothing more or less to it than that.

Still, I paused when we reached the border between trees and sand. The lagoon was full and big, the blue above it cloudless. The open expanse felt exposed, a place where even the sky could see what I was doing. For a moment I hesitated, started to turn around. Cleo had no such compunctions, however, and raced out onto the sand.

"Cleo," I called. "Come back!"

But Cleo didn't listen, caught up in the joy of sand and water and space to run. The beach was her favorite place on the island and she was never there as much as she wanted to be. She danced about, her small feet leaving tiny cloven marks on the wet sand, her back legs kicking high in the air. Beyond her, the water danced in the sunlight, a mirror of her happiness. The channel was full and frothing; the drawbridge was up.

Nothing to be afraid of, I thought. My father worried too much. I stepped out onto the sand, let it slip between my toes. We'd had a week of hazy cloud cover, and that endless blue above me turned hesitation into euphoria. I broke off a knobby bit of sea asparagus, and crunched it between my teeth. My favorite boulder had been warmed by the sun, and I lay down on top of it, feeling its friendly solidity against my back. I closed my eyes and let the sunshine play across my lids. There was plenty of seaweed on the beach, I told myself; I could gather food in a little while.

I don't know how much later it was when the sound woke me, deep and growling. I jolted up and looked around. Everything was the same except the channel, which was flat and calm. I had never seen it like that before. All I could do was stare. The sound grew closer, rumbling up the channel.

"Cleo!" I called, and this time she came. We scrambled up into the woods just as a boat entered the lagoon.

I had seen boats from my perch on the bluff. From a distance, they had looked like birds skimming over the water, friendly even, but the noise of this thing up close was huge. The smell of it filled the air, thick and slick, wiping out the scents of salt and sand. From my hiding place, I could see a man at the front of the boat.

A *pirate*, I thought, and my skin went cold.

The boat roared across the lagoon, the noise stopping as it reached the shallows. The trees around me shivered in the sudden silence. The man stood straight, seeming to listen, too. I watched him from behind my tree, even as I willed myself to be invisible. He was wiry and small, with tanned skin and white hair that stuck out from under a bright red cap. When I concentrated, I could smell his sweat, different from my father's, and the scent of something like bread dough.

The man jumped over the side of the boat into the water, grabbed a rope off the front, and slogged over to one of the larger rocks. He tied the boat up with easy efficiency, and then patted the top of the rock's craggy surface. He didn't seem like a pirate, at least not the ones I'd read about.

Beside me, Cleo trembled with excitement. I kept my hand firmly on the back of her neck, trying to calm both of us, but with a quick shake of her head she broke away and capered down the beach toward the man.

"Daisy!" he said, and opened his arms. Cleo ran to him, and my eyes widened as the man knelt down, rubbing the top of her head.

"Look at you," he said to Cleo. "Such a big girl now. They must be feeding you well."

Cleo bleated happily and the man rubbed the top of her head a little harder. "Hush now," he said. "There's a bear swimming out in the big water. We don't want to let it know you're here."

The man's eyes scanned the perimeter of the beach, searching for something. *Me*, I thought. *He's looking for me.* I froze in place, becoming part of the trees. Then the man seemed to hear something from behind him; he glanced back at the channel. It was starting to move again, the first ripples showing on its surface. He stood.

"I gotta get going," he said to Cleo. "Tide's changing." He went to the boat and pulled something out. His back was to me so I couldn't see what it was, but I could tell by the slope of his shoulders that it wasn't light.

I watched as he carried his load up to just above the high-tide mark, where the seaweed lay in crazy strands. He straightened and gave one more scan of the beach. With a sigh, he turned and gave Cleo a pat on the rump.

"Head on home now," he said. He untied and started his boat, then headed into the just-frothing water of the channel.

I waited until I couldn't hear the motor anymore before coming out of the trees. Cleo ran up and nuzzled my hand, but I didn't pet her. I just stood, staring at the high-tide mark. At the black plastic box, nestled amidst the seaweed.

It made no sense. The man was no mermaid. There had been no party. I didn't understand.

But then suddenly I did—and just like that, everything was different.

THE LIE

I wonder sometimes how I could have ever believed in mermaids. I never would have accepted something like the Easter bunny—I knew too much about chickens and who they let take their eggs away. But I had seen flowers bloom into fruit, like straw turned into gold. I'd seen the way sea anemones seemed to die and be born again with every shift of the tide. I'd found seashells that spiraled into themselves, and my father had told me that those elegant shapes once housed animals. In such a world, mermaids did not seem impossible.

There was another thing, too. For good or ill, my father and I lived close to the earth. My childhood was suffused with wonder—along with the stone-hard knowledge that our lives depended upon what we could make or find or grow. For me, those mermaid boxes were about more than just food. They gave me the feeling that someone magical knew we were there and was taking care of us. Someone beyond my father, bigger than the island. I very much needed to believe in that. I think we all do.

But all I knew that day on the beach was that my father had told me a lie. I didn't stop to ask whether that lie was for me or him or both of us. Whether his stories were to make reality go away or bring it closer. All I knew was that if mermaids didn't exist, then everything else must be up for grabs, too. I turned and headed for the cabin, my feet slamming against the dirt.

"You lied, Papa."

My father had been facing the stove. He whipped around at the sound of my voice, his eyes red.

"Where were you?" he asked. "I looked everywhere. I thought I'd lost you."

I was shaking with outrage. "There are no mermaids," I said.

He looked at me, the shock on his face pure and clean.

"You went to the beach." His words fell onto the floor and cracked open. Even with everything that was happening, everything else that had changed, his trust in me had been so complete he hadn't even thought of it.

The realization knocked me sideways. I stood, stunned at the pain on his face. I had been heading in a single, retaliatory direction, but now everything inside me was a jumble. It was like being caught in the channel midtide. I was furious at my father's deception, but I burned with shame at the depth of my own betrayal, too.

He had done a terrible thing. I had done a terrible thing.

It was impossible to hold both those thoughts inside me. I was too grown-up in some ways, but still a child in too many others. I didn't want to think about what I had done. I just wanted the purity of my anger, the way it had felt when I came stamping up the trail to the cabin, a flaming torch of righteousness.

"Is that why you didn't want me to go?" I snapped. "Because I might see the truth?"

"No," my father said quietly. I waited for more, but there was nothing. Just the soft and broken smell of sadness, coming off him in waves from an ocean deeper than I had thought possible.

I needed to get away. I needed room for my thoughts to settle. I started to go outside to put Cleo in her shed for the night.

"No," my father said, putting a hand on my arm. "Stay inside."

I didn't want to, but the shame held me tight as lies. My father went out the door. I could hear him murmuring softly to Cleo, and then the click of the shed latch. When he came back in, I was up in my loft.

"Dinner?" he asked, but I didn't answer. I didn't know who to be mad at anymore. I listened as he rustled about the kitchen, but in the end I never smelled any food, just the flame of a candle when it got dark, and then nothing.

I lay in bed. Outside, I heard Cleo bleating. I wanted to go to the shed and be with her, but I knew I couldn't. I couldn't add one more bucket of pain to my father's ocean, no matter what else had happened. So I lay awake, listening as Cleo's cries turned from frustrated to heartbroken. Eventually she quieted and I was left alone with my own thoughts, which tangled and spun until exhaustion pulled me into sleep.

I woke to a scream, shooting its way into my dreams. I sat upright, my brain spinning. The sound was too high-pitched for my father, too loud for an owl. It came again, an icy wail of fear.

Cleo.

"Papa!" I yelled, tossing aside my covers. The screams continued, interspersed with deep-pitched blasts of noise, hoarse and rough, unlike anything I had ever heard.

My father caught me as I reached the bottom of the ladder.

"What's happening?" I asked.

We ran to the window. The moon was full, lighting up the clearing. Something shaggy and huge was circling the perimeter, as if the darkness between the trees had turned solid and begun to move. Every once in a while the thing would shake, and water droplets would fly. I could hear Cleo in the shed, her hooves scrambling against its sides. In their cage, the chickens were a blur of feathers and shrieks.

"What is that?" I asked.

"A bear." My father's face was white.

The creature came into the clearing, and I could see muscles moving under its thick fur. It passed by the chicken coop and gave it a casual glance, as if appraising it for later. Then it went to the shed and circled it once, twice, Cleo growing more frantic with each revolution, her hooves pummeling the walls. The bear stood on its hind legs. I heard wood splinter, heard Cleo's scream reach new heights as she leapt from the enclosure.

"Papa!" I cried out.

Cleo was running, darting right and left, trying to get to the cabin or the woods or just away, but the bear was unrelenting, cutting off her exit each time, moving in closer and closer. Cleo was terrified, her eyes huge, looking for safety. She had almost reached the cabin, but the bear made a quick move to the right, blocking her. She reared up, her hooves raking the air. The bear stood, too, and pulled back one paw. The first swipe cut her scream into silence. And then there was just the bear, and the moist, soft sound of eating.

I stood by the window, stunned.

"Papa," I said, "why didn't you do anything?"

Outside, the bear growled in satisfaction.

"How did it find us?" My father was asking the air, not me.

But I knew then. It was my fault. I had taken Cleo to the beach. We had called the bear. And there was no place inside me big enough to hold that knowledge.

THE INTRUDER

The bear didn't leave immediately—our island was a fully stocked smorgasbord with nobody else in line. It spent the next day cleaning Cleo's bones, then made its way through the chickens and the eggs, one by one, until all that was left was the rank odor of bear. The smell came in under the door, around the sides of every window, through every crack in the walls. I stopped eating.

My father stayed by the window, hands clenched. I'm not sure if he moved for days. We had no weapons; we'd never needed any. I had seen pictures of guns in books, but they'd seemed as fantastical as witches, or trolls under a bridge. In our cabin we had an ax for cutting wood, but the one time my father looked in its direction, I ran and stood in front of the door.

"No," I said, terrified.

He relented, and went back to watching the bear. After a while he spoke again, his voice dull and factual.

"It's a female. If we're lucky, she'll have a den somewhere else; she'll go back to hibernate. If she has babies, she'll stay with them and she won't come back here for years."

Then there was nothing left but waiting.

Cleo was gone. I didn't know what to do with the suddenness of it. Mice were killed that way, gripped in the talons of owls at night, sailing off screaming into the dark—but not things I loved. The world had been one way and then, with a swift slap across my face, it was another.

I had fallen out of a tree once, when I was first learning to climb. It hadn't been far, but I'd landed on my back and the ground smacked the breath from my lungs, leaving me suspended, neither here nor there, for one long, crystalline moment. Cleo had raced up, licking my face until I'd finally inhaled and life had swooped back into me with a rush. But now there was no Cleo.

I wanted to scream. I wanted to cry. I wanted to hit my father, the walls, myself. I wanted to do something, anything that would let the pain out, but there was nothing.

Once the chickens were finished, the bear turned to the apple trees. Then it shoved over the fence to the vegetable garden with a desultory slap of its paw and rooted through the potatoes and the carrots. We watched as our provisions for winter disappeared, sucked down into the seemingly endless appetite of the bear.

When the clearing was truly cleared, she lumbered up onto our porch. From up in my loft, I could hear her sniffing at the crack in the door, and I froze. She soon grew disinterested, however. There was no need for the effort it would take to get inside; our woods and beach were full of food. She disappeared into the trees. We couldn't see her anymore, but I could smell her anytime I opened the door.

"She'll leave when there's nothing left to eat," my father said. "It could take a while."

We waited, day after day, my father and I circling each other in the confined space, our need pulling us together while everything else pushed us apart.

Every morning, I awoke determined to tell my father that I was the reason the bear had come. To tell him I was sorry. But every time I climbed down the ladder and saw him staring out the window or looking up at the bottles, there was a part of me that still wanted to blame him. His secrets. His lie that had ruined everything.

My fault. His fault. My fault.

My father paced the cabin, his eyes moving back and forth in quick darting motions. The clothes began to hang loose on his body.

I wish I could say that I knew what my father was feeling, or that I tried to guess. Grief makes a tunnel of our lives, and it is all too easy to lose sight of the other people in the darkness with us—to wish they weren't there, so their loss would stop rubbing up against ours. My father and I desperately needed open space, clean air for our pain to move into. But all we could do was wait.

"Do you want to burn a scent-paper?" I asked my father. Anything to bring a different smell into the space.

"No," he said, moving to stand in front of the drawers. "I need to protect them."

From me? I wondered, but I didn't say anything.

We had always been careful with our food stores, but normally we had fall to prepare us for winter, and we'd already been behind on foraging that day I had gone to the beach. The thought of eating still made me retch, but I knew that eventually my body would demand its due, and we did not have enough—even if the bear left us with anything. I spent days staring at the pantry, dividing food into days. Not enough.

Then, one morning, something was different. I could smell it in the air when I opened the front door—an absence as welcome as all the rest of the absences were awful.

"She's gone," I told my father. He came and stood beside me, then nodded.

The temperature was cool, veering toward cold. We had lost most of autumn to the bear. My father got the ax, just in case, and we walked the trail, past where the salal bushes had been stripped of almost all their berries, past trees with their mushrooms scuffed into dirt. We walked to the beach and saw the bear's footprints, heading to the water. Disappearing.

We were free.

Except, of course, we weren't. The bear had taken more than Cleo, more than our ability to make it through the winter. It had ripped the fabric of what made us two and now we were not even one plus one.

THE MESSAGE

The island as I had known it—my place of wonder and delight and safety—was gone. Cleo was dead. For weeks, the grief had crammed itself into my thoughts and muscles. Now that it had been given space it turned huge and reckless. It didn't want to be quiet anymore.

It was a terrifying thing, far bigger than me. Bigger, I knew, than anything my father could handle. So I went deep into the woods and set the howls free. I sucked in air and slammed it out again, and yet for all my caution, my sobs held the same refrain every time—*hear me, hear me, hear me.* I wanted my father to take this pain and put it in one of his precious bottles, make it go away. I wanted him to love me, even though it was my fault that Cleo was dead and our island was ruined.

But my father was so closed off that speaking to him felt like throwing pebbles against the window of an empty house. More and more, he went off by himself to search for things that no longer existed.

"Do you want company?" I asked.

He shook his head. Looked up at the drawers.

"All I wanted was to keep you safe," he said, but whether he was referring to me or the bottles I didn't know.

"Papa," I said.

But he just grabbed his foraging basket and headed out the door.

I stood in the cabin, sensing everything that was no longer in it. As I often did to settle myself, I went to the pantry to check how much, or rather how little, was left. It was then that I caught sight of my father's machine on the top shelf.

~

The machine was lighter than I'd expected, the cloth wrapping soft and gray, so faded that the white swirls woven into the fabric seemed more like smoke than thread. I set the fabric aside and lifted the lid, half expecting it to crack off as punishment for my transgression, but it just slid up soundlessly to expose the hundreds of tiny holes.

My hands shook. I'd figured out what this machine did, but I still had no better explanation for it than magic. And magic, I knew, came at a price. I wondered if the machine could *take* as well as give. When I considered my father's relationship with the scent-papers, it seemed entirely possible.

I listened for the sound of footsteps on the path and heard only the quick chirping of the birds. I inhaled once, taking the smells around me into my lungs, my mind, then I lifted the machine with both hands, aimed it at my face, and pushed the button. The machine breathed in, clicked, whirred. I felt air slipping through my curls, toward the holes. I didn't move until the paper had almost completely scrolled out, then I lowered one of my hands and let it fall, like a leaf, onto my palm.

I looked at that paper for a long time. Then I gently took one of its edges and waved it in front of me. I could smell an ever-so-slightly younger version of myself in the air, and for a moment I sensed why my father might want to protect his creations.

I wasn't him, however.

I got out one of the empty bottles. I put my nose in the opening, but there was nothing there, just a quiet blankness. It was waiting.

For me, I thought.

I put the scent-paper inside my stolen bottle and took out the small wooden box that held my father's supply of wax. I wished there was red, but I found only green. I melted a bit, watching the drops fall onto the rim around the stopper, sealing it tight. I put the bottle in my jacket pocket, replaced the machine carefully in the pantry, and then I slipped out the cabin door, closing it behind me.

It was freezing outside after the warmth of the cabin. I followed the trail until I found the start of Cleo's and my path to the bluff. It was easier to spot now, and as I followed the familiar route through the salal bushes, I missed Cleo with a pain so sharp I thought a branch had stuck me in the side. I stopped.

Maybe I shouldn't do this, I thought, but I was sick with grief, sick of grief.

I kept going until I reached the edge of the bluff. I stood there, the wind cold on my face, the water far below. I reached into my jacket pocket and felt the smooth glass against my fingers. I drew my arm back and threw the bottle out into that awful, exhilarating expanse. I counted *one, two, three, four* and then I heard the splash.

"I am here," I said to the sky that would never answer, to the people I couldn't see. "I am here."

I did the same thing the next day. And the next and the next. I knew I shouldn't be using the machine at all, let alone so often, but I didn't care. I didn't want to be cautious anymore.

Each scent-paper I made, each bottle I sent out into the water, felt like release. A tiny lessening of pressure. Maybe I had been right—maybe the machine did take something from the person who used it. But by the next morning, the feelings would be built back up again, and I would wait anxiously until my father left. Until I could use the machine and feel myself falling into my own palm.

Then came the day when I opened the lid and pushed the button and nothing came out. The machine clicked and whirred, clicked and whirred. No paper. Just an endless, frustrated inhalation through the holes.

Was it possible to use up magic? The machine kept going, breathing in as if it would suck up the whole island.

Panicked, I closed the lid with a snap. The sound died.

What would my father do if he found out? He hadn't used the machine since our failed attempt to make a copy of one of the scent-papers, but if he changed his mind, if he tried to use it, he would know what I had done.

I quickly wrapped up the machine in the long, gray piece of fabric and put it back on the shelf, making sure it was exactly where I had found it. Then I closed the door of the pantry, tight.

THE BOTTLE

Everything was leaving. The paper in the machine, the food in the pantry, my father's mind. One day, he would set out all our stores of food on the table. The next, he would take down the remaining bottles from the drawers, arranging them in rows, counting each one before carefully putting them back. He no longer burned the faded scents. He clung to them as if they themselves were sustenance. I watched him, wondering if I was the only one who saw the way the balance was tipping.

"Papa," I said. "We need to get help."

"We have to keep them safe" was all he said, and now I knew for sure that he meant the scent-papers.

But what about me? I wondered. What about keeping me safe? Whatever was outside our island, it couldn't be as bad as the certainty of starvation. The mermaids had never brought us boxes in the winter. My father had always said it was too cold for them to have a party. Now I understood that it had to do with storms and the inability of boats to make it through the channel. There would be no help before spring. If we wanted rescue, we would need to make it come to us, but my father was unwilling to draw any attention to our island. Not as long as the bottles existed.

Every day I would go to the bluff and look out at the bigger world.

Winter blew down the strait, making the water froth. The islands in the distance were inky black, without a trace of other people. I knew I couldn't rely on luck to save us.

At night I lay in my loft bed, thinking. The whispers of the scent-papers in the drawers were almost completely gone, their stories quieted. Perhaps my father was wrong, and they did not want to be saved.

But perhaps they could still save us.

I waited a few days until my father finally left the cabin and wandered off toward the woods. As soon as he was out of sight, I set to work. I slung a foraging bag over my shoulder and climbed the ladder high up among the drawers. It felt perilous up there, the air heavier and hotter. My palms were slippery against the rungs. I had a plan, but for a moment I still wasn't sure what I was doing.

As I was reaching out toward the top-most bottle I looked down, and suddenly I saw our world, spread out below me like the open pages of a book. The loft my father had built for me, with the quilt made from squares of clothes I had worn over the years. The woodstove where my father had taught me to cook. The plank table where he'd taught me how to write. Our shelves of books. The chair where we had read them. The baskets we'd made on winter evenings, weaving together strands of cedar bark by the fire.

It was our life—a full and breathing thing. Not a memory, caught in a bottle. I knew then that I would do whatever it took to save it.

I leaned forward carefully, taking the bottles from one drawer after another and placing them in my bag, their red-wax seals disappearing in its depths. When the bag was full I tidied up, leaving the wall just the way I had found it. Then I descended the ladder, listening to the soft clink of glass against glass.

It would take many trips, and I would have to do it quickly, before my father realized what I was doing, but I was determined. I hoisted my bag and set off for the bluff, making my way along the trail, the bushes whispering caution against the legs of my pants. *Stop stop stop stop*. I didn't listen.

When I reached the bluff, I set down the bag at my feet. Standing on the edge of the rock, I drew out a bottle, feeling the stiff wax seal around its top. I wondered for a moment what fragrance it had held, what miraculous memory it once contained. Then I shook my head, lifted the bottle high, and threw it as far as I could. There was a long silence, as if the air was holding its breath, and then a splash. For a moment my heart seized as an entire world vanished. I would never know why Jack had loved it so, or why my father would do anything to protect it.

But more than I wanted those worlds, I wanted ours. So I threw the bottles, again and again, until the bag was empty.

It took two days to make my way through the red-wax sealed bottles, and it was pure luck that my father did not open the drawers during that time. On the third day, I opened a drawer that had been hidden behind a string of herbs my father had hung, long ago, and never taken down. He used to joke that it was watching over us, just like we watched over the scent-papers.

I tried to be gentle as I removed the string from its hook, but the herbs were brittle and crumbled to the floor. I could smell dusty oregano and thyme, soft and a little sad. I leaned against the ladder and opened the drawer. I was about to slip the bottle in my bag when I paused. The wax seal was blue.

I stared for a moment. I had never seen a blue-wax seal before. I didn't know why my father had never taken this bottle from the drawer, nor shown it to me. It had lain there, hidden, all this time. For an instant I thought of leaving him this one, but they all had to go, or there would be no point. So I put the bottle in my bag and headed out. I had to be strong for the both of us, I told myself.

It's amazing how easily we can cast ourselves in the role of hero.

I stood on the edge of the bluff, looking out at all those islands, and once again I threw the bottles, one after another, until only the blue one was left. The water below me was littered with bobbing glass, bits of red like little fish floating in the sea, moving away with the tide. I wondered, as I had with my own bottles, who might find them, if there would be any smell remaining when they did. Would anyone think to burn them?

There was no point in thinking those things this time, however. These were not messages. I could have buried them, hidden them, but I knew the bottles needed to be irretrievable. Only then would my father be willing to get help.

I lifted the last bottle from the pack and touched the blue seal that ran around the stopper. The wax was old and starting to crack, but it had never been broken. The temptation to open the bottle and see if there was any scent still left inside made my hands shake. *What are you?* I wondered. *What makes you special?* I leaned in, listening, as if it might answer. I thought I almost caught a whisper.

It was then that I heard footsteps coming down the path.

My mind spun; I had only seconds before he would find me. I gripped the bottle in my hand. I had to be fast; I had to get rid of it or all of this was for nothing. My eye caught on the blue of the seal. I didn't want to do it. I had to.

My father broke through the edge of the trees. I raised my arm.

I could feel him coming up behind me, uttering an anguished howl even as I flung the bottle. He threw himself past me, hands reaching. He never even looked for the edge of the bluff.

The bottle arced into the air, his body lifting after it, and in an instant they were both gone. I heard a splash far below in the black water.

"Papa!" I screamed as I leaned over the ledge, scanning for him amongst those stupid bobbing bottles. His head surfaced. His expression was agonized, but his eyes met mine for a long moment. Then he looked at the water and cliffs around him. I knew what he was doing. *Assess the situation, Emmeline. Eliminate the variables. Determine the best course of action.*

Or maybe he was looking for the blue bottle.

"Papa!"

He looked up again. His skin was already changing color with the cold.

"Lagoon," he shouted, pointing to the right, around the curve of the sheer wall of the island.

"I'm sorry," I sobbed. "I'm sorry."

"I love you," he mouthed. Then he began to swim.

"I'll meet you!" I yelled. Although I think even then we both knew.

AFTER

I waited at the lagoon all afternoon, my eyes fixed on the channel. The waves growled and churned, refusing to calm no matter how hard I set my thoughts on the roiling water, willing it to grow soft and welcoming. I knew in my brain that it didn't matter. My father and I had talked many times about the temperature of that water. About how long someone could last in its embrace. If the first shock didn't get you—didn't make you open your mouth, gasping for air and letting in water instead—the cold would. Extended exposure was always fatal, my father had said, even in the summer. This was winter. And even if he could have made it all the way to the channel, those tides and rocks were never going to let him through in one piece. My father was a scientist; I knew these things.

I waited anyway.

⌒

The sky darkened until all that was left was smells, and as I sat there breathing in the scents of salt water and damp sand, smells I had known all my life, I realized with a flash of panic that my nose was already overwriting those olfactory memories with new ones. Ones that didn't contain my father.

When you change a scent, you change the memory, he'd always said. I hadn't truly understood until now.

With every inhalation, my father was disappearing.

No, I thought. I stood up, gave one last frantic look across the lagoon toward the channel, then turned and ran up the trail.

I threw open the cabin door and shut it tight behind me, trying to seal the precious smells inside. His scent was still there—in the air, in the fabric of his shirts, even in the pages of our books. I shoved my nose into each and every object I could find, knowing as I did so that his scent was already slipping from them like water through a sieve.

I thought of all the scent-papers I had created of myself. All those white squares, dropping into my hand. I had never made a single one of my father—there had never been a reason to. He was my father; he would always be there.

"Selfish," I whispered into the silence of the cabin. "Selfish. Selfish."

I looked around. The upper drawers of the walls were all open, right down to the one where the blue-wax bottle had hid. The machine was unwrapped and on the table.

He knew, I thought.

The horror of it was more than I could stand. I picked up the machine, that sleek and beautiful thing. It had started all of this.

"I hate you," I screamed. I threw it on the floor, again and again, until all that was left were tiny pieces of metal. Trash, not magic.

I picked up the fabric that had always protected it and tossed it into the fire without thinking. A fragrance, indolent and spicy, unfurled into the room, mingling with its smells, changing what was left of my father. I slammed the door of the woodstove shut, but it was too late.

I spent the next two days curled in our big chair, the book of fairy tales clutched tight against my chest. A part of me thought if I didn't change anything, then maybe everything would go back to how it was. My father would walk through the door, shaking the water from his hair and laughing about an off-season swim. He would be the man of my childhood, the one who would stop our foraging to show me the shining path of a snail. Not the man he'd been these past months. Not the man flying into the water.

I tried to ignore the bottles still left in the lower drawers. *If it weren't for them, I would still have my father,* I thought.

And yet, I knew what was inside those green-wax bottles. Our life, waiting for me.

After three days, the missing of him became so loud in my head that I couldn't stand it anymore. I started opening the drawers. I just held the bottles at first—wondered which day each scent-paper had captured. What we had been doing. The last of the food disappeared, but I no longer cared. I sat, wrapped in the blankets from my father's bed, holding one of the bottles against my chest until the heat of my body warmed its cool surface. Then I would swap it out for another.

On the morning of the fifth day, I woke up in the chair, the world cold and tilting around me. The smell of my father was almost completely gone from the room. I managed to get the fire going again, then went to the drawers. As I took out a bottle, the paper inside shifted, and I could hear my father's voice. *I am here. I am here.*

I got a knife and broke the seal. The scent was still there, but barely, like trees through fog. A faint glimpse, nothing you could navigate by— and I needed navigation. I walked across the room, opened the door of the woodstove, and tossed the paper in.

It took a moment. I almost thought it wouldn't happen and that this would be the punishment for all I had done—but then it was there. I was in the middle of a warm and sunny afternoon, the fragrance of late summer draped around me. I could smell a basket of ripe apples on the table. I remembered the knife, the smooth spiral of the peel as my father separated it from the fruit.

Here, little lark. He let the peel fall into my tiny hands. *A toy you can eat.* He was smiling.

I dropped to my knees. I could feel his arms, smell his animal warmth, the salt water and pine pitch in his beard.

I was already reaching for the next bottle before the fragrance was gone.

After that initial splurge, I tried to ration myself. But as my muscles weakened, my resistance went with them. One bottle a day turned into two, then three, then five. I was never going to leave. Even if I could figure out how to get help, or how to overcome that horrible channel, it was too late. I just wanted to be with my father again.

So I opened the bottles and lit the papers, one after another. I even found Cleo in one of them, and strangely, it was that one that made me sob.

Days passed. I could feel myself turning into air. The fragrances of the scent-papers became my lungs, the blood in my veins. I found it easier and easier to lose myself in them. My father had taught me to track a scent, but now I went inside the smells, wandering among them like trees in an unfamiliar forest.

Once upon a time, Emmeline, they whispered.

I wanted to live in the stories those fragrances told. When I realized that it would be too much effort to keep standing up to get them, I took down all the bottles. I needed to save what energy I had to keep the fire going.

Now the bottles lay around me in a field of glass and bits of broken green wax. I was already holding the next one, although the murmurs of the previous scent-paper still lingered—an ordinary day, right at the cusp of spring, violets waiting under the ground. My hair had been washed; the wood in the stove was a little green. Details I hadn't cared about at the time. I pulled the fragrance into me, then felt it leaving, fading. I pulled harder.

"Emmeline!"

The voice came from far away. It wasn't the first voice I'd heard coming out of the scent-papers, but this time something wasn't right about it. I pushed it away, burrowed deeper into the smell of new growth and damp wood.

"Emmeline!" It came again, closer—outside the cabin, I realized. I sat up slowly, knowing the voice was not my father's but hoping anyway. The room wobbled and the fragrance began pulling at me anew.

Don't go, it whispered.

Footsteps sounded on the porch. The door opened and the scents inside were swept away on a blast of fresh, cold air. I saw the mermaid man walk in, but he didn't have a black plastic box this time. He didn't have my father, either.

PART TWO

The Cove

WONDERLAND

The mattress was soft, the sheets stiff.

Not my bed.

I lay there, eyes closed, holding my breath. The moment I let the smells in, let my eyelids open, the world would be different, wrong. It would be what I had made it—and so I told myself I would not open my eyes. I would not breathe through my nose. I would not know where I was.

I tried to roll over, wanting to curl up in a ball and disappear, but a weight on my legs kept me from moving. I inhaled reflexively and smelled damp animal fur. *Cleo?*

I gasped, half hoping, but in response I heard only hoarse breathing. *Not Cleo.* I froze, my skin sizzling with panic. A warm exhalation brushed my face, and I inhaled air full of deep, musky tones. *Bear?* A tongue lapped across my cheek.

I kept my eyes shut, and screamed.

"It's okay, *ma cherie*." The horrible animal was gone, a voice in its place, the words tilted slightly upward. *A woman*. A palm rested against my cheek. I could smell yeast, flour, sugar.

"That was just our dog," she said. "He's outside now."

The hand moved across the top of my head. As she stroked, every strand of my hair remembered my father's fingers slipping through my curls as he read to me. Instinctively, I pulled the front of my shirt toward my face, yearning for the last fragrance from the scent-papers. But the fabric in my hands was soft, thin.

Not my shirt. I inhaled an empty scent of not-quite flowers. No pine pitch and sea salt. No applewood and flannel. *No*, I thought.

"Your clothes are in the wash," the woman said. "They were full of smoke. They'll be fresh and clean soon, don't worry."

No. No. No.

He was gone. A hole of grief opened beneath me and I fell in.

I don't know how much time passed. I knew the woman came in and checked on me, put her hand on my cheek, my shoulder.

"Emmeline?"

I couldn't answer.

Hours later she returned. "Emmeline." Her voice was different this time, calm but firm. "You need to open your eyes now. You need to eat."

Behind my closed lids, all I could see was a black watery ocean of bottles. *Let me jump in with you, Papa.* I didn't care how cold it was, how dark the world would have to stay, if only I could be with him.

"You're safe here," the woman's voice said.

Safe. What an odd word.

Smells don't care what the mind or heart wants, however. Scents will find their way around the darkness of closed eyes, slipping past barricades of thought. The body is their accomplice. We can live without food for weeks, and water for days, but try not to breathe and the lungs mutiny.

And so, bit by bit, on the backs of those traitorous breaths, in snuck the fragrance of something baking in an oven. The smell of onions, softening over heat. I tried to keep the scents away, but still they slipped inside, warm and welcoming as summer.

People lie, Emmeline, but smells never do, my father had told me. I could still see him, standing by the chicken coop, teaching me how to find new eggs.

Follow this. His finger tapping my nose. *Follow this.*

I don't want to leave you, Papa.

But in the end, there was nowhere else to go.

I opened my eyes.

It's hard to explain my shock at seeing a real, female human being for the first time. I'd seen photos and illustrations of other people, but they'd existed in books, had smelled only of paper. Their voices had been variations of my father's as he read aloud. If I'd thought about it at all, I would have thought other people were simply smaller or taller or rounder versions of him.

But this woman in front of me *moved* differently. She wore a loose blue dress, with a big apron over it. Her white hair was pulled up on her head, and her skin was tanned from the sun, with plenty of lines around her eyes and mouth. She seemed old and not at the same time, her hands strong but knobby as tree roots.

"There you are, *ma cherie*," she said, smiling. Then, as if realizing I might need a moment by myself, she added, "I'll get you some food. It's time for you to eat."

I looked around after she left. The walls of the room were smooth and blue. No drawers. No bottles. No glowing wood. The window across from the bed looked out to water, and the light coming in held the silver of late winter, bright as it had ever been on the bluff. I felt exposed, away from the protection of the woods. I pulled my knees to my chest, ignoring the room, staring at the door.

The smell of cardamom preceded the woman into the room, soft and comforting. A memory opened—one of the scent-papers from a red-wax bottle, with the fragrance of a sultry place that had wound itself around me, kissed my skin. *Cardamom,* my father had said. *They hide like treasure.* He'd shown me pictures of pods shaped like tiny boats, spilling out black seeds.

"Here," the woman said, holding out a plate in one hand and a glass of something white in the other. "No one has ever turned down one of my rolls."

The smell from the plate made me dizzy. We'd made bread on the island, but this scent was rounder, more delicate, with something heavy yet silky woven into it. I pulled one of the rolls off the plate. It was brown and sticky, and when I took a bite it filled my mouth with sweetness. I had tried sugar before, but only as a rare treat from the mermaid boxes. This was as much sugar as I'd ever had in a whole season all at once. My teeth buzzed; saliva rushed across my tongue.

I looked up at the woman, my eyes wide, and she smiled.

"I'm glad you like them," she said. "And now that we're looking at each other, let me introduce myself. I'm Colette. My husband's Henry—he's the one who found you. This is our home."

She handed me the glass. I put it to my mouth and sipped, then gagged. I was accustomed to water and the bright clear green of spruce tea. This was thick and cold, soft as the scum that would collect at the edge of the lagoon.

"It's milk," the woman said.

So that's what it tastes like. It had been a recurring image in one of my storybooks—the glass of milk given to a child at bedtime. It had seemed like such a treat.

"I'm sorry," I said. My stomach roiled, and I worried I might be sick.

Colette left and brought me a glass of water. It tasted of metal, not at all like the cool stones that had lined our well, but it was better than the milk. She sat on the edge of the bed while I drank, staying long after I was done. I looked around the room, trying to avoid the message lingering in the taste of the water and the sight of that open sky outside the window.

You are not home.

I turned my head away. To my left was a dresser with a small lamp on it. Next to the lamp, I saw a bottle with a green-wax seal. I started at the sight.

"You wouldn't let go of it," the woman said. "Henry says it was the last one in the cabin." She watched me closely. "People have been finding these all over the beaches. Everyone's been wondering where they came from. There was even an article in the *Daily Sun*. But most of them have red seals."

I remembered standing on the bluff, throwing my father's bottles into the water. My father's face, looking up at me from the waves.

"Don't tell," I said to Colette. "Please."

She looked down. My fingers were tight on her wrist, but if it hurt she said nothing.

"Okay," she said.

I let go. She picked up the bottle and handed it to me.

"Here you go," she said.

She left the room—to work on Henry's lunch, she said—and I lay there with the bottle in my hands. The desire to open it, to burn the paper and smell my father, was almost overwhelming, but that scent-paper was all I had left. It was proof of everything we had been—and of everything I had done to us. It was the best and the worst of me.

DODGE

It must have been close to a week before I left that room. Colette put a bucket next to the bed so I could relieve myself, and I was stunned at the energy it took to move even that far. Mostly I slept, but whether that was for my body or my mind, I couldn't say. All I remember is that slowly the room seemed to get brighter, and my arms and legs remembered they were made of bone and muscle. People are like that—given a chance, we come back, whether we want to or not.

This new world was a strange place, however. On the island, I had read fairy tales about houses made of candy, and animals that could talk. Our walls had been filled with bottles that held time. My father had told me how the roots of trees spoke to one another, deep beneath the soil.

All that was more believable than what I now encountered.

"Would you like to take a bath?" Colette asked one afternoon.

For me, *a bath* was a cold, wet cloth. A bar of soap and a scratchy towel to dry off with. Hair washing was rare and involved a jug of water and a bowl—one to wet my hair, the other to catch the runoff. As for the water itself—well, that came from a well or off the roof.

Instead, Colette led me to a bright white room with shining walls. She pushed back a curtain to reveal a tub, slick and white. I looked around for a bucket, but Colette turned a handle, and an endless torrent of cool, then hot, water poured out of the wall. I watched, fascinated and terrified, as it filled the tub. I couldn't imagine how all that water stayed inside the walls, or what might happen if you made a hole in them by accident.

"Want to get in?" Colette asked, smiling. "You don't want it to cool off."

I looked at her.

"I'll wait outside," she said. "Tell me if you need anything."

The door closed behind her and I stood staring at the water. I'd been in water that deep before, but it had always been cold and full of salt. This had a different smell—steam, and the same sharp, white scent I'd smelled on Colette's hands. Something else, too. I followed my nose to a bar of soap on the lip of the tub and picked it up. Its fragrance was sweet, and a little sad. It reminded me of something I'd smelled in one of the red-wax scent-papers, but this time it felt wrong—thin, not even alive.

I didn't want these unknown smells, but I knew what soap and water were for. I took my clothes off, my body still shaky from weeks of starvation followed by a week in bed. I sat on the side of the tub and put in a foot. The heat welcomed my toes, then my leg. I slid down until only my nose was above the water. The warmth surrounded me; I couldn't believe how good it felt. I looked at my body, pale skin in a white tub, almost invisible. I wanted to stay there forever.

The water had turned cold when Colette came and knocked at the door.

"Are you all right in there?" she asked.

"Yes," I said.

I toweled off, dressed, and went to the kitchen, where Colette sat me in a rocking chair. I looked around at the pots hanging on hooks, the plates and bowls on shelves, the apples in a wire basket. I knew what all those things were.

"How about some tea?" Colette asked.

I nodded. *You can do this*, I told myself. *It's not so very strange.*

Colette turned her wrist and flames flared out of the top of a big white box. I screamed and ran for my bed. I lay there for hours, clutching my father's green-wax bottle. I pretended he and I were in the cabin again, but it was a comfort enclosed in glass. It would never be the same, and I could never go back.

Over the days that followed, I learned many things. In this place, stoves did not require wood, and heat did not require fire. Clocks cut the day into equal parts, and barometers turned weather into numbers. Colette and Henry flipped switches and night went away; they held small boxes to their heads and talked to people who weren't there.

The smells of these new things were different, too—spiky and agitated, as if they moved too quickly to let life accumulate. By the end of each day, I was desperate for the scent of island dirt beneath my feet, the smell of applewood smoke and oatmeal and the runaway's tobacco.

I fit nowhere. There was no call here for foraging or bow drills. Colette made her tea with a bag, not spruce tips. All the skills that I had been so proud of mattered not at all here, and the ones I needed, it seemed, were indecipherable. At night I would go to sleep and retreat to the island in my dreams, hoping to find home, only to wake up screaming.

Henry, the mermaid man, had white hair, but he moved with the lithe energy of someone much younger. He spent his time working nearby, the sound of his hammer providing a steady rhythm to the day. When he was inside the house, he was a quiet presence. I'd seen him watching me, waiting for my questions. My father used to do that with the chickens when they were agitated, standing in their coop until they settled. The memory stung, sharp and fizzing; would I ever get used to that absence?

"How did you find me?" I asked Henry finally. I had put it off, suspecting the answer.

He looked at me, as if deciding something. Then he said, "Old Man Jenkins lives out on the islands, too. He found your father's . . ."

Colette had come out of the kitchen, and shook her head at him slightly. He coughed, looking abashed.

"I'm sorry, Emmeline," he said.

My fault. My fault. My fault.

"I had to wait for the right tide to get through your channel," Henry said. "It was hard waiting, thinking of you out there all by yourself."

I focused on my hands in my lap. I didn't want to think about those days. I felt Colette's hand on my shoulder.

"I remember when your father brought you here," she said.

Her words made me look up. "What?"

She nodded. "You were a little thing, barely walking. Your father was wrestling with something—we could see that. But a lot of people who come out here are, you know?

"What was clear," she added more forcefully, "was that he loved you. He knew how to take care of you, too. I never would have let him take you to that island if he hadn't."

Henry nodded. "We don't mind a hankering for solitude out here, but we don't hold with cruelty," he said. "And once you two were on the island, we could tell you were doing okay by what he asked for."

"What do you mean?"

"He'd leave me notes in the empty boxes. Tell me when you wanted something special."

The blue rain slicker. The books and the chocolate. *Cleo*, I thought, and looked outside, so they couldn't see my eyes.

"I think maybe that's enough for today," Colette said.

There had been a time in my life when I had felt grown-up, capable. Now I was too scared of the world outside to leave the house. I stayed in my room mostly, telling myself the stories from my father's book of fairy tales. The girl in the red cloak, running through the trees. The genie waiting in the bottle, growing more powerful with time. The children, lost in the woods with only breadcrumbs to help them. I spoke the words in my mind, as if they could tell me how to navigate this place I'd found myself in, but the best they could do was help me forget. Still, I returned to the stories, wishing for something that would never come. An ending that had already happened.

It was the dog, Dodge, who brought me back. At first, I was too frightened to be near his coarse fur and sharp teeth—too much like a bear, even if Dodge's fur was golden, his muzzle white, and his eyes a calm, melting brown. I would stand in the doorway of the kitchen or living room, unable to enter until Colette rousted him and put him out on the front porch.

Then one day, when I neared the kitchen, he simply rose to his feet and went to the front door, waiting to be let out. As if he understood. Colette opened the door and I heard his body thud down on the painted boards of the porch.

I went to the window and watched him. He fell asleep again, his breathing becoming smooth and even. Then, suddenly, his head lifted, his nose on full alert. Standing on the other side of the glass, it took me a moment before I, too, smelled the odor of a motor and saw Henry's boat turning into the harbor. While I stiffened at the smell, Dodge got up, ambled down to the dock, and waited as Henry tied up the boat. I watched as Henry bent and ran his hands over Dodge's back.

They walked back up to the house together. When they got there, Henry opened the door but Dodge didn't come in. Henry looked back, head cocked.

"Staying outside, old guy?" he asked. Dodge looked up and saw me in the window, then lay down in front of the door. *Protecting me*, I realized.

After that, I started watching Dodge all the time. I saw the way he knew by scent alone when Colette's bread was done cooking, or a squirrel was a hundred feet away, or the wind had changed direction. Before he even saw them, he recognized each of the five fishermen who kept their boats in the cove. Most he would go greet, tail wagging, but one he stayed away from.

Over the following days, Dodge became my translator of the world outside the house. Through his nose it became safer, and soon I found myself wanting to inhale the air around me as he did, as something pure and alive and full of messages.

One afternoon, I looked out and saw Dodge on his feet, staring out across the water, every muscle in his body taut. Even though I was inside, I could smell the shift. A bit of metal, a heaviness to the air. I remembered the feel of it, the way the trees seemed to pull into themselves, the scent of quick sap.

Storm, I thought.

"You should let Dodge in," I told Colette. She looked at me, surprised.

"There's big weather coming," I said.

"Really?" The sky outside was clear.

"He knows it. Look at him."

Colette glanced at Dodge and checked the barometer.

"Well, aren't you two something," she said. She opened the door, and this time when Dodge entered, I didn't leave.

That evening, the rain lashed at the windows. Henry and Colette talked softly in the kitchen, their words an indistinguishable murmur, while I sat in the living room with Dodge beside the fire. Colette had given me a big book she called an atlas. She said it would show me the whole world. What I saw was flat pages, shapes divided into colors.

"This is where we are," she'd said, pointing to the edge of a mass of green, right up against a vast expanse of blue. "I was born here." She tapped on a name, *Montreal*, far on the other side. "I met Henry here." Her finger slipped down, through a thicket of tiny shapes, to the words *New York*. "I was walking in a big park, and there he was."

She smiled, falling into memory. "He said he wanted to get away from everything. There was a caretaker job at the end of the world. He asked me to come with him. I was ready for a new adventure, and I wanted to be with him, so I said yes, for the summer."

She laughed. "I guess I stayed, eh?"

I'd listened to the affection in her voice, wanting to fall asleep inside it and never wake up. A love like that seemed so simple, so real. But it wasn't mine. I knew that. My father's love had been tangled and full of secrets, locked away on an island.

"Where did I live?" I'd asked, and she turned the pages until she found one that looked like the others, but with everything bigger, more detailed. A puzzle of blue and green—inlets and islands, she explained, pointing to a speck in the middle of the page, lost amidst the others as soon as she removed her finger.

I could never find my way home, I thought. Even if I did, there was nothing there for me.

Now I sat in front of the fire, the atlas open in my lap, staring at where my island might be. At my feet, Dodge snored in his sleep. He smelled of the outdoors, of wet wool and trees and rain. I got down on the floor and carefully put my hand on his back. His eyes opened and he lifted his chin, resting it on my foot. We stayed there in a circle of our own for a long time, while the wind played in the downspouts and the logs crackled in the fireplace.

During a lull in the storm, I could hear voices, drifting in from the kitchen.

"What should we do?" Henry's voice.

"We keep her."

"But what if someone is looking for her?"

"How would we find them, Henry? We don't even know her last name—they were Emmeline and John. He paid you in cash. She says her birthday is the first day of spring."

"We could advertise."

"And bring every crazy person and pedophile in the country to our door? Thank you, no."

"A private detective, then."

"We don't have that kind of money, Henry."

The kitchen got quiet. I heard the sound of Colette walking across the room, the shift of Henry's chair. In a softer tone, Colette said, "It's been more than ten years since they got here, and no one's come looking. Maybe there's a reason."

"What'll we tell people?"

"She's a relative, come to visit. Simple as that. She takes our name."

There was a long pause. I held my breath. Colette was stirring something on the stove, the wooden spoon rhythmic against the sides of the pan.

"She's a child, Henry." I heard the yearning in her voice. "She's been through enough. Let's let her be."

"Okay," Henry said finally.

***

I sat in the living room next to Dodge, my fingers curling in his soft fur, thinking of what they'd said. When I lived on the island, *Emmeline* was all I needed for a name. My father had been the feeling of his arms around me. My birthday was the scent of violets. Now none of that was enough.

Who am I, Papa? Who were you?

But then I felt the question change, get rough on the edges.

Why didn't you tell me?

THE SECRET COVE

That night, when I went to my room, Dodge followed, settling down on the floor next to my bed. I could hear him breathing, the sound filling the space between me and the bottle on the dresser, and I realized this was the first time I would sleep in that room with something other than memories to keep me company.

I listened as his exhalations turned to snores. I had a choice to make, I understood—go back or go forward. In the end, it was simple. *Back* had been reduced to fairy tales in my head, a scent-paper that would burn once and be gone. There was nothing left but forward. I put the bottle in the dresser drawer.

The next morning, Dodge and I got up and went toward the kitchen. As we passed the front door, Dodge went over and scratched to be let out.

I could feel the heat of the house around me, the bottle waiting, holding my past. Dodge turned and looked at me, then scratched again. I reached for the knob and opened the door.

After weeks inside, I had forgotten the cleanness of the air after a good rain. The storm had washed the world into silence. The evergreens lining the edge of the cove were so soaked they appeared black; beyond them, the clouds reached down toward the ocean, gray meeting silver. In the small harbor were two long wooden walkways; attached to one of them was Henry's boat, white against the dark water.

I walked down the stairs in my bare feet and lifted my face to the sky, letting the mist coat my skin. I could smell dirt, damp wood, the welcoming green of trees.

"Ahoy, Mistress Emmeline!"

I opened my eyes and spotted Henry working on his boat. He waved, carefully casual, as if I came outside every day.

Behind me, I heard Colette bustling toward the front door.

"Old man, did you leave this thing open? You're letting in the cold—" She stopped when she saw me. "Well, look at you, all outside and adventurous." I heard the smile in her voice.

She ducked inside, and reappeared carrying a pair of boots and a rain jacket. "Best to put these on, though."

She sat down next to me on the bottom step as I pulled on the boots, which were a bit too big. "Welcome to our cove," she said, and motioned toward the wooden sign hanging over the boardwalk: *Secret Cove Resort.* "It's not much, but it's all ours."

I looked down the boardwalk and saw a string of little cottages, painted in impossibly bright colors—yellow and blue and peach and red. They stood like a burst of laughter against the evergreens that rose up the slopes behind them.

"Henry does love a paintbrush," Colette said.

My focus, however, was on the tall, dark hills. They seemed endless, wild, and capable of holding anything. "Bears?" I asked, keeping my voice low.

"You're safe here."

I turned back and scanned the harbor. Colette followed my gaze. "The fishermen have already come through and gotten their boats," she said. "They won't be back for hours—and we won't have any guests in those cottages until the summer."

My shoulders relaxed, and Dodge came up and bumped against me.

Colette chuckled. "Don't worry. Dodge can show you around—and I'll be right here if you need me." She put her hand on my back and gave me a gentle push.

"Go explore," she said. "Nothing can hurt you here."

My father had said much the same thing, once upon a time.

Dodge and I set off down the wooden boardwalk. I kept my breathing shallow, my nose alert for any sign of danger, but Dodge seemed unconcerned. He wandered along in front of me, favoring one hip as he went.

As we drew nearer to the cottages, I could see the way they stood on barnacled stilts, their feet in the foamy water of a high tide, their roofs alive with green moss. Their bright colors had made me think they were somehow separate, but I saw now that they would always be part of the cove, part of the woods.

The cottages were silent, full of anticipation, and my boots made soft clomping sounds along the wide, worn planks. My breathing evened out. I peeked in one of the windows and saw an old rocking chair and a bed with a red and white patchwork quilt. I thought of our cabin on the island, alone now and waiting. Would someone else discover it? Would they find our drawers in the walls, smell the runaway's tobacco?

Go forward, I told myself. *Not back.*

I kept walking.

Dodge and I followed the curving boardwalk around the cove to where it stopped near the entrance of the harbor. There were two large buildings there, one red, one blue. Henry must not have gotten to them yet, I figured, because their paint was faded almost to nonexistence. The red building was basic—long and two-storied. A couple of spiky plants I didn't recognize grew wild in two wooden barrels that flanked the door. The blue-green scent tugged at my memory, but I couldn't place it, so I kept going.

The blue building was plain as well, its windows bare. I looked through one of them, and in the darkness I saw something white, floating below a tall ceiling.

A *ghost*, I thought. I jumped back and looked for Dodge, wanting to see his reaction, but he was staring fixedly at the harbor entrance. I heard the sound of an approaching motor, and smelled the odor of gasoline—sharp and yellow. There was only one fisherman who used gas in his boat instead of diesel, the one Dodge never went to greet. Now the boat would pass right by us as it came into the harbor. Dodge growled softly, low in his chest.

I didn't need to be told twice. I tugged on the handle and the door to the blue building opened with a screech.

"Come, Dodge," I said. We slipped inside, and I shut the door safely behind us.

It took a moment for my eyes to adjust. The bones appeared first, huge white curves hanging from the ceiling in graceful arcs. Nearby were smaller creatures, with tiny skulls and hands with long, long fingers, and a table spread with yet more skeletons, organized by shape and size.

I realized I'd been holding my breath. When I inhaled, I froze, stunned. I knew that smell.

It was the fragrance of the sea gone dry, all salt and no seaweed. Dust and old leather and older wood. An undercurrent of the blue-green smell from the plants in the barrels outside. Without warning, I was deep in memory, standing with my father as he pulled a scent-paper out of a red-wax bottle and we entered another world.

Once upon a time, Emmeline, Jack met a wizard who could turn the ocean into bones.

Now here was that scent again. Not from a bottle, but in this room. It *lived* here.

I had spent so many years wanting to be a scent hunter, wanting to meet the elusive Jack, and see the places where he had gone. And now for the first time, I had a location that matched a red-wax scent.

"Found you, Jack," I said into the darkness of the room.

But then I remembered—Jack wasn't the only person I knew who'd been at Secret Cove.

Who were you, Papa? I asked that empty room.

Dodge and I walked back along the boardwalk, my brain still spinning. I didn't see the figures coming toward me at first, and when I did, it was too late to hide.

There were two of them, a man and a woman. The woman's pants hugged her so tightly I thought at first she had blue legs; as she walked, her shoes made clattering sounds on the boards. The man next to her was tall. On his shoulder he held a strange black contraption with a single eye that gazed out at the world.

Cyclops, I thought.

The woman spotted me. "Hello!" she called out. "Do you live here?"

They came closer. The woman's lips were so red I was afraid she was bleeding; her eyelashes were thick as sticks. A fragrance swelled around her, complicated and full of flowers that had never been alive. The smells climbed on each other, permeating the air until I wanted to bat them away with my hands. Beside me, Dodge had gone still.

"We're doing a story on Secret Cove," the woman said. The man raised the contraption on his shoulder, its eye scanning across the cove. I wondered if it could capture you, like my father's machine. I stepped back.

Behind me, one of the cottage doors opened. I turned and saw Henry walking toward us, a hammer held loosely in his hand. "Who are you?" he asked the couple.

The woman stopped, her face turning pink; she touched the man's shoulder and he lowered the machine. I moved quickly to the side of the boardwalk, watching.

"My apologies," the woman said, extending a hand toward Henry. "I'm Terry Anderson from CTV. We do a show called *Hidden Hideaways*? Maybe you know it?"

Henry shook his head. The woman's eyebrows furrowed slightly, but then she smiled.

"Anyway," she said, "we drop in unannounced on places we think could be the next big thing. I saw a photo of your cove—in that *Sun* article about the bottles?—and as soon as I saw it I just *knew* we needed to do a story. It's taken me a while to get it together—you sure are remote, aren't you?"

"Yes," Henry said.

"You must be Henry, the owner?" When he nodded, she continued, "And this beautiful girl, is she your daughter?" I saw her glance between me and Henry, taking in his white hair, her expression skeptical.

"A relative," he said.

"I'd love to include her." Terry motioned to the cameraman, who started to swing the machine in my direction. "If you don't mind, of course."

"She's not much for pictures," Henry said, stepping in front of me.

"Are you sure?" Terry said. "She's just lovely."

"I'm sure."

"Well." Terry shrugged her shoulders. "In that case, we'll just have to take advantage of the light and get those darling cottages on film. You don't mind, do you?" She smiled disarmingly. "Our viewers are going to eat this up, Henry. We're going to change your life. Although you might have to fix up your road a bit first. Our car is half mud at this point."

It was a long afternoon. The two interlopers walked the length of the boardwalk, and Terry insisted on interviewing both Colette and Henry. Her voice was like her fragrance, filled with too much activity.

"So, you redid all these cottages yourself?" she asked. The man turned the black eye of the machine toward Henry. So far, no paper had come out of it, I noticed.

Henry nodded. The woman waited, but he said nothing.

"How about your customers?" Terry asked, turning smoothly to Colette. "This must be a gorgeous place in the summer."

Colette's eyes were warm and inviting. "We've got some wonderful guests; they come every year."

"I know it's off-season, but do you get bottle hunters?" Terry asked, excited. "We keep reading about the bottles showing up on the beaches around here. Wax seals, papers inside—but no messages. A real mystery, wouldn't you say?"

I was standing to the side, almost hidden by one of the porch supports. *Please no please no please no,* I thought.

Colette shot me the briefest of looks, then smiled at Terry.

"We've never needed a fuss to get business," she said.

"Well, you certainly won't now," Terry declared. She turned to talk directly to the machine. "Make your reservations today, folks, because Secret Cove isn't a secret anymore. Signing off—this is Terry from *Hidden Hideaways* on CTV. May all your vacations be fairy tales."

THE BOARDINGHOUSE

We watched the story on the television in the living room. I still couldn't wrap my head around the way it showed you people who weren't there, places you couldn't touch.

"Where are the smells?" I'd asked Henry the first time he'd showed it to me, and he chuckled.

"Now, wouldn't that be something," he said. I'd opened my mouth to tell him about my father's machine, but then remembered it lying in pieces across the cabin floor, and said nothing.

In the days since I'd discovered the building with the hanging bones, I'd examined every machine in Henry and Colette's house. I'd found ones that captured faces or voices, or played music, but none of them was like my father's.

I thought of him, standing in our cabin, catching the scents of our life on a piece of paper.

How does it work, Papa?

Science and magic, Emmeline.

Every thought about my father was like that now; every memory shifted into a question. My thoughts were on a constant prowl, riffling through my past, looking for clues.

"Why did my father go to the island?" I asked Henry the night after I found the blue building.

He shook his head. "I honestly don't know, darlin'. I'm sorry."

I'd figured he would say that, but it didn't make the answer any easier. This was my search, that much was certain, and I had precious little to go on besides memories and the scents of a room full of bones.

Now Henry and Colette and I sat on the couch, watching the glowing screen of the television, waiting. Dodge stayed on the floor, his chin on my knee.

"There it is!" Colette said suddenly, pointing to the screen. Our brightly colored cottages encircled the water like wildflowers. Henry looked gruff but lovable; welcome shone in Colette's eyes.

"Down a long dirt road lies a little piece of magic." Terry's voice came from the box as the camera's focus roamed over the curve of the cove, the boats in the harbor.

"It's so beautiful," Colette said, giving Henry a kiss on the cheek. He smiled and took her hand. I watched them as if they were a fairy tale I could read.

The calls started the next morning. By the end of the week, Colette was using a recorded message so she wouldn't have to keep picking up the phone. It took me a while to get used to her disembodied voice floating through the house like a ghost: *This is the Secret Cove Resort. We're sorry to tell you we're fully booked for the summer, but . . .*

"What's going to happen to our regulars?" Henry asked as we ate breakfast.

Colette was making notes in the reservation book, frowning. "I held their slots, but it's going to be tricky."

"Things are gonna change," Henry said. He got up and went to the window. The cove was hushed and peaceful, the fog so thick that even the fishermen had stayed home. Thin white wisps wove through the branches of the trees, muffling everything.

Colette put down her pencil and looked at him. "I know, I know—but we could use the money."

Henry stiffened, but after a moment he came back to the table and sat down next to her. "I've been thinking about redoing the boardinghouse," he said. "I could take a look, see what I'd need to do."

"That would be wonderful," Colette said, relief washing through her words.

The kitchen grew quiet. After a while, Henry stood up and put his dishes in the sink.

"Guess I'd better get to work," he said.

"Should we get the Internet?" Colette asked as he was leaving the kitchen. She saw him pause. "People keep asking, that's all."

"No," Henry said firmly. He turned and looked at her. "You saw what happened to the Big Cove Lodge. George calls it Screenville now. I'll do the rest, but not that."

He left without another word. Colette washed the dishes as she watched him tromping down the boardwalk. I'd made this happen, I thought. My bottles had brought that woman to our cove, and now Henry was sad and Colette looked worried. My fault. Again.

After a while, Colette came over and sat down at the table across from me.

"We're going to need your help, *ma cherie*."

I stared at her, uncertain.

"There's going to be a lot of people here this summer," she said.

I shook my head no.

"I know," Colette said, "but you can help me clean cottages and change sheets—and it'll be good practice talking to people before you start school."

"School?"

"Yes. You'll like it. There'll be kids your own age, books."

I shook my head. The thought of a group of kids made me freeze. I was barely used to Henry and Colette. And what would I do without Dodge to tell me whom to trust? Something told me dogs didn't go to school.

Colette smiled, but there was sympathy in her eyes. "We don't really have a choice, I'm afraid. I talked to the folks at the school district. We can keep you out for this spring, but come fall you'll have to go."

I tried to keep the panic from my face.

"Don't worry," she said, "you'll be fine."

The phone rang again.

Even though there was too much to do before the summer guests arrived, Colette set aside a couple hours every morning for lessons with me. I didn't tell her that this was exactly how my father had started each day, and that every time she and I sat down at the kitchen table and opened a book, it broke my heart.

"You know a lot," she said encouragingly. "Especially about science. Your father did a good job."

Except he never told me what really mattered, I thought.

In the afternoons, I worked with Henry in the boardinghouse while Dodge kept us company. It was cold in there, but I liked the steady rhythm of the labor. I learned how to hold a paintbrush. How to clean eighty years of grime off windows. How to drive a straight line of nails. It was a relief to feel the solidity of a hammer or a brush, to know that this thing in my hand existed and would be there tomorrow. That it was what it was and nothing more.

Mostly, we were quiet, but sometimes I could get Henry to tell me stories about the cove.

"Are those your whale bones?" I asked one day, pointing with my paintbrush toward the blue building next door. A couple drops of creamy white paint fell to the floor. I grabbed a rag to wipe them before they dried.

"Ah," Henry said. "The whale museum. Those are the professor's. People used to bring him skeletons they found. He'd clean them up and donate them to museums."

The wizard. "Where is he?" The words came fast. Maybe the professor could answer my questions.

"I don't know." Henry looked over at me, curious. "He used to come every summer, but not for years now. He was an old guy—I keep the bones, just in case, but . . ."

I could almost feel the door of opportunity shut. Another clue lost, I thought. It felt like every time I got a chance at a real story, it disappeared. In the end, truth seemed no easier to catch than the scent of violets. My father used to show me how their smell could be there, so clear and beautiful, and then vanish, only to return a few minutes later, as strong as it had ever been. You couldn't control it. You couldn't hold on to it. I'd thought that was a wonderful thing, back then.

Henry dipped his brush in a can of bright white paint, and started on the window trim. I listened to the quiet swish of the bristles against the wood.

"Why did *you* come here?" I asked after a while.

He angled his brush around a tricky edge. "I was tired of people," he said, his eyes focused on his work. "There was a war. I'd had to do some things I wasn't proud of, and didn't want to ever do again." He looked over at me. "This place can heal you, if you let it."

I ignored this comment; I wanted the kind of healing that came from information. "Who else lives out on the islands?" I asked.

"I thought we were done with the interviews." But he smiled as he said it. He took the paintbrush from my hand and gave me a hammer. "There are some loose floorboards," he said. "Check the nails, okay?"

"Please," I said.

He sighed, picked up his brush again, and talked while he painted. "Well, there's Old Man Jenkins. Back when he was twenty, he built a canoe and went exploring. Bought an old floating shack from a fisherman for forty bucks. Still lives there, 'cept he's too old to paddle into town anymore. I take him supplies every once in a while."

"Did we live close to him?" I asked. My hands roamed over the floorboards, feeling for the sharp edge of a raised nail. Found one. Waited for the answer.

"No," Henry said, and I could almost hear him calculating distances in his head. "Your nearest neighbor would've been Mary. She lived a couple islands over from you. Her husband died in a logging accident, but she stayed on her island. She's got three kids, too." He shook his head in admiration.

There were other kids. I could've had friends. I wouldn't be so scared now. And then—*we might have survived.*

I hit the raised nail with the hammer, hard.

THE SHEETS

As summer approached, the talk of preparing for the new guests grew more heated.

"That chair in number two is so ratty," Colette said.

"It's Jerry's favorite," Henry countered. "He always says that's his place to sit after a day of fishing."

"It smells like it, too," Colette noted.

She planned a trip to the big city to pick up supplies. It was a long drive, and she would have to spend the night.

"Want to come along?" Colette asked me.

I looked up at her, horrified.

She laughed. "I'm going to stay in a hotel. Go to a restaurant." She said these things as if they could be enticing.

"No thank you."

"You know, Emmeline, you can't hide forever."

Apparently, she'd forgotten whose daughter I was.

Early the next morning, Colette got in the big, clanking truck and set off down the dirt road. She returned two days later with bags of sheets, bottles of cleaning supplies, and a chair that held the smell of plastic in the weave of its cloth. Henry helped her move it into number two the next morning, but he went straight out to his boat afterward.

"He'll be okay," Colette told me. "He just has to get his head around things. He's not one for change, but we need this and he knows it."

Out on the water, I heard the puttering engine cut off. I could barely see Henry sitting there, just beyond the cove, his head tilted toward the sky, his hand dipped toward the water. I knew just how he felt.

When the guests finally arrived, they brought chaos with them. The children ran and screamed; the grown-ups lounged and laughed. Henry got a young man from town to take over his deliveries, and now his boat was always full of people who wanted to go on bottle-hunting excursions, or do something they called *sightseeing*. Each time the boat returned, I would run to a spot where I could see the people disembarking, check their hands for red-wax bottles, but it appeared there were no more to be found.

Maybe the wax seals had cracked, the water slipped in. Maybe they'd made it down, down to the bottom. Maybe the one in my drawer was truly all that was left. Some days the thought brought me relief, other days panic. I kept it all inside. It was safer there.

Henry tried to be excited about all the activity at the resort, but I could see it wearing on him. Behind the scenes, Colette was a blur of action. At the end of each day, she and Henry would sit in their chairs in the living room, eyes dozing shut, until somebody banged on the front door and asked for soap or ice or complained about something called cell reception. Colette was right—the two of them couldn't do all this alone.

So I cleaned.

In spite of my apprehension, it wasn't a bad job. When guests checked out, I would go into their cottage, shut the door, and tidy up for the next group. Dodge would come with me and watch as I mopped the floors and changed the sheets. I didn't like the stuff I had to use for the floors, which smelled nothing like the pine tree on the bottle, but I enjoyed making the beds—it turned into a guessing game of sorts. As I took off the rumpled sheets, the smell of the people who had slept in them would lift up into the air. There was the round, almost sweet sweat smell of a child who had spent a day happily exploring, or the sharper-edged odor of one who'd gone to bed unhappy. With the bigger beds, I came to understand the way the scents of two people could mingle as effortlessly as rainwater, and to recognize the times they stayed apart, the smells resolutely separate. Sometimes there were those unreal perfumes, jumbling and talking too loudly—but underneath them I could always find the person. Sadness, like the dark purple juice of a blackberry. Fear, like the metallic taste of an oncoming storm. Love, which smelled like nothing so much as fresh bread. In an odd way, the game wasn't that different from reading the smells of our island. Scents were always about what was growing and what was dying. What would last through the next season. This was just with people instead of trees or flowers or dirt. Maybe I could read them after all. The thought gave me hope.

For the longer-term guests, I would go in once a week and change the sheets and towels while the occupants were out and about. Those cabins felt different, filled with belongings. A small red shoe under a bed, a bright blue hat with *Just Do It* written across its brim. Bottles and tubes sprawled across the bathroom counter. I read their labels—*sunscreen, pain reliever, anti-aging serum*—apparently my father wasn't the only one who kept magic in bottles.

There was something unsettling about being among other people's possessions. The lives in those rooms felt exposed. I thought again of our cabin as I had left it, the book of fairy tales dropped next to the chair, the pieces of my father's machine scattered across the floor, the empty scent-paper bottles. What story would they tell a stranger?

One morning late in the summer, I was in the yellow cottage, lifting up a pillow to take off its case, when underneath it I saw something pink, carefully folded. I picked it up to get it out of the way, and it loosened in my hands, draping down long and silky, releasing a scent of vanilla and cinnamon. Lingerie. I'd seen a beautiful woman on TV wearing something like it.

As I was standing there, trying to refold the slippery thing, the door opened. A woman stepped inside, freezing in place as she saw me.

"What are you doing with that?" she asked.

I dropped the nightgown and it floated to the floor like seaweed moving in the ocean.

"I was just changing the bed," I stammered. My skin was on fire.

"Give me that," she said, her face every bit as red as mine. As she came closer, I smelled the buttery-white scent of coconut, a hint of sweat. I picked up the silky thing and handed it to her, shaking. Even as I did so, my nose automatically inhaled again and I noticed something. There was no human scent on the fabric, no fragrance of dreams and warmth. They'd been here a week. It didn't make sense.

"I'm sorry," I said, "I'm sure it's still clean. I just swept the floor."

She looked at me. "I'm going to wear it, you know," she said. "It just hasn't been the right . . ." She stopped. "Oh, for God's sake, I'm not discussing this with you."

She went into the bathroom, locked the door. Turned on the water in the sink and let it run. I stood there for a moment, unsure of what to do. I didn't know what had happened, really, but the one thing I did understand was the scent of loneliness that waited beneath the coconut and sweat on her skin.

I finished making the bed, as neatly as I could. Later, when I knew she had gone, I slipped back into the cottage and left a wild rose on her pillow, pink against the white fabric.

The next morning I saw the woman and her husband, strolling along the boardwalk. Her hand was tucked in his arm, his head bent down toward hers. The rose was tucked in the brim of her straw hat.

A stupid smile overtook my face. Perhaps I *could* understand people after all. Perhaps school wouldn't be so bad.

I was wrong.

SCHOOL

The old truck clattered up the dirt road, and I watched as everything I knew slipped away with alarming rapidity. My fingers gripped the door handle and I could feel every jolt in my feet, my spine, my brain. The trees, tightly packed on both sides of the road, surged around us like breaking waves. We rounded a curve, and I gasped as I felt my body press against the door.

Colette glanced over at me. "I'm sorry," she said. "I was going to take you into town—get you used to everything before school started. But then the guests came, and . . ."

"It's so fast," I said, unsure whether I meant the truck or everything else.

Colette tapped at a circle on the panel in front of her. "Look," she said. "Not too bad."

The circle had a single pointer, hovering at fifteen. Fifteen was how many minutes there were in a quarter hour. More hours than half a day. Older than I was. What it had to do with a truck, I had no idea.

"It'll be smoother once we hit the main road," Colette added as the truck dipped into a rut with a gut-wrenching lurch.

When we finally reached the top of the hill, the woods disappeared. I looked down on an open bowl of land covered with stacks of what looked like sticks. When we got closer, I realized they were trees. Hundreds upon hundreds of them, stripped of their branches, piled up. I could smell the scent of sap and sawdust filling the air where once there had been branches, trunks, bark, green.

"What is that?" I asked Colette.

"The mill," she said. "It used to be a lot bigger."

I couldn't imagine *bigger*. My father and I had cut wood, certainly, but a tree at a time, and only when there were none that had not already fallen. This place looked like our lives after the bear was done with them.

Colette and I descended into the bowl, skirting its edge to the far side, where the dirt gave way to something smooth and black, and the wheels sighed in relief. Just like that, the sides of the road were lined in trees again, as if what we had just passed had never existed.

"Not too long now," Colette said.

We reached another break in the trees and there was the town of Port Hubbard, a set of dirty white buildings crowded together like barnacles on a rock. Colette ticked off names as we passed—grocery store, coffee shop, hardware store—as if they meant something to me. I let my eyes unfocus and everything became a blur. I wondered how long it would take to break off each barnacle of a store, let the trees come back.

"Here we are," Colette said a few moments later, forcing me back to the real world. I saw a patch of grass and a rectangular building with evenly spaced square windows. It was the most boring thing I had ever seen.

"All right," Colette said, and I could hear the extra brightness in her voice. "We've got an early appointment so we can get you settled in before the other students arrive. Shall we go meet the principal?"

No, I thought—but even I knew when a question wasn't a question.

"Okay," I said.

The principal's office was in the center of the building, its door almost hidden behind a tall counter, as if it didn't really want to be found.

"I'm sorry, but there's no money for special attention," the principal was saying to Colette. "I've got K through twelve here, all in one building, and more budget cuts than students. You say she just turned thirteen . . ."

On the first day of spring, I thought. Colette had brought in a cake one evening after dinner. There had been candles. She'd showed me the date on the calendar. I hadn't had the heart to tell her that Dodge and I had followed our noses to the edge of the woods and found violets two days before. I'd put my face in them and cried.

". . . that would put her in eighth grade," the principal was saying. "We'll start her there and see how it goes."

I sat in a chair, barely listening. I had learned that sometimes it was better to let go of words and listen to smells. The principal's were sturdy, unexceptional—scrambled eggs and soap that didn't have flowers in it.

"She's extraordinary . . ." Colette began.

"I'm sure she is," the principal replied.

I breathed in the scents of faded couch cushions, old tea and older grief, rough and dry as sandpaper. The principal tapped her pencil, looking up at the clock.

"Okay then," she said. "We'll take it from here."

Colette hesitated, looking at me. I had known she was going to leave, but the loss struck me suddenly. If I watched her go, I would break, so I shut my eyes hard.

"Emmeline?" Colette said. I kept them closed. "Maybe it's too soon . . . ?"

"She's thirteen years old. She'll be fine." The principal's voice was firm. There was a long silence.

Finally, I heard Colette stand. "I'll be back at the end of the day, Emmeline. You can tell me all about your adventures." I felt her hand, soft on the top of my head. Smelled the scents of coffee and fresh bread; felt them leave with her.

"Caroline," the principal called out, and I heard bustling footsteps behind me. "Can you take this young lady down to room seven?"

"Is she blind?" a woman's voice asked tentatively. I opened my eyes, stared at her.

"Oh!" she said, then recovered. "Well okay then, let's go."

⁓

We went down a hall that smelled of hot oil and potatoes. The corridor was easily three times as wide as any of the wooded paths on our island, but I felt the walls closing in on me all the same.

After about forty paces, the woman opened a door on the right, and ushered me in. The room was square and white, with narrow windows along one side and a big black desk at the front. Facing the desk were rows of strange little tables, each one attached to a seat like the shell of a hermit crab.

"Sit anywhere you'd like," the woman said. "The others will be in soon." She put a piece of paper on the big black desk and left.

I went to the back row and slid into a chair in the corner, waiting. After a few minutes, I could hear voices bouncing off one another and starting to fill the halls. The door opened and in came a flood of noise and bodies. Boys, long limbed and smelling of sweat and too much energy. Girls, drenched in lemon or flowers or strawberries, except the scents weren't actually any of those things. They were like the saturated colors I'd seen in magazines. Too sweet. Too strong. It made me rub my nose.

"Whatcha doing, new girl?" A boy stood next to my desk. "Going on a booger hunt?"

I didn't know what he meant, but the odor that came off him was like the flare of a match, tight and excited. In my mind, I could almost hear Dodge's low growl of warning.

⁓

The room filled up, girls and boys jostling for seats. The match boy sat in front of me, scooting his desk back so I had to pull my feet in, but the chair next to me stayed empty. The teacher arrived, a thin, brisk woman with dark eyes.

"All right," she said, inhaling on the word. "Welcome back, everybody. We all know each other by now. Are we ready for another year?"

I heard muffled groans. The teacher picked up the paper the other woman had left on the desk and scanned the room.

"Emma*leen*?" the teacher said. I watched the others, waiting. "Emma*leen*," she repeated, walking up one of the aisles and stopping when she reached me. "We don't have time for games here. You're supposed to answer when I call your name."

"That's not my name," I said, confused.

"What is your name, then?"

"Emme*line*. Like *Once upon a time, Emmeline*." I could see my father's smile, hear his voice, rolling around the rhyme.

There was a burst of laughter. I looked about, startled by the wide, un-believing faces of the kids in the seats.

"Weirdo," the boy in front of me said. The words invaded the memory, curled its edges.

"That's enough, Dylan," the teacher said sharply. She turned to me. "All right, Emme*line*," and she pulled out that last syllable like it was a potato stuck in the ground, "now that we've had our pronunciation class, can we start our school year?"

I slipped deeper into my chair, staring at her back as she returned to her desk.

I had thought, perhaps, I could handle school. I'd read people's scents like I'd read the bedsheets in the cottages and everything would be okay. But that room was filled with so many smells, so many needs and fears and secrets. The teachers cycled through—math and English and history—and I tried to listen to what they were saying, but the words had to make their way through all the other messages floating in the air, and I couldn't concentrate. The teachers asked me questions, and the glee of the boy in front of me grew with each of my fumbled responses. Finally they gave up.

"We'll let you settle in," they said, one after another, and even in the clamor of scents I could smell their disappointment.

At lunchtime, when the other kids shouted their way down the hall toward the odor of hot oil and potatoes, I turned my head in the opposite direction. I caught the scent of grass and followed it outside. I saw small children, climbing on something that looked like a metal memory of trees. To one side was a row of the blue-green plants that grew in front of the boardinghouse—*rosemary*, Henry had taught me. I went over and sat down, letting their fragrance sweep the morning away.

Please don't make me go back inside. Please don't make me go back inside.

I wanted to run, to find the road, a boat, go back to the island. I didn't care what was or wasn't there. I just wanted the silence of the trees, the comfort of my loft.

One of the girls from my class walked across the playground toward me, half a sandwich in her hand.

"Hey," she said, sitting down, smiling, "where are you from?"

I couldn't read her well; she was one of the strawberry girls—the smell seeming to come from her lips. The cloying sweetness took over the air like a wave of pollen.

"Secret Cove," I said.

"Before that," she prompted. When I didn't say anything, she lowered her voice.

"Everybody knows you came from the islands. What was it like?" Her eyes were bright as she leaned forward, but she didn't look dangerous. I inhaled deeply, searching for the scent of who she really was.

"What're you doing?" the girl asked, pulling back.

My thoughts scrambled. Panicked, I picked a sprig of the rosemary.

"Here," I said, offering it to her.

"What?"

"You can rub it between your hands." I fumbled. "It'll balance out the pink."

"What?"

"The strawberry . . ."

"You're telling me I smell bad?" The girl stood up. It was strange, I realized—anger was actually a good counterbalance to pink, too.

"Sorry for trying to be nice, freak," she said.

And then she was gone.

I sat there, shaking, until the bell rang and a teacher rounded up the smaller children.

"Do you know where you're going, honey?" she asked me, and I could have cried at the softness in her voice.

She took me with her, leaving me at my room. I didn't realize my mistake until I saw the other students look up from their desks and notice the little kids in the doorway. I saw the strawberry girl lean over and say something to the boy next to her. I heard the whispers running up and down the aisles of the classroom like gritty sand through my fingers. Saw the grins.

"How was it?" Colette asked that afternoon when she picked me up.

I looked at her face, still tired from the summer. I smelled the damp wool scent of worry. I couldn't go back to the island, I knew that; Colette and Henry were all I had. What would happen if I became too much for them?

"Fine," I said. "It was fine."

FISHER

In the second week of school, the red-haired boy appeared.

"Look who came out of the woods!" the kids chorused as he entered the room.

The boy ducked his head and walked quickly to the only available seat, the one next to me. He sat down, and I saw that he wore long sleeves, even though the day was hot for September and most of the kids had on T-shirts. I could smell nervousness on him, but beneath that was the scent of alderwood smoke, clean and honest.

The boy looked over and saw me watching him. He watched me back for a moment, and then he cocked his head. His eyes were astonishingly green. Like trees in the spring.

"I'm Fisher," he whispered.

"Emmeline."

He didn't laugh. I smiled. It was as simple as that.

⌒

Like me, Fisher was an almost silent presence in the classroom, but his silence was the most active I'd ever seen. He was like a squirrel or a mouse—constantly watching everything around him. It was a skill he took with him wherever he went. I knew what that was like, although I used my nose instead of my eyes.

"What do you see?" I asked as we sat on the side of the playground one day during lunch. We'd found it was easier to be outside—anywhere, really, except the cafeteria, which felt like a beach full of hungry seagulls. It was there that I'd learned Fisher was a year behind.

"He's so slow he can't even make it to school half the time," Dylan had joked. Fisher had turned red. I felt sorry for him, but a part of me swelled with relief to find someone else who was odd like me.

Now Fisher pointed over to the swing set on the playground. A little girl was working her legs hard, but not getting much momentum. A boy about her age was waiting, shifting his weight from side to side.

"That boy there is going to shove the girl on the swing."

"How do you know?"

"Look at his mouth."

The little boy's lip curled, just on one side.

"Now check out his hand."

I looked. At the boy's hip, his hand curled into a fist. I caught a whiff of something, sharp and hungry.

"I can smell it," I said. "I mean, I can see it."

The boy pushed the girl and sent her sprawling. She started crying, and the teacher came over, dusting her off and ushering her away. The boy sat on the swing and started pumping his legs.

"The teacher's scared of him," Fisher said. Then, "What do the smells tell you?" he asked abruptly.

I listened, but heard only curiosity in his voice.

"Everything," I said finally.

Fisher nodded.

"You know, I found one of those bottles once," he said. "The ones on the beaches?"

I didn't move.

"I smelled something on the paper, but nobody else believed me."

My heart beat fast and heavy at the same time. "What did it smell like?"

"Like nowhere I'd ever been." A faint smile crossed his face.

Red wax, I thought.

I tried to calm my breathing. He'd smelled what no one else could. I couldn't tell him how the bottles got in the water, not without explaining a lot of other things I didn't want anyone to know, but I basked in the knowledge that here was someone who thought the way I did.

"What happened to the bottle?" I asked.

"My father took it." Fisher shrugged. "He said I wrecked its value by opening it."

It was becoming apparent that my scattered academic background was going to cause a lot of trouble for the teachers. Add to that my utter abhorrence of participating, and most of them found it easier to ignore me, which suited me just fine. The one exception to this rule was the science teacher, Ms. Boyd, who seemed to have taken it as her personal mission to make me feel special—which, of course, only made things worse with the other kids.

One Monday she came into the classroom, the smell of excitement buzzing on her skin.

"We're going to travel to France today," she said, "and learn about some truly amazing animals." She looked all the way to the back of the room, found my eyes, and smiled.

"They have some of the best noses in the world," she continued. "They can find truffles, hidden underground."

"What's a truffle?" one of the kids asked.

"It's a kind of mushroom."

"We have mushrooms all over the place." Dylan was unimpressed.

"This is a special kind," Ms. Boyd said. "Just this year, a single two-pound truffle sold for three hundred and thirty thousand U.S. dollars. See how important a good nose is?"

There was a collective gasp in the classroom. Again, Ms. Boyd smiled at me. I took in the warmth of it, pulled it close.

"What kind of animals?" Dylan asked, leaning back in his chair.

Ms. Boyd opened a big book and held it up. I couldn't quite see the illustration.

"Is that a *pig*?" said the strawberry girl, turning and staring at me with jaw-gaping delight. I'd hoped she would forget our encounter on the playground, but it was clear that wasn't going to happen.

Ms. Boyd realized her mistake, but there was nothing she could do. From that point on, I was *Miss Piggy. Dirt Sniffer.* Snuffles and snorts followed me down the hall and haunted my chair in the classroom. By the end of the week, it felt as if there was nowhere I could go.

"I know a good place," Fisher said that Friday.

At lunchtime, he took me down the corridor and opened a door that said *Library.* I saw rows of books, rising to the ceiling like drawers of secrets.

"Oh," I said, relaxing for the first time since Miss Piggy had entered my life, and Fisher smiled.

"Let me show you the computer," he said, and led me over to a row of three boxes with screens like a television. Fisher sat down in front of one and his fingers typed out a series of letters. The word *Google* came up in front of us.

"Look," he said. "Magic." He entered the word *cat* and then he showed me images and movies of cats and puppies until a woman came over and told him that the computers were for research, and we reluctantly allowed ourselves to be ushered away.

That weekend, the computer was pretty much all I thought about. Here was a machine more magical, more powerful, than my father's. It didn't have scents, but like them it could take me anywhere, and unlike them or television, I got to say where I wanted to go.

I had almost given up on the idea of ever learning anything more about my father, or where I came from. Now, however, I saw a chance.

⌒

Fisher wasn't in school Monday morning. I hadn't realized how much I counted on the emotional armor of his friendship until it wasn't there, and by midday, I was overwhelmed. I threw my lunch in the trash and fled to the library.

Other kids were on the computers, so I had to wait. I wandered through the aisles of books, stopping in the little kids' section, when I saw several books of fairy tales laid out on a low table. I checked every cover, looking for gold writing, for the princess and the crumpled man, but none of them was the one I had grown up with. Even so, it was calming to be near the volumes—though I knew that if anybody from my class saw me, I'd have even more to contend with.

When a computer was finally available, I went over and looked at its blank screen. It reminded me of the time my father had given me my own scent-paper. I hadn't known what it meant, what it could do. I'd learned what I needed to know by playing scientist.

Eliminate the variables, Emmeline.

I typed in my name. The first thing I saw was the title of a book: *Emmeline, the Orphan of the Castle*, but it had been written hundreds of years ago. There was an image, of a woman with a stern chin and dark eyes— but she'd lived a long time ago, too, in another country.

The only thing left was the meaning of my name: *work*, and somehow that didn't surprise me at all.

What else could I try? *Jack? John?* I typed in *scent-paper*, but all that gave me was something called do-it-yourself craft ideas that involved steeping paper in tea leaves and water. I tried *whale bones* but that became a different science lesson quickly enough.

I needed more. A clue. One good word—but I didn't have it.

Fisher was back in school that afternoon. I was going to tell him what I'd been doing, but I realized it would be difficult without revealing what I was looking for. I wasn't ready to risk the possibility that he would find it all too strange and no longer want to be my friend.

He was quieter than usual, and when he was taking notes I saw that he held his hand in an awkward position.

"Where were you?" I asked him as we were leaving school. "What happened to your hand?"

"Got caught in a doorjamb," he said. "Stupid, huh?"

There was something about his voice that made me want to ask more questions, but before I could, I heard footsteps behind us.

"Hey, Miss Piggy," Dylan said, coming up next to me. He snorted and pawed the toe of his shoe in the ground.

"Stop it," Fisher said, his voice tight.

Dylan tugged on one of my curls. "They even look like pig's tails."

I didn't move.

"Want to smell my shit, Piggy?" Dylan said, tugging again, harder.

"Don't touch her." Fisher's words were so hot that the air around them seemed to smoke.

"Whoa," Dylan said, stepping back.

"Just leave her the *fuck* alone. All of you."

Whatever had come over Fisher retreated quickly, and while it scared me, at least no one touched me after that—not physically, anyway. Nothing could stop the snorts and snuffles and whispers, however. I was too tempting a target, even with Fisher nearby.

The rumors didn't stop, either; they just changed. My father had been a disgraced politician. He was an escaped murderer with a thing for children.

I was a kidnap victim, a clone he was protecting from evil government researchers, a changeling.

The kids threw the rumors out like lit matches, to see what would catch. I stayed silent, listening to the fizz and spark of their words, pretending I was water, putting them out.

IN THE WOODS

Colette took a shine to Fisher. That's what she called it—*taking a shine*. It made sense; I'd seen the way she rubbed her one silver vase until the dark smudges left and the bright came through. She was like that with Fisher, too.

"You live near us, don't you?" she'd said the first time they met, as she was picking me up after school. Before the term began, there had been talk of my taking the bus, but she was still there, every day. It was yet another thing for the kids to tease me about, but I didn't care. That truck, and Colette inside it, meant safety at the end of the day, and I was grateful for it.

"Yes, ma'am," Fisher said. "My dad keeps his fishing boat in your cove."

Colette looked at him more closely. "Is your dad Frank?" she asked.

"No, ma'am. Martin."

"Oh," she said, her eyebrows rising slightly. She put the key in the ignition and then turned back to him. "Would you like a ride to our place, Fisher?" she asked. His nod was accompanied by a smile.

After that, he came home with us almost every afternoon, and I noticed Colette baking more than usual. Cardamom rolls. Oatmeal cookies. A spice cake, as fall settled heavily around us, pressing the flowers back into the ground with sheets of rain.

"I'm just trying out recipes for next summer's guests," she said.

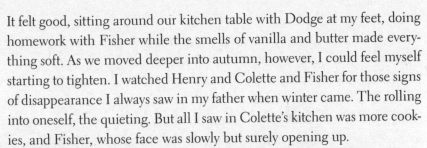

It felt good, sitting around our kitchen table with Dodge at my feet, doing homework with Fisher while the smells of vanilla and butter made everything soft. As we moved deeper into autumn, however, I could feel myself starting to tighten. I watched Henry and Colette and Fisher for those signs of disappearance I always saw in my father when winter came. The rolling into oneself, the quieting. But all I saw in Colette's kitchen was more cookies, and Fisher, whose face was slowly but surely opening up.

He helped me with history; I helped him with science. He taught me how to write a paper; I told him stories from my father's books. Whatever had held Fisher back in school, it clearly wasn't his brain. For my part, I caught up with the other kids in class. I still never raised my hand or answered a question, but I was passing my tests, which narrowed my problems down to the other students.

There were times—like when a kid would pass by me, pulling up the front of her nose to make it look like a pig's snout, or when another one started an answer in history class with a casually innocent *once upon a time*—that I hated my father for what he'd made me. A freak. The girl who lived through her nose. I'd loved our island, believed in the wonder of its smells and bottles. But I had come to understand that my father had created that world—and now I fit nowhere else.

I didn't know how to sit still for six hours. I didn't understand eye shadow, or tampons, or the way the girls could giggle their way into a boy's consciousness. I knew how to wash my hair with a single cup of water, and cook tiny crabs in hot oil—and now I felt like one, every day.

It's your fault, Papa.

"I'm no good at this," I told Fisher after the twentieth time I stupidly responded to a gesture of friendship, only to have it snatched away in a burst of laughter.

"Watch their faces," he said. "Never trust a smile that doesn't make it to their eyes."

"How do you know all this?" I asked.

"How do you know how to smell?"

"I learned."

He shrugged. "Me, too."

The exchange was not uncommon—we talked about everything except where we came from. Every afternoon, Fisher left Colette and Henry's home promptly at four thirty and headed up the path through the woods, but in all those months he never once invited me to his house and I never asked to go. Ours was a friendship built on instinct; we were young enough to think our pasts didn't matter. Or maybe we just didn't want them to.

I was wrong about a lot of things back then.

Bit by bit, the days grew longer. When we were done with homework, Fisher and I would play cards, or take Dodge exploring around the cove, Fisher in his brown cloth coat, me in my red rain jacket. The air would be filled with the scent of new leaves and the hope of more light. We'd wander down the boardwalk, Dodge checking out the waterlogged smells, while Fisher and I looked in the windows of every cottage, and I told him about the guests who stayed there.

Each time we went a little farther, until one day we passed the boarding-house and arrived at the blue building where the big white bones hung from the ceiling. Since my conversation with Henry, I hadn't gone inside the whale museum. I didn't know what I thought about it. All I knew was that it never felt like answers.

I watched as Fisher peered in through a window, his hands cupped around his eyes so he could see better. His red hair was a burst of color against the white skin of his neck; he looked like a bird, all concentration and quick curiosity.

"Are those whale bones?" he asked, turning to me, his face alight.

Dodge nudged at my hand, and I opened the door to let us inside. The curved bones shifted in the breeze, ethereal, otherworldly. I waited to see Fisher's reaction.

"It's like a fairy tale in here," he said, gazing up. "It's amazing."

I didn't realize I'd been holding my breath until I let it out. The smell came in with my next inhalation, and it felt as close to home as I'd been in months.

                                                      ~

When we weren't exploring the boardwalk, we'd go along the tide line, or up into the woods. On one such day, Fisher led me off the trail, farther into the forest. He picked up a downed cedar bough and handed it to me. I could feel the caress of its fanlike foliage.

"Find as many of these as you can," he said. "Branches, too."

"Why?"

"You'll see."

The winter storms had left us plenty of material. We gathered a stack of boughs and another of branches. With practiced efficiency, Fisher took the branches and arranged them into something that looked like a little triangular house, lower in the back than the front. He took some of the boughs and layered them to make a deep carpet inside, then took the rest and laid them across the branches to form a roof.

"What do you think?" he asked, stepping back.

"It's beautiful," I said.

We crawled inside, the scent of sap and cedar all around us.

"It's like a nest for people," I said. "You could sleep in here."

"Why did you say that?" he blurted out. He sounded angry.

"I'm sorry," I said, confused. I waited for him to say something else, but his earlier excitement had gone quiet.

"Did you know that trees talk to each other through their roots?" I asked after a while. I held the words out like an offer, a door, but he didn't say a word. We sat in silence, letting the green in the air heal what it could.

                                                      ~

Later, Fisher set off up the trail into the woods, and I headed down to the cove. I was about halfway back when I heard heavy footsteps. We'd left Dodge behind that day because his hip had been bothering him, and the lack of his familiar, watchful presence hit me sharply. Maybe it was just Henry coming to find me, I told myself; I was getting home later than usual. Still, I stepped off the trail, behind a tree, and pulled my red rain jacket tighter around myself.

The footsteps drew nearer, then stopped.

"I know you're there," said a voice, deep and amused.

I emerged slowly and saw a man with a clean-cut beard and hair so dark it looked like the underside of the sea. He wore tall fisherman's boots and a thick rain slicker. A lingering odor of gasoline surrounded him, sharp and yellow.

There's only one fisherman who uses gas instead of diesel, I thought, wishing again for Dodge.

"You're Henry's girl?" the man asked.

I nodded, inhaling, searching for clues, but the smell of gasoline was blocking everything else.

Do what Fisher told you. Watch his face.

"Funny we haven't met," the man said. He held out his hand. "I'm Martin."

"Fisher's father?" I asked.

"Yes," he said. I saw a smile travel slowly up his cheeks, almost to his eyes. Almost.

Never trust a smile that doesn't make it to their eyes, Fisher always said.

Martin stood there, waiting, his hand outstretched. I shook it, stiffly, then stepped back so he could pass me on the trail. When he moved on through the woods, I turned and bolted back to the cove.

THE RESORT

Though I never spoke to Fisher about my encounter with his father, I found myself noticing things I hadn't before. The way he checked the clock as we sat at the table doing homework. The way he hurried out the door and up the hill as soon as we heard the sound of the returning fishing boats.

I knew what it was like to be constantly aware of your father, but there was a difference between me and Fisher. I'd been scared for my father, for what might happen to us, but I had never been scared *of* him.

"What would you think about working here this summer?" Colette asked Fisher one afternoon. "We've got more guests coming this year, and we're going to need some extra hands."

For a moment I saw excitement in his eyes, but then he looked out the window at the harbor. "I don't know," he said.

"We'd pay you, of course," Colette said.

"I'll ask," he said, but he didn't sound hopeful.

His father came to the front door the next afternoon. Fisher had already left for home.

I smelled the gasoline odor even before Martin arrived and sprinted to my bedroom, where I stood in my doorway, listening. Dodge pushed himself to his feet and went to stand next to Colette as she opened the door. I pulled my head back out of sight.

Their voices were low, too low for me to make out the words, but I could feel them. Colette's, soft as flour. Martin's, like the sounds of footsteps bent on a destination. Back and forth they went, two, three, five times, until finally I heard the smile that wasn't a smile in Martin's voice and the front door closed.

I came out of hiding. Colette turned and saw me; her eyes were fierce, but pleased.

"Great news," she said. "Looks like Fisher will be joining us this summer."

School finally ended, and the relief I felt could have filled a whole sky. I had three full months of freedom, and I didn't even care if they were filled with resort guests. I was away from the rumors, the tests, the small brown bags left on my desk, always with a note in different handwriting: *smell this.* I had learned not to open them.

By the end of the first week of summer, Fisher and I were a brilliantly efficient cottage-cleaning team. I mopped floors while he cleaned bathrooms; we changed the sheets together. We could be in and out of a cottage in half an hour. We worked so harmoniously that we barely needed words. Most of the guests assumed we were brother and sister, although we didn't look at all alike.

With two pairs of hands doing the work, we had time to help Colette in other ways. She'd decided to start selling coffee and baked goods, and so our mornings started early, with yeast and cinnamon and cardamom. The guests would come and knock on the kitchen window with a mug from their cottage, and we'd fill it with steaming coffee, handing over warm rolls wrapped in paper napkins. I loved watching their faces relax as the aromas reached them.

In the afternoons, when our cleaning rounds were done, Fisher and I worked on Colette's vegetable garden. We would dig and weed, and I would smell life growing again.

"We are mighty growers of food, Emmeline!" Fisher would say, holding up vegetables like trophies. "We will eat like kings."

It was the happiest I had been since the time I believed in fairy tales and my father was my hero. I did my best not to remember that I would have to go back to school. But as with all things I tried to ignore, fall came too soon. I stepped out of Colette's truck that first day of classes, and it was as if a tide receded around me, leaving me exposed once again.

I had hoped that the summer might temper the kids' desire to torment me, but when that didn't happen I tried to make myself small, unremarkable. I learned to keep my curls short, my eyes down. I never went in the cafeteria, and I avoided the bathroom at all costs.

I crossed off each school day on my calendar, and threw it away in June.

Summer. School. Summer. School. Time and tide moving in and out with the years. I was fifteen, then sixteen. The bullying never changed, although the methods did. The ubiquity of technology had found its way even to our little edge of the world. Some of the kids had gotten cell phones, and rumors and teasing, once the domain of notes and whispers, could now travel at lightning speed. I would sit at my desk and watch their fingers, tapping underneath their desks. Feel the insults flickering through the air.

Dylan had managed to keep his seat assignment, just in front of mine, and as his body grew, he expanded farther and farther into the space around him. His legs stretched across the aisle, blocking my access, while his eyes took their time with my body. Assessing. Approving of one part, not of another. His jokes thickened, took on the stench of hormones and hair gel.

He would whisper them to me when Fisher wasn't around. When it came to those taunts, it was as if we had a pact, Dylan and I. Neither of us wanted Fisher to hear them.

"Can you smell what I've got for you, Miss Piggy?" Dylan would say, his voice low and grinning, his hand reaching down under his desk, toward his lap, making sure my eyes followed. He'd say the nickname like an endearment, made intimate by years of repetition. I hated it.

Fisher was my sanctuary, but things were shifting there, too. One afternoon, as he was helping Henry fix a leaky cottage roof, I noticed muscles in Fisher's arms that hadn't been there before. His voice had deepened. He'd always smelled like trees, but now the scent was more roots than sap. Even as I shied away from Dylan, I found myself yearning for Fisher, wanting to tangle myself up in the fragrance of him. It was confusing as much as anything.

The resort had kept changing, too, more and faster each year. Though the media had long ago forgotten the mysterious bottles, Secret Cove had its own momentum now, and by my fourth summer it was barely recognizable. There was a small grocery store and four more cottages. The whale bones had been donated to a museum, and the old warehouse converted into a restaurant that smelled of fish and chips. The boardinghouse provided summer lodging for the young men and women who cooked and waited tables. Henry no longer took people out on sightseeing trips; a company called Wild Blue Adventures started leasing dock space and offering whale and grizzly bear excursions, and a kayaking group led expeditions to the smaller islands. Day-tour buses pulled up regularly at noon, unloading their human cargo.

"No damn reception," I heard the tourists say, one after another, cell phones lifted high, as if offering landing spots for small birds. They would meander down the boardwalk, checklists in hand—*see a live whale/bear/ salmon; paddle a kayak*. They ate at the restaurant, went out on boats, took pictures of themselves, and left. At the end of each day, our numbers were reduced to only those people staying at the resort, and relative quiet descended. I remembered my first summer at the cove, when the cottage guests had terrified me. Now I was relieved when it was only them.

Most of the young men and women who worked at the resort were college students from the bigger cities, looking for a summer adventure. On their days off, they would go out in the kayaks, voices clear and confident as they called out to one another. They didn't pay much attention to me and Fisher—we were still in high school, local, and always stuck to ourselves, anyway—but I was fascinated by the ease of them. They were sea creatures that swam through life; they didn't cower, waiting for the peck of sharp beaks like I did.

The summer I was seventeen, Colette hired a girl with long blond hair and an easy smile. She came from the big city, and carried the shine of foreign places. Everyone was in love with her.

"You live here, don't you?" she asked me one day as I was coming out of a cottage, my arms full of sheets.

"Yes," I said, not sure if that was a good answer.

"You're lucky," she said. "It's beautiful." We heard the sounds of the boys coming out of the boardinghouse, heading for the restaurant.

"What's the city like?" I asked, trying to hold her there. She carried the scents of sunshine and apples, and I wanted to stay near them.

"The city? It's big and fast, but you can do whatever you want. There are so many people, you can just get lost." She smiled. "In a good way, eh?"

The boys looked our way, and called out. "Jessie, you're gonna be late!"

"Gotta go," she said to me, and jogged off down the boardwalk. The effortless motion reminded me of someone, and it took me a while before I realized: Jack the Scent Hunter.

How long had it been since I'd thought of him? How long since I'd thought I could be like that myself? I could barely remember the feeling, and yet there it was, lingering like a scent caught inside the pages of a book, waiting.

Colette had handled the resort's expansion with equanimity, even enthu-
siasm. Henry was a different matter. He seemed to become less himself
with each summer season, each busload of tourists. Colette watched him
carefully.

"Jeff says he can't do the deliveries to the islands anymore," she said over
coffee one morning. "What do you think about taking them on again, old
man? It's only once every couple of weeks. We've got a boardinghouse full
of young folks who can keep the resort going while you're out on the water."

Henry sipped his coffee, but I could see he was thinking.

"You could take Emmeline," Colette added.

Henry shot me a quick, troubled look. "Emmeline lives here now," he
said firmly. "She doesn't have to go anywhere."

Their words bounced back and forth, as if I wasn't there in the middle
of them, and suddenly I was so tired of everybody talking about me. Island
Girl. Miss Piggy. The Girl that Henry Saved. For years now, I'd been scared
of so many things. I'd made myself as small and invisible as possible, and yet
there was a time in my life when I'd climbed to the top of the tallest trees,
searching for scents on the wind. When I'd foraged and known every plant
on my island. When I had been a scent hunter.

"I'll go," I blurted out.

The kitchen was quiet for a moment.

"Fisher, too, then," Henry said. I wasn't sure if I was offended or relieved.

"Please," I said to Fisher as we changed the sheets in one of the cottages.

"No," he said. He tossed a clean pillowcase toward me.

"He won't take me unless you go, too." I didn't say, *I don't know what
I'm doing.* I didn't say, *I'm scared to go without you.*

"It's not . . ." he started.

"Please," I said.

I didn't know what I was asking for, but he gave it anyway.

THE END OF SUMMER

A few days later, we set off in Henry's boat, a small vessel, maybe fifteen feet long and open to the sky. The weather was calm and clear, the islands tiny in the distance. Henry stood at the front, his hands on the wheel, glowing with the joy of being out on the water. Fisher stood next to him, and I watched his body relax, lighten with each mile away from the cove.

I sat on the bench seat, feeling panic lapping at my feet, getting ready to rise up and roll over me. I'd told myself I was ready to go back to the islands. I had thought I'd forgotten the day Henry brought me to Secret Cove. My body remembered, though, and as we entered the strait and the boat began to buck its way through the currents, I felt my breathing turn shallow. I smelled the diesel, the cold water, the biting scent of fast air, and suddenly I was twelve again, curled tight in the bottom of the boat as we flew across the waves, away from everything I knew.

You'll be okay, little one. Henry's voice, calling out to me over the roar of the motor. *Hang in there.*

Little lark, I'd wanted to tell him, but I hadn't, and nobody had ever called me that again.

I faced away from the exhaust, opening my lungs, forcing in clean, salty air. *This is what now smells like*, I told myself. I let Henry and Fisher's conversation fade while I watched the islands in the distance. Slowly but surely they grew closer, rising out of the water, veiled in evergreens. I could feel the pull of them deep in my muscles. I wanted this place with every fiber of my being, and I was scared of it in equal measure.

After more than an hour, we left the chop of the strait and the rocking of the boat calmed. We slipped into an intricate maze of gray and green islands, their sides steep around us. White birds flew over our heads, then wheeled about and disappeared. The only sound was our engine.

After a while, Henry took a right turn down a slim passage and throttled back on the motor until we were barely coasting. The surface of the water quieted into a mirror; it looked as if we were moving through two worlds, with trees living equally above and below the surface. A seal head emerged, and its liquid brown eyes watched us pass. I could smell magic in the air again, and I wanted to sob with the relief and pain of it.

This is who you are, the trees said.

"Oh," I said, so low I didn't think it was even a sound.

After that, we went out every couple weeks or so to do the deliveries, and every time I looked for my island, desperate to see it, not wanting to see it at the same time. I noticed that Henry seemed to take us close to every rocky outcropping but mine, as if my island was a heat source you had to approach slowly, getting used to the temperature before you touched it. Sometimes that made me frustrated, but mostly I was relieved. I needed the time.

Something was happening to me on those trips. At school, even at the cove, my senses were always sharp, spiky, alert to every buzz of a machine, every nuance of conversation. I could feel the grate and shred of them. But when Henry aimed the prow of his boat toward the islands and the sky opened up in front of us, all of that changed. I could feel my mind lighten.

With miles of nothing but water in front of me, my thoughts expanded, slowed, gaining altitude without speed. I could track a whale by a far-off disturbance on the surface; I could feel the day move across my skin. And I could smell. Oh, I could smell.

"Look!" I'd say to Fisher, pointing out an eagle's nest high in a tree, or a group of sea stars clinging to an underwater rock. But then in the next instant my nose would pick up the scent of cedar wood smoke in the distance, or I would see a steep gray cliff that looked like my bluff, and I would fall into memories. My father—working at our table, watching the bear from the window, swimming away from me. I'd step out of my body, and the world would disappear.

Fisher and Henry let me work through it on my own. Henry focused on teaching Fisher how to navigate tides, how to hear when the boat was low on fuel or the motor was skipping. The sight of them standing next to one another at the wheel was my lodestar.

"You doing okay, Em?" Fisher asked one day as we were tying up the boat.

For something was happening between us, too. When we were out on the water, we spoke in gestures more than words, his hand on my arm, his breath on my cheek. Out there, in the midst of all that air, our scents wove together and had their own conversations. It was as if the more space we had, the less we needed it between each other. I remembered the way Colette's voice had sounded when she'd talked about meeting Henry—the love so simple and easy. I thought I'd never know anything like that. But here it was.

It wasn't until the second to last day of summer vacation that Henry took us past the entrance to a narrow, steep-sided channel that curved quickly out of sight.

"That's it," Henry said, watching me closely. "That's your island."

"How do you get in?" Fisher asked, looking at the frothing water.

"You have to time it just right," Henry said, turning to him. "You can only get through at the highest slack tide of a full moon, and you can't do it in a boat any bigger than this." His voice warmed with the pride of his accomplishment. "You only get one chance a month, maybe two in the summer when it's light longer. Winter's almost impossible."

I thought of my father, trying to swim through that chaos—if he'd even made it to the channel at all—and felt the unintended punch of Henry's words in my stomach.

My fault.

I stared at that entrance and thought of the lagoon inside it, the beach that no one had run across for years. The berries growing heavy on the bushes. The cabin waiting at the end of the trail.

"It's like a fortress," Fisher said, marveling.

"Does anybody live here now?" My words came out cracked and strange.

"No," Henry said. "No one's touched it."

You poor thing, I thought. *Left here all alone.* I could feel the pull of it, like a hand grabbing mine. *Come find me.*

"It's just a couple days until the full moon," Fisher said. He sent me a look of careful inquiry.

"Another time," Henry said with a smile. "You'll be back in school by then."

Even after all these years, the prospect of school still filled me with dread. I looked at my island, and suddenly all I wanted was to be there, hidden among the trees.

It was later than usual when we started our return to the resort. Henry had taken a long, slow circle around the group of islands that surrounded mine, as if understanding I needed the time.

Fisher, however, grew increasingly anxious as the afternoon faded. When Henry handed over the wheel, he pointed the boat toward the cove and sent it flying across the waves.

We were almost to the cove's entrance when I saw a fishing boat coming in, the scent of gasoline heavy on the wind. Fisher shot it a quick look and throttled up the engine, but the boat had a clear view of us. I saw Martin at the wheel, saw the astonishment and anger on his face as he stared at his son.

"Fisher," I asked, "did he know . . . ?"

Fisher shook his head.

We got to our mooring spot first. Fisher was out of the boat and heading up the hill before I even had a chance to say good-bye. Henry watched him go, concern in his eyes.

The other boat docked.

"Martin," Henry said, as Fisher's father walked up the dock toward us. He said nothing as he passed, but I smelled an odor, bitter as burnt coffee, trailing in the air behind him.

Fisher didn't come to the resort the following day. Colette tried calling his house, but there was no answer.

"He's probably just grounded," she said, but I could hear her hesitation.

It was the last day of the season. School started the next day. The guests and the summer kids who worked at the resort were gone, leaving Colette and me with the insurmountable task of getting all the cottages buttoned up for winter.

"We can't get to it all today," Colette said. "But let's see what we can do."

Without Fisher, I had my hands full. I didn't have much time to think, and to be honest, I didn't want to. The odor of burnt coffee and gasoline lingered in the back of my mind, even as I spent the day in a fog of pine-scented cleaners and laundry detergent. I made my way through one cottage after another, trying to focus only on the work in front of me. I didn't want to think about school. I didn't want to think about Fisher. If he was in trouble it was because of me. I was the one who made him go out on the boat in the first place. He hadn't wanted to, and he'd tried to tell me, but I hadn't listened.

I finished the red cottage and moved on to the blue one. The guests had left the kind of mess that I knew meant there would be no tip in the envelope on the dresser. There had been young children, and I found toothpaste on every surface in the bathroom, even some on the bedroom wall. In the kitchen, there were pots on the stove with two-day-old macaroni and cheese stuck to the bottom. There were more dirty dishes in the sink, in the bedroom. Mismatched socks were hidden under the chair cushion and left sopping wet in the bathtub. I had learned better than to throw them out—these were the type of people who always called the next day: *Son bereft. Favorite socks. Please send.* No offer to pay for postage.

But they'd left something else, too.

I was shoving my mop under the bed with more vigor than necessary when it hit something and sent it sliding. I crossed to the other side and spotted the corner of a hardbound book, saw a bit of flowing white dress on the cover. Heart racing, I bent down and pulled it out from under the bed. There was the princess and the crumpled man. The gold lettering—*Fairy Tales from Around the World.*

My book.

As I ran my hands over its surface, however, I realized that this was a newer copy. I flipped through the pages, the edges flowing smoothly across the pad of my thumb. Some muscle memory seemed to scream at the change.

There was no gap in the middle.

I didn't move, as if the book were a rabbit that might startle and run. Carefully, I reopened it, checking each story until I found the one I had never seen before. I sat down on the floor with my back against the bed, and began to read.

THE NIGHTINGALE

Once upon a time, there was a nightingale that lived in the woods. Her song was so beautiful that it could take people back to all the things they wished they had done, and all the things they wished they could be. Even the Emperor in his golden city heard tales of it.

"Bring the bird to me," he said. "I want to hear her for myself."

The courtiers and soldiers and cooks from the kitchen were all sent out to search. They brought back the small brown bird, which sang so sweetly it made the Emperor cry. After that the nightingale was kept in a golden cage. She was let out twice a day, with twelve silken ribbons attached to her legs, and each ribbon held by a trusted servant.

The bird became famous, and people sent gifts in her honor. One day a package arrived. In it was a mechanical bird, encrusted with rubies and emeralds and sapphires. When the Emperor turned a key, it sang a song, complicated and beautiful, but always the same.

"This is better than the nightingale," the music master said, clapping his hands in delight. "The nightingale never sings the same song twice, but with this one we never have to guess what is coming."

While they were marveling over the jewels and the intricacies of the song, *however, the little brown bird escaped from her cage and flew away. No one noticed.*

Some months later, however, the jeweled bird stopped singing. It was taken apart, but the gears were worn, and the Emperor was told it could only play a song once a year. Heartbroken, the Emperor fell into an illness so deep that everyone thought he was dead, but the little brown nightingale came in through the window and sang so soulfully that death went away and the Emperor awoke.

The Emperor wanted to keep the bird, but the nightingale said she would never live in a palace again. She would come and sing for him sometimes, but he must never tell anyone. Then she flew back to the woods, where she sang for the trees and the sky.

And once again her song made the travelers stop on the path, and remember the things they wished they had done, and the things they wished they could be.

THE STORIES

For the first time in four years, I couldn't wait to get to school. I didn't know what the nightingale story meant, but it was a clue. It had to be—why else would my father have cut it out of my book? Maybe this time I would find an answer. I just needed to get to the computer in the library.

I was dying to tell Fisher, but he didn't come down to catch a ride to school in the morning. When I got to the classroom, he wasn't there, either. I spent the morning alternating between anxiety and impatience. I'd worry about Fisher, then I'd check the clock, trying to speed the hands toward lunchtime and the library. Then I'd worry about Fisher again.

For once, I didn't care about the other kids. Dylan passed me a note, and I absentmindedly opened it to find a handwritten fairy tale, graphic in its descriptions of what the prince did to the sleeping princess after he woke her up. I read the first paragraph and tossed it into the trash can, leaving him gaping.

When the lunch bell finally rang, I sprinted to the library and claimed the computer. When the Google page showed up on the screen, I typed in *Nightingale*, watching each letter as it appeared so I wouldn't make a mistake.

The list of links was long and unhelpful. There was a Wikipedia page describing the actual bird itself, with paragraphs filled with multisyllabic terms like those in my father's science books. There were Web sites for a security system, a restaurant, and something called an Experimental Marketing Agency. I looked through each one, but saw nothing I could connect to my father.

I even found an audio recording of a nightingale, and clicked the Start button. The clear, liquid notes filled the room like raindrops, causing the librarian to shoot me a stern look.

I went to the images next, photo after photo of little brown birds on tree branches or in nests—their tiny bodies unremarkable, but lovely all the same.

Lunchtime was almost over, and the tenth grader waiting behind me had begun tapping her pencil on the table in irritation. I was getting nowhere. Because I didn't have any other ideas, I clicked the Next option at the bottom of the screen.

And there it was. Two-thirds of the way down the page, a photo of a sleek silver box, about the size of a fat paperback. The image was small, but I would have known it anywhere.

My father's machine. I clicked through to the source. But just as the words *John Hartfell* appeared on the screen, the end-of-lunch bell rang. I let out a small groan of frustration.

The librarian came over.

"I need to read this," I said, desperation clear in my voice. "Five more minutes."

The librarian shook her head. "You've got to go back to class. I could print out the page for you, though."

"Please," I said, and went to stand by the printer, waiting impatiently until the paper emerged. I grabbed it and sprinted back to the classroom. The teacher wasn't there yet; the kids were milling about. Dylan glowered at me as I hurried down the aisle to my seat.

"I *worked* on that fairy tale," he griped. I instinctively dodged the hand that reached out to grab my ass as I passed. I had other things to think about. I sat down and started to read.

JOHN HARTFELL DISAPPEARS
THE DAILY SUN
SEPTEMBER 26, 1999

The mastermind of last year's phenomenon, Nightingale, has been reported missing. John Hartfell had been at the center of a firestorm of controversy . . .

A hand ripped the paper away midsentence. I looked up, stunned, to see Dylan's face close to mine. His breath smelled like boiled ham and cold French fries.

"Whatcha got there?" he asked. He lifted the page, ready to read.

No. I thought. *No. No. No.* I didn't know what else the article would say—all I knew was that Dylan couldn't have it. I looked around. The teacher still wasn't there.

"Give it back," I said, standing up.

Dylan stood up, too. The class turned as one to watch. Dylan moved in closer, his breath all over me.

"Or what?" he asked, and grinned. He lifted the paper into the air, managing to brush my breast on his way.

The feel of his hand cracked something inside me. I hated those hands. I hated his stupid notes, his horrible smells, his certainty that whatever was mine was his. I had dealt with it all for four years. Now I stepped forward and slammed my knee, hard, right into that precious package he always said was waiting for me.

"Shit!" he said, buckling over.

"Fuck you, Dylan," I said.

"Emmeline?" The teacher had finally entered the room.

Dylan crumpled onto his seat. I yanked the paper from his hand, flew past him and the teacher and all the rest of the gape-mouthed kids. I got to the classroom door and turned left. I could hear the angry clatter of the teacher's shoes. If she caught me, she'd send me to the principal's office, or back to the classroom. They'd read the article. They'd make me apologize to Dylan. Just the thought of it filled me with fury. I reached the exit, pushed open the door, and ran.

~

It was eight miles back to Secret Cove, but I kept running until my lungs burned. I had to get out of there.

Finally, I realized that people in passing cars were looking at me and I slowed my pace. When I got to the dirt road, I heard the distinctive sound of Colette's truck. They must have called her, I thought. I stepped off the road and hid in the trees. I would tell her everything later, I promised in my head. But first I had to understand it myself.

Once Colette had gone past, I jogged toward the resort, keeping my steps light and muffled. The cove was empty, the fishermen's boats still out. Henry's, too. Dodge was lying on the porch, and he lifted his head when he smelled me. I looked around one more time, then went over and put my arms around him, feeling the warmth of his body. It was the first moment of calm I'd felt since I saw the image of my father's machine on the screen of the computer.

"What am I doing, Dodge?" I asked. I pulled the paper from the pocket where I'd shoved it, and this time I read the whole article.

> The mastermind of last year's phenomenon, Nightingale, has been reported missing. John Hartfell had been at the center of a firestorm of controversy since the news broke early last month that Nightingale did not preserve scents as had been claimed.
>
> Nightingale has been called the Polaroid camera for smells. It is based on a revolutionary development called Headspace Technology, which made it possible to capture a scent in the wild and re-create its chemical equation in a laboratory.
>
> With HST, Hartfell saw a possibility to build a technology that could capture and re-create a scent in the same machine, preserving

it for posterity, just as Polaroid cameras take and develop a photo at the same time. Unfortunately for Nightingale's thousands of users, the challenge was not met. While a Polaroid picture fades over years, Nightingale's scent-photos have proved to fade within one.

The outrage has been overwhelming.

Tamara Lewis filed a lawsuit against the parent company, Scentography. "I lost my whole wedding," she told reporters. "They promised I would have those memories forever. Now I have nothing."

Reports are also circulating of a class action lawsuit.

Hartfell went missing three days ago, along with his infant daughter. Hartfell's wife and business partner, Victoria Wingate, went on television on Tuesday, begging for him to return.

"I don't care what you did, John. I forgive you. Just bring our little girl home."

Chief of Police Marlin Stern says they are tracking down all leads, but so far have turned up nothing.

I put the paper down. The magical machine of my childhood was a flawed piece of science. My father was a failure. I had a mother.

It was the mermaids, all over again. Nothing I had known was true. Nothing was real.

Dodge just looked at me with his endless brown eyes. He would forgive me anything, I thought. Dogs are better than people that way.

We both glanced up at the smell of diesel, the sound of a motor. Henry's boat, we both knew it. I couldn't talk to Henry, not yet. He would listen; he might not even ask any questions. But in that moment there was only one person I wanted to be with. Fisher. I didn't know where his house was, but I knew he always took the trail that led up the hill from Secret Cove. If I followed it, maybe I would get lucky.

I looked down at Dodge. He was getting so old. The fur of his face was almost entirely white. I wanted to take him with me up the trail, but I knew he couldn't make it. I kissed him on the top of his head.

"Don't tell," I said, and headed for the path.

The path was uphill, and my legs were already tired when I began. I hadn't eaten since breakfast, but going back to the house for food meant I'd probably run into Henry. Something told me he wouldn't like where I was going. I breathed hard instead, letting the oxygen power my muscles.

I'd never been so far up the path. I came across a deserted cabin, the roof caved in on itself, young trees growing up through its center. Someone had tried to clear a garden there once, but the woods were reclaiming that space as well.

Keep going, Emmeline, I told myself. *Go find Fisher.*

I started walking again, but the smells were all around me, full of early September, the woods just beginning to think about sleep, thick with rain and wet dirt and damp leaves.

When I was young, my father used to tuck me in every night. He'd climb up the ladder to my loft, wrapping his big warm arms around me and arranging the blankets. I always thought fall was like that, nature tucking everything in. Nothing had ever felt so safe.

Who were you, Papa?

The article had given me a name, but bigger questions were hammering in my brain now. *Why did you take me? Did you love me? Why did you keep me from my mother?*

I was so deep in my thoughts that I almost tripped when the path stopped suddenly at the edge of a dirt road, about as wide as ours, but more deeply rutted.

Which way?

I stood there, scanning back and forth, hoping for a clue. All I saw was a mass of trees and a road that had as much chance of going in the wrong direction as the right.

Follow your nose, Emmeline.

They were my father's words, but the voice in my head was mine.

I inhaled, shallow, then deeper, letting the scents of the woods and the road come to me. That was when I smelled the alderwood smoke. The scent was coming from my left, so I turned in that direction, walking on the flat parts of the road between the ruts.

Ten minutes passed before I saw the house, a forlorn-looking thing, its once yellow paint peeling and faded, the porch sagging on one side. There was a rusted car in the side yard, and the surrounding trees grew close to the walls and roof, as if trying to hide it. The smoke coming out of the chimney held that alderwood scent, though. I was in the right place, even if it felt wrong.

As I started up the short driveway, I heard the sound of a car coming up the road behind me. At almost the same time, the front door opened and a woman came out on the porch. She was too thin and too pale, but I could tell she'd been beautiful once. Her eyes were the same incredible green as Fisher's, her hair a faded version of his red. She saw me and stopped, uncertain. Stuck between her gaze and the approaching car, I had nowhere to hide.

The woman said nothing. The car rounded the bend and I saw it was actually a big red truck. Fisher's father was at the wheel, with Fisher next to him in the passenger seat. The shock on Fisher's face when he saw me made me wish I'd stayed back at the cove with Dodge. I'd come here for me; I hadn't thought what it might do to Fisher.

They pulled into the driveway.

"What's this?" Fisher's father asked, getting out of the truck.

Fisher's mother shook her head. "I don't know," she said. "I just saw her when I came outside."

Fisher's father turned to me, looked closer.

"You're that friend of Fisher's, aren't you?" he said.

I nodded. There was no point in lying; we'd met.

Fisher had gotten out of the truck and was standing behind his father. He smelled of fish.

"Maridel," Martin said. "You're always complaining we don't have company, and here it is, delivered to your door. You should ask the girl to dinner."

"Colette will be expecting me," I said, glancing at the strained expression on Fisher's face.

"You must be hungry," Martin said. "We'll give Colette a call; I'm sure it will be fine." He started into the house, confident that I would follow.

Fisher's eyes met mine.

I'm sorry, I mouthed. He shrugged, and in that motion I saw a memory—my father, folding into himself when winter came.

THE DINNER

Once inside, Fisher's father walked straight toward the back of the house.

"I'm going to take a shower," he said. "I'll be ready by dinner."

Fisher's mother went to the kitchen and returned with a beer, heading off in the direction Martin had gone. I heard a shower turn on, smelled water—cool, then warm, then hot. I looked around the living room at the lumpy blue couch, the red and yellow woven rug on the floor, all of it faded, all of it meticulously clean.

On her way back through the living room, Fisher's mother showed me the telephone on the table by the couch.

"You should call Colette. She'll be worried." Her eyes flicked over me, to the hall, to the kitchen. She was a fragile, birdlike person, all red hair and green eyes and constant, vigilant movement.

Reluctantly, I picked up the phone and dialed, watching as Fisher followed his mother into the kitchen. He hadn't said anything yet and I tried to read him as he passed—the smell of him, the expression on his face. All I got was fish and emptiness.

"Hello?" Colette's voice came through the receiver.

"It's me," I said.

"Thank God," Colette said. "Where are you? The school called; they said you ran out in the middle of the day. Nobody knew where you went."

"I'm at Fisher's."

The flow of her sentences stopped abruptly. "What?"

"Can I stay for dinner?"

The silence on the other side of the line was long and considered.

"Are you okay?" she asked.

"Yes." *No.*

"We need to talk, Emmeline." Her voice was firm. "What happened today—"

"I know."

A pause.

"I'll have Henry come pick you up at eight," she said.

"Okay." I could almost smell her through the phone line—cinnamon, overlaid with the scent of worry.

I hung up and went to stand in the doorway of the kitchen, watching Fisher and his mother. They worked automatically and in silence, Fisher helping his mother with an easy efficiency. No wonder he'd made such a good cottage-cleaning companion. They handed each other utensils without words, their movements small and careful, no clattering of knives, no banging of pots. They were a team, and in a way it made me jealous, although I knew I had no right to the feeling. Besides, this was a different kind of team.

The shower was still going.

"Maridel!" We all jumped at the sound. Fisher's mother opened the refrigerator, got out another beer, and disappeared.

"Are you coming back to school?" I asked Fisher when she was out of the room. I needed him to talk to me.

I couldn't say the other thought in my head.

Are you going to be okay?

He shook his head. "I don't know."

"But that's not fair."

"No," he said flatly. "It's not."

"I was already a fisherman when I met this woman here."

We were midway through a dinner of roasted chicken and mashed potatoes, the comforting smells turned brittle by the strain in the air. Fisher's mother passed the bowls often, always making sure her husband's plate was full. Fisher's father was on his fifth beer. He seemed to be the only person in that room who wasn't counting the empty cans.

"Maridel was the most beautiful thing I'd ever seen," Martin went on, leaning back in his chair. "That long red hair, those big green eyes. I saw her standing on the side of the road; gave her a ride into town. She told me she loved the sea, too—could help me fish. She was the perfect woman, I thought, and I'd found her, like in a fairy tale."

He told the story with great relish, his hands and face moving, filled with energy. It was hard not to stare.

"So we got married," he said. "But when we went out in the boat, she threw up every time we left the cove. The only thing that woman ever caught was me. And the fish went to shit. They know when a liar's been on your boat."

"Martin," Fisher's mother said quietly.

"It's true," Fisher's father said. His eyes narrowed. His upper lip raised, just one side. *Contempt.*

I knew what to look for; Fisher had taught me. *Nothing good comes from half a face.*

"You know the kicker?" Fisher's father shifted his weight forward, closing the distance between us. "My son always said he hated the ocean, too. I took him out once and he acted like I was trying to kill him the whole time. *Fisher,*" he said, and laughed. "That name sure didn't work."

He took a long swallow from the can in his hand. The three of us waited.

"How was school today, Emmeline?" Fisher's mother asked. Fisher shot her a quick look.

"I wasn't even sure if he was mine sometimes," Fisher's father went on, as if she hadn't spoken. "I mean, look at him."

Fisher's mother sat up straighter in her chair. Fisher went still. They were mirror images of each other; Fisher's father was right about that. There wasn't a bit of his dark eyes or hair in Fisher.

Martin kept his gaze on me while he pulled out a pack of cigarettes, chose one, and lit it. He inhaled and blew the smoke out across the table.

"But a vow is a vow," he said. "Besides, it turns out Fisher likes the water just fine. Now that we've got that cleared up, I've finally got me a real helper." He turned his gaze toward Fisher, and the look was so cold it crackled.

Fisher tensed.

"What about school?" I blurted out. Fisher's father turned back to me and I instantly wished I'd kept my mouth shut.

"Fishermen don't need school," he said. He took another pull on the cigarette. "They just need to know fish."

"Martin." Fisher's mother again.

"What?" The word snapped like a branch in a storm.

Fisher leaned toward me. "Doesn't Colette want you home by seven?" he said.

I nodded, grateful for the lie.

"Can you drive her, Fisher?" his mother asked.

"We're low on gas." Martin's face was set.

"We can't just send her off into the woods," she murmured.

Fisher stood up. "I'll walk her down," he said. Martin started to rise.

"Fisher," he said, and I saw his right hand flex, once.

Fisher turned to him, his eyes hot. His mother leaned forward, her chair scraping on the wooden floorboards. Fisher stepped back.

"Let's go, Emmeline," he said, and pulled me toward the door.

I looked back at Fisher's mother as he tugged me away, but her eyes were on her husband.

We stood in the driveway, Fisher fiddling with a flashlight, trying to make it work. The air had turned chill while we were inside, and the sky was dark with clouds.

"I'm sorry," I said. "This is my fault."

"It's not," Fisher said.

From the dining room came the sound of a plate dropping on the floor.

"We should go," he said. He gave the flashlight a hard knock and it flared to life.

We walked down the road in silence. The trees loomed on either side, thick and dark. I would have walked right by the trailhead, but Fisher turned down it without needing to look. Within three feet we were in total darkness, and Fisher reached the flashlight behind him so it illuminated the trail for me.

"Don't you need it to see?" I asked.

"I'm okay," he said.

I let the words hang in the trees for a moment, white lies tangling in the branches.

"Are you?" I asked.

"Yes. No."

"What *was* that back there?"

"That was my father."

The pieces were falling into place now, so much later than they should have. Fisher's long sleeves, his absences from school, his flares of anger. "But can't you do anything? What about the police?"

He pushed a branch out of the way. "She'll never take a stand against him, Emmeline."

"But . . ."

"Let's just get you home," he said.

The longing hidden in that last word broke my heart.

We walked in silence, my mind whirling. I'd made Fisher go out on the boat with Henry and me; I hadn't listened to what he was trying to tell me. Then I'd come to his house because I needed him. By thinking only of myself, I'd set a match to a pile of tinder I hadn't known existed.

And yet, I *had* known. That was the thing. I'd been raised on fairy tales, stories about fathers who left their children in the woods, and evil step-mothers who talked to mirrors. All the pieces were there. But even with everything I'd seen since I'd left the island, I hadn't had the imagination to let those characters walk off the pages into real life. I hadn't wanted to know.

"Here you are."

Fisher's voice cut through my thoughts. I looked up to see him gazing down at the cove. All the lights were on in Henry and Colette's house. The clouds had disappeared while we were in the woods, and the moon lit the ripples of the water. A full moon, I realized suddenly. I could almost feel the pull of the tide.

Come find me.

Fisher turned to go up the hill. I couldn't let him go back to that house. I knew now what waited for him.

My fault.

"Don't go back," I said.

"Where else can I go?" His voice was cold, ironic. Grown-up.

And then suddenly I knew.

"The island," I said. The words came out fast, unthinking, as if speed could carry them past logic or consequences.

"What?"

"We can go together," I said. "We can take care of ourselves. I know how."

He paused. I could see him thinking, saw the yearning start in him. He looked at the moon, and his eyes widened.

"The channel . . ." he said.

The hope in his words pushed me forward. "We could do it, Fisher."

"But what about a boat?"

That stopped me. I hadn't thought that far. But I couldn't turn back now. I took a deep breath.

"We'll take Henry's," I said. "He only uses it for deliveries, and we just did them."

Had it only been two days ago? The world had changed so utterly since then. For a moment I thought of that other life, out on the boat with Henry. The way he'd shown me my island, given it back to me.

"You'd do that?" Fisher asked. He looked me straight in the eyes. "Take the boat?"

He wasn't asking me to choose, but it was a choice all the same. *No,* I thought. *I can't do that to Henry.* But I nodded.

"Okay," Fisher said. His feet were set, solid. "I have to go back first, though. I have to tell my mother."

"No," I said. "We don't have time." I needed to keep moving forward or I knew I'd back out.

"I'll hurry," he said, and set off running up the hill.

RUNAWAY

I watched until Fisher disappeared into the woods, and then turned back to the lights of the house, my heart sinking. What was I doing? For almost five years now, Colette and Henry had taken care of me. They'd sheltered me when I was terrified, cared for me without words when affection was all I could hear.

I thought of Colette, picking me up every day after school. Henry, teaching me about the world through paintbrushes and hammers. I was about to betray them, and I'd seen the consequences of that before. I'd sworn I'd never do it again—but I had to protect Fisher.

My brain went into rationalization mode. My father had had only me, I told myself; my betrayal had left him alone. Henry and Colette had each other. They would be okay. They might even understand—once upon a time, Colette had been a traveler, and Henry had run away once, too, searching for peace and safety. They would be okay. I said it like a mantra.

Sure, said a voice in my head. *And Martin's probably not beating his wife right now, either.*

The only thing I knew for certain was that Fisher would be next, and I was to blame. It was worth all the costs if I could save him.

"Oh my darling child," Colette said as I walked in the door. The love in her voice almost broke me. Maybe, I thought for one beautiful moment, if I told them everything, they could help. Do something.

But as I was opening my mouth, Henry came down the hall, truck keys in hand. His eyes did a quick scan over me, checking my face, hands. "You okay?" he asked.

I understood then—they'd known about Martin. Of course they had. And they'd done nothing. I didn't know which made me angrier, their knowledge or my lack of it. I grabbed the wave of that fury, let it wash away the words I was going to say and sweep me away from them.

"I just want to go to sleep," I said, heading for my bedroom.

"Emmeline, we need to—"

I closed my door and leaned against it, my heart hammering. After a while, Colette went back to the kitchen, taking the scents of cardamom and bread dough with her. Dodge made his slow way down the hall and scratched at my door. I couldn't let him in. I was afraid I'd cry.

Henry and Colette stayed in the kitchen for a long time, their voices murmuring. I lay down on my bed, waiting for them to go to their room, to sleep.

As I lay there, my restless mind spinning, my body feeling the pull of the tide, I gradually came to understand that I wasn't doing this just for Fisher. I needed to go to the island for myself. In reality, the idea had been simmering in my head ever since I'd started doing deliveries to the islands with Henry. It had been a fantasy then, but now that I'd found that article, I think a part of me knew I'd have to go back—to the lagoon, our cabin— to see if the man in the story bore any relation to the father of my memories. I needed to set the versions one on top of another and see where the edges matched.

But that would never happen if I couldn't get out of the house.

To distract myself, I set my mind to details, plans. It was only September—when we got to the island there would be plenty of food to gather. Henry had said no one else was there, and with any luck the cabin would be in good shape.

I let myself relax into the memory of my own childhood competence, into the prospect of those tall, forgiving trees. I refused to think about what it would be like for Henry and Colette to find my empty bedroom. I refused to think about what it would be like to forage on the beach without the sound of my father's laughter.

After what felt like forever, Colette and Henry went to bed. I listened as the night settled into silence. When I finally heard Henry's deep, rhythmic snoring, I loaded some clothes in my backpack, then added the article and the green-wax bottle, shoving them deep inside. Carefully, I opened my door. Dodge was asleep in the hallway outside, but he was so old now that his sleep was more like a fall into a deep well. I looked at him for a moment, then stepped gingerly around him and made my way to the kitchen.

We needed basics—flour and rice and salt—and I packed a couple grocery bags, then slipped the boat key from its hook by the door. Glancing out the window, I saw Fisher's silhouette crouching at the base of the porch steps. I put on the backpack, grabbed the food, and went to the front door.

Just go forward, Emmeline, I told myself as I heard it click shut behind me.

Fisher's face looked like I felt. "You okay?" I asked.

"She wouldn't come," he said. He swallowed, a liquid sound. We hugged each other.

"Okay," he said. "Let's go."

The journey out of the harbor was agonizing. We couldn't risk turning on the motor; we had to paddle, and the boat wasn't designed for that. We moved forward ponderously, no matter how much Fisher and I leaned into our strokes. We'd positioned ourselves on either side of the boat, but if we didn't paddle at exactly the same moment, we wandered sideways, and the tide we would need later when we tried to run the channel was no friend now. I could hear the front edge of it running through the rocks on the shore. I had always loved the music it made, the conversation between stone and water, but not now. We were in a race with that tide, and those rocks told us we were losing.

I felt the sharp, squishy pain of blisters forming in the curve between my thumb and index finger. The muscles in my neck screamed from the constant craning. I looked over my shoulder, searching Henry and Colette's windows for a light.

"Should we . . ."

Give up. Go back.

"No."

I shut my eyes then and listened for Fisher's strokes, staying with them, putting every ounce of my energy into my back, my arms, my hands. As we slowly moved forward, I could begin to feel the boat rocking slightly with the current of the bigger water beyond. The scent of trees started giving way to water, to salt.

Then, with one thrust of our paddles, we were out. I opened my eyes and could just barely see the islands in the distance, a slim black line between the glittering water and the dark sky. It surprised me, how much you could see at night when there was nothing—no trees, no hills—between you and the moon.

The tide grabbed the prow of the boat and started pulling it south, along the coastline. Fisher turned the key and the engine roared to life. He cranked the wheel hard, steering us out across the current and toward the islands. As we shot eastward, I kept my face to the wind, pressing it into the blast of clean air and moisture.

Don't look back, I told myself.

The moon lit the water as we raced across the strait. The world was a palette of silver and black, all contrast and mystery. If we hadn't been watching the surface so closely for errant logs, we might not have seen how the slowly brightening sky was turning the tips of the waves from silver to white.

It wasn't until I could see the trees of the first row of islands that I looked back. Just once, I promised myself. I scanned the rippling waves for boats, then paused. The horizon *itself* was moving, the edge of the water lifting up and down in bursts.

"Fisher," I said, pointing behind us. "Look."

He glanced over his shoulder. "What do you see?"

"Slow down."

"Really?" Fisher asked. We'd been racing for over an hour.

"Yes. Look back."

Fisher ramped back the engine while I waited, watching as the line of the horizon turned into dots and dashes—and then something slim and black and white lifted out of the water in a soaring arc that looked like nothing but celebration.

"Dolphins," I said, laughing. "It's dolphins."

Hundreds of them, streaking toward us, faster than our boat could ever go. They overtook us, wave after wave of flashing tails and gleaming backs. For what must have been ten minutes we stood, stunned, as the dolphins flowed around our boat. Finally, the last wave passed and we watched as they traveled on, leaving a foaming white trail for us behind them.

"I think we can call that a welcome," Fisher said.

We got to my island just before high tide. Even within the dark maze of the archipelago, there was enough light to see the rocks along the sides of the channel, the water pushing over them in angry bursts. There were more underneath the surface, I knew. On the day my father drowned, I'd spent hours staring at them, trying to learn every detail of the water as it rushed over the barely hidden rocks.

"What do you think?" Fisher asked. I looked at the surface of the water; there was still a strong current.

"Not yet," I said.

We waited. The sky lightened, bit by bit. We could see the froth of the waves diminishing with each minute. And then, as easy as a last breath, the water in the channel slowed, then stilled. The drawbridge lowered. The island invited us in.

"Now," I said, and Fisher started the motor. The walls were steep and dripping, the trees turning from black to green with the approaching sunrise. The water foamed in haphazard circles, as if confused by the sudden lack of movement. Bull kelp floated around us like strange sea creatures, long and languorous tails obscuring our vision.

We kept going, trying to stick to whatever the *middle* of the channel was when everything was a curve or the jag of a rock. We heard a long, rough scrape on the bottom of the boat, then one on the side. Fisher's hands were tight on the wheel; my eyes strained as I looked for movement on the surface. We inched around another curve, then another and another. A moment later we passed rocks I recognized, and then there it was.

Home.

THE RETURN

Fisher whooped as we left the channel behind, the sound reverberating across the hushed lagoon, sending birds flying. I stood next to him at the wheel, my heart pounding as I stared at the beach.

It hadn't changed, the oval of water still the welcome it had always been. The last of the high tide almost covered the beach, leaving seaweed draped along the upper edge like forgotten scarves.

Mermaid party, I thought, and memories collided inside me. I breathed in the fragrance of seaweed and cedar and mussels and salt that was my island, smelled the diesel exhaust mixing in, and suddenly I was twelve years old again, hiding in the woods, watching a white boat come into the lagoon and break my childhood in two.

But I was the one in the boat now. A stolen boat. Shaking off the thoughts, I jumped to the sand and tied the rope around a boulder. Fisher leaped down beside me.

"We made it," he said, pulling me into a hug. He held me close and his warm scent was comforting, home. I could feel it starting to filter into the smells of the beach around me.

Once you change the scent, you change the memory, my father's voice whispered.

I pulled away, and Fisher looked at me, confused. I didn't know how to explain what I was feeling. For almost thirteen years, I'd lived on this island alone with my father. Now here I was again, without him, my mind full of the story in the article, my arms around a boy whose smells had never been here before. Each thing I did was changing everything I'd had.

I gazed past Fisher at the bushes that lined the beach, heavy with berries. The memory of my father hung in the air. A breeze brushed the needles up in the trees until they sounded like footsteps on the trail.

"Foragers feast," I said, grasping the first idea that came into my head. I needed to move.

"What?"

"Let's find some food."

We gathered for an hour, and I watched Fisher the whole time. Just having the channel between him and his father seemed to calm him. His long fingers moved neatly among the berries and the roots of the sea plantains. He never crushed what he took, and he left plenty for later. He was comfortable, assured, like he'd always been when we harvested in Colette's garden.

As he worked, the smells of the island gradually began to reach out to him, the dark night of salal berries lingering on his fingertips, the spiciness of the sea asparagus mingling with his breath. When the tide receded and the clams started their waterworks, one burst of liquid caught him full in the face. He stood up, laughing, wiping the water away, but the smell of salt and sea stayed in his hair like a mark of approval. One scent at a time, the island was taking him in.

Whether I still belonged here, too, I couldn't tell. Because of me, my father was dead. Now I had returned, carrying stories that could kill the memories that remained.

"Should we make sure the cabin is okay?" Fisher asked after a while.

"Sure," I said. But my feet were slow on the trail, which seemed to have little interest in aiding my passage. The salal bushes had grown over the past five years, their coverage so dense that I had to rely more on instinct and memory than sight. It was as if they knew what I brought with me.

The closer Fisher and I got to the cabin, the more my mind was filled with images of what we might find—the roof caved in, squirrels making homes in the beds, the drawers, the pantry, the stuffing of the big chair. Maybe someone else had gotten a boat through the channel, found the cabin, and burned it down; I'd heard of vandalism like that.

Or, perhaps worst of all, everything would be just as I'd left it the afternoon that Henry came and took me away. I didn't remember much of my final days on the island, but I could still see my father's machine, smashed to pieces, the empty bottles scattered like straw.

I didn't deserve to be here, for so many reasons. I scanned the woods for a welcome. The trees were silent. I couldn't even hear the birds. The only thing I could smell was the scent of my own nervousness, sharp and acrid.

"Let me go first," I said to Fisher as we got close, and he nodded and stayed back.

I pushed through the last of the bushes, leaving the gloaming of the trees, and stood at the edge of the clearing. The vegetable garden in front of me was rampant with weeds, the once-careful stack of wood fallen into chaos, a sapling growing up through its midst. The woods were claiming back the land, bit by bit, but on the far side of the clearing I saw the cabin standing straight and true, its roof solid—so much the way it had always looked that for a moment I had the crazy hope that somehow my father was still inside. *My* father, not the one in the newspaper article, not the one from those awful last months on the island.

I could feel Fisher waiting behind me. I shook my head, then walked across the clearing, the long, damp grass whispering as I moved through it. I went up the stairs and stood, my hand on the doorknob. I closed my eyes. I didn't want to see.

Breathe in, Emmeline. My father, standing by the chicken coop.

Who were you, Papa? The thought interrupted the memory, but my father's voice stayed the same. I could feel myself yearning toward it, even with the article in my backpack, a sharp, folded reminder.

Let the smell introduce itself, he said.

I opened the door. The cool, dusty scent of time and absence met me there.

Now, open the back of your mind. Listen to the story.

The smells came to find me. I caught a hint of wood smoke and tobacco, dried apples and something else. Something out of place.

I opened my eyes.

I saw the wall of drawers, each one closed and orderly. The loft with my bed neatly made, the woodstove ready to be lit. Everything clean and loved and in its place, just as it had always been. I breathed in again and recognized the faintest slip of a fragrance—sawdust and paint and cinnamon rolls.

Henry, I realized. He had done this, for me, without knowing when or if I would ever return. Or maybe he had known, better even than I did.

And I had stolen his boat.

"Henry," I said into the room. "I'm so sorry." And then, "Thank you."

I took my father's last bottle from my backpack and walked over to the wall, opening the drawer that had once held the bottle with the blue-wax seal. I put mine inside. I thought I heard a sigh from within, but I couldn't be sure.

When Fisher finally poked his head in the door twenty minutes later, he found me sitting on the floor. I couldn't bring myself to sit in the big chair yet. The width of its arms would tell me how different I was from the girl who had sat there with her father.

I watched as Fisher gazed around the cabin. I wondered how it looked through his eyes.

"How is it?" he asked.

"Okay," I said. "Strange."

"Do you want to go back?" he asked hesitantly.

"No." We had come this far. I wanted to stay.

I didn't say what we both knew. The afternoon was well under way; the next high tide was coming in a few hours. It would be the last chance to get through the channel for a month. Our last chance to leave, and anyone else's last chance to come.

Fisher sat down on the floor next to me. "My mom said she'd tell my dad I went to school. That should slow him down."

"Henry and Colette will know we took the boat," I said. My throat clenched at the thought of them finding my room and the dock empty.

"They'll have to find another boat small enough to make it through the channel," Fisher said. "That'll take a while."

I thought about how the inside of the cabin felt when I first saw it. I remembered those trips in the boat with Henry, the way he had slowly brought me closer and closer to this island.

This place will heal you if you let it.

There was a chance Henry would understand why I'd come here. He might be able to convince Colette to give us some time.

I didn't even want to think about Fisher's father.

"Maybe we'll get lucky," I said.

We were quiet for a while, Fisher continuing to survey the cabin. "You really lived here?" he said finally, marveling.

I nodded.

"What're all those for?" he asked, pointing at the drawers. The open curiosity on his face made me want to tell him, but I couldn't. I remembered my father, opening a drawer, bringing down a bottle, showing me a new world. Then I remembered the clink of those bottles in my foraging bag as I climbed down the ladder, heading for the bluff.

"It's getting late," I said. "We shouldn't be here. This is the first place they'll look."

We went and hid within earshot of the clearing, crouching in the under-brush. My nose scanned the air, searching for a scent of gasoline, while our ears strained for the sound of a motor. Time passed. The woods dark-ened. The noises around us grew huge, but in the end, they were never more than the cracklings of birds and squirrels in the bushes. My legs started to fall asleep and I settled on the ground, feeling the damp work its way through my pants. Fisher sat next to me, our shoulders touching. We waited.

"Why'd you come to my house yesterday?" Fisher asked quietly.

I thought of myself, bumbling into his home, setting so many things in motion.

"I wanted to make sure you were okay," I said. I shifted position and felt the cool air slip between our shoulders.

"Was that all?"

I should have known he could read me. He read everyone.

"I found something," I said, and as the light disappeared almost entirely, I told him about the article and Dylan and running away from school.

"You kneed Dylan in the nuts?" I could hear his smile in the darkness.

"Yeah."

"Good for you." He started to laugh, but stifled the sound. "So what do you think? About the article?"

"It's my father," I said. "I'm sure of it. I just don't know what it means yet."

All I knew was that nothing was the same. The last time my vision of my father had shifted so dramatically, when I'd learned about the mer-maids, he'd still been there—to yell at, to hold back the whole truth, but to be there nonetheless, sleeping in the bed below my loft.

Now all I had was words on a piece of paper and memories to test them against. And those memories were shifting under my feet.

Fisher and I sat in silence. I could smell the trees hushing into sleep, the island giving itself over to the rustle of night wings. I waited, listening for Henry and Martin. Listening for my father.

The air grew colder. Fisher and I moved closer and closer toward each other, until he put his arms around me and I burrowed close, grateful for his warmth. My breath found its way into the curve of his neck and his into the curls of my hair. We fell asleep like that, and woke with the first light of day. The woods were still.

"They're not coming," Fisher whispered.

THE ISLAND

It was almost too much to take in—the relief that Martin hadn't found us, followed by the realization that we were now responsible for keeping ourselves alive for at least a month, and maybe a winter. We went back to the cabin and faced the twelve empty shelves of the pantry. I tried to forget the last time I'd seen them this way.

"What do we do?" Fisher asked, his jubilation sobering.

Aside from the limited supplies I'd packed, and some packets of yeast, sugar, and matches that Fisher's mother had stuffed in his pockets, we were starting from scratch. There was everything to do. Clams and mussels and seaweed and berries to harvest. The woodpile to sort through, and more to cut. Trails to clear.

Even though it was daunting, these were tasks I understood—things you could do with your hands, your muscles. Given the option of facing Fisher's father, or school, or this, the choice was clear. I picked up a gathering basket from the corner by the woodstove and handed it to Fisher.

"Here," I said. "Let's get started."

I shoved the memories into the back of my mind, grabbed the other basket, and we set out.

I had spent all that time in school hiding what I could do with my nose. Now I stopped worrying about being teased and followed its lead. I used my skills to find us mushrooms and patches of huckleberries; I got us back to the cabin when we lost our way on an overgrown trail. I sniffed out the dryness of the usable logs in the woodpile, the damp and slippery scent of rot in the others. For the past five years, each inhalation had been tinged with the fear of being caught. On the island, I was beginning to feel like myself again. In those moments, my nose tucked into the bark of a tree or lifted to the sky, I was with my father in a way that was clean and easy. The best of me. The best of him. It made the man in the article go away.

"You're different here," Fisher said.

He was, too. I watched as the constant vigilance fell away from him. It left his eyes first, turning them alive and wondering. His mouth relaxed. His stride loosened. When he hefted the ax to split logs, the muscles in his arms released a pent-up energy that seemed to shimmer in the air. He had always smelled like trees, but now it was the smell of new growth, those green tips that came in the spring.

"You going to help or just watch?" He grinned, holding out the ax. I took it, got in position, and swung it high, bringing it down on the log, feeling the force of the blow travel up my arms. I had split wood as a child, but this was different. I was taller now, my body stronger. I sank the ax head into the cleft I had formed and the log broke in two.

That evening we lit a fire, the warmth and light of it filling the room. We made a stew of mussels and clams, flavored with wild onions and sea asparagus, and ate it from wooden bowls that fit in our hands like promises. I steeped spruce tea and watched Fisher as the steam reached his nose.

"Maybe we can do this," he said, smiling.

"Maybe we can," I said.

I kept busy; we had to work to survive, I told myself. I let my muscles rule the days, but in the evenings the thoughts came in. Each night after that first one in the woods, we slept in the cabin, me in the loft, Fisher in my father's bed. I lay there, listening to breathing that was not my father's, waiting for the familiar whispers of scent-papers that were no longer there. What would they have told me back then, if I'd known what to listen for? Who was the man inside them? Had any of them held the scent of my mother?

In my mind, I placed the stories of my father next to each other, pages in a book that made no sense. My father was my hero. He was a liar. He loved me. He'd kidnapped me. I had killed him. That last one was the only one I knew for sure.

I didn't understand how it was possible to feel so right and so wrong in a place at the same time. The island itself was unchanged—its rules and beauties the same as they'd always been and always would be. It was me that was different, who couldn't decide how or where I fit. I yearned to be the child who'd lived here, but I wanted to understand my father, and that would mean leaving childhood behind. I wanted to tell Fisher what I had done, but I didn't know how to start. Perhaps, in the end, I didn't want to.

And so, each night as Fisher and I buttoned up the woodstove and headed toward bed, I walked past the question in his eyes and went up to my loft alone.

We'd been on the island almost two weeks when I felt the first of the fall gales coming, an early one. The air grew heavy, then loud, the wind smashing like fists at the cedar shakes of the roof. The downspouts moaned. Fisher started pacing, his feet loud against the floor.

"It's just a storm," I said. He didn't answer. A branch sheered off a nearby tree and landed with a crash on the porch. Fisher jumped, instinctively putting up an arm to block his face.

"Shit," he said.

He paced for hours, leaping at each sudden noise, fists tensed at his sides. When the storm finally passed, he dropped down in the big chair and closed his eyes, as exhausted as the wind-smashed trees outside. I sat on the floor, put my head against his knee.

"Tell me," I said. "Please." I held out the words like open hands.

It took a while, the story finding its way up from some strange and subterranean place, slipping through the cracks of his fatigue. "He didn't hit either of us at first," he said finally. "But you could feel it coming. Even when I was little, I knew."

I thought of my father, his arms around me as we read. Even later, when everything fell apart, I never once believed he would hurt me.

Fisher shifted in the chair. "My mom had a vegetable garden, and she taught me how to work it. At first it was just a place to keep me with her, but by the time I was five, I really was helping. I loved being there with her. She made me feel like I could grow things."

He stopped. I caught a scent gathering, a darkening like the dirt that lives underneath mushrooms.

"I remember my first tomatoes," Fisher said. "I'd gathered them all by myself. There were so many I had to hold up the edge of my shirt to make a bowl. I was so proud of them." I heard the shake of his head. "My father was standing on the porch steps, and he asked me what I had. For one second, I actually thought he wanted to see. So I held out my shirt, and there were all those gorgeous tomatoes, and I said, 'Look what Mom and I made.'

"And then he just hit me. Right in the face."

It was quiet in the cabin. I waited.

"She'll never leave," he said. "I've asked her over and over."

I thought of my father, refusing to leave the island, even after the bear had eaten everything we had.

"Why wouldn't she come with me?" Fisher asked.

I climbed into the chair and put my arms around him. I didn't know the answer. I didn't think I ever would.

It was as if a door had opened after that. Not wide, but enough to catch a glimpse. Things we'd never told each other started slipping out as we made dinner, or cleared a trail, or walked along the sand at the lagoon.

"My father used to tell me stories about Jack the Scent Hunter . . ."

"Sometimes I slept in the garage . . ."

"I had a goat . . ."

"He won't let my mother drive . . ."

"There are no mermaids . . ."

"I want to kill my father."

I stopped; I couldn't force the words out. *I did.* I didn't know how to tell him what it felt like, to do what he was imagining. The way that you never took only one life; you always took two—the person you killed and the person you thought you were.

Tell him, I thought.

"There was a bear," I said instead.

As our minds followed our stories toward each other, our bodies followed suit. His hand found the small of my back as I stood making tea. My fingers reached into the waves of his red hair to pull out a twig. That evening I smelled his scent on my fingertips, the way it met mine and made a fragrance that felt whole.

I was the one who threw the bottles in the water, I wanted to tell him. *Everything fell apart because of me.* But then he took my face in his hands and kissed me.

Tell him, I said to myself. *It's not right unless you tell him.*

But I was seventeen years old, alone on an island with a boy I had loved since the first time he sat down at the desk next to mine. So I closed my eyes and kissed him back, and then we both went up to the loft.

THE BLUFF

I woke in the morning, our scents tangled in the sheets, our legs wound together like tree roots. I knew that as soon as I moved, this new smell of us would find its way out of the blankets and disperse into the ordinary life of the cabin. So I stayed still, cocooned in the covers. The walls of drawers rose above me, and I wished for my father's machine, so I could make a scent-paper of this moment while it was still pure and only us.

Fisher stirred, opening his eyes with a smile.

In so many ways it was the fairy tale I'd always wanted—two children in the woods, taking care of one another. We spent our days filling the pantry, contented, ignoring any thought that in the end we might not need the stores we were collecting. Food seemed to fly into our foraging baskets. We found a downed tree, already dry and perfect for chopping. Over time, the sky turned cloudy, heading into fall. We couldn't see the moon, and we didn't care. No moon meant no light. We had to go to bed early—to save the candles, we would say, reaching for one another. When Fisher was sleeping next to me, my mind calmed, let go. I could forget the article, and those last weeks on this island with my father. I was creating new memories, all my own. I lost track of time, happily and willfully.

"Hey, Em!" Fisher said, coming into the cabin one afternoon. "I found something."

"What?"

"It's a surprise. I have to show you." His green eyes were bright.

I put my coat over the T-shirt I had slept in and followed him out. The air was changing, the openness of the trees and dirt tightening in preparation for colder weather. It was strange to smell the woods slowing down, getting ready for sleep while everything inside me felt so open and alive.

I breathed in, the cool air tickling the inside of my nose, colored by the fragrance of us that was still hiding in my shirt. For the first time in my life, I was looking forward to the shorter days of winter. I smiled as I watched Fisher's excitement lengthen his loping stride.

Fisher led me past the dormant vegetable garden, but instead of turning down the now well-maintained trail to the lagoon, he headed in the opposite direction, pushing through the overgrowth. My breath caught. I knew what path we'd pass going this way, but if it was as hidden as the rest had been, there was a chance he'd missed it.

He hadn't. He stopped and stood, grinning, at the turnoff for the bluff.

"I found the coolest place," he said.

Every memory I had been avoiding came crashing back into my head. I saw myself, running down this trail, my foraging bag full of bottles. I saw myself on the bluff, hand raised.

My fault.

I should have told Fisher the truth before, told him I wished that trail had never existed. But I hadn't, and now he'd discovered the only place I never wanted him to see. I reached forward and grabbed his arm.

"You've already been there, huh?" he said. "I guess it was too much to hope. Still, we should go—"

"No."

He stopped and looked at me, the joy draining from his face.

"Tell me," he said.

The secrets sat there, waiting in my throat. I couldn't imagine what this island would be like, what Fisher and I would be like, if they came out. Words were like scents that way; they changed the very air you breathed.

I shook my head, once.

His eyes, so open and expressive, went flat. "I told you everything," he said. "Things I never told anybody."

I looked at him. Three hours before, we'd been in bed, his skin warm against mine. In my happiness, I'd convinced myself I'd given him every-thing, but that was a lie. I'd kept this from him because I didn't want him to know what I'd done. I'd wanted to be only myself, not what had hap-pened before. As if that is ever possible.

But there was more to it than that, I knew. This one memory, that face in the water looking up at me, belonged only to my father and me. In a strange way, it was the one thing that hadn't been touched by someone else's stories or smells. It was all I had left. That, and a scent-paper I'd never burn.

"I can't," I said to Fisher. "It's mine."

He stared at me for a moment, the hurt of it slapped across his face.

"Keep it, then," he said.

He turned and went back down the trail, leaving me alone.

I took the other path, the one to the bluff, pushing my way through the whispers of the overgrown bushes.

Stop. Stop. Stop.

But I didn't stop, any more than I had five years before, when I had run that path with a pack full of bottles. The leaves scratched at my hands and face, but I kept going until I stumbled free of the last gasp of underbrush and the bluff was before me, cold and gray, the sky and water beyond it endless.

So many nights I had come here in my dreams; I knew every line in the stone, every scent of the sky and water. I could smell the leaves turning to dirt in the ground, just as they had been back then. I could smell my fear, see my father flying by me. Time was rounding in on itself.

I forced myself to the edge of the bluff, and looked down at the water. I made myself stand there until I saw his face.

And then I was doubled over, sobbing.

I don't know how long I was there. I cried my way back through Fisher and school and the cove and those last days in the cabin without my father. I cried until I couldn't stand, until I couldn't sit, until I felt the stone, cold beneath my cheek.

It was the smell that pulled me back—diesel—and the sound of a distant motor. I rose to my feet, feeling the shake in my muscles, scanning the water in front of me. A few moments later, a small boat came into view, rounding the edge of the island, two men standing at the front. I ducked down. I didn't know the boat, but I recognized Henry at the wheel, saw Martin standing next to him. And suddenly, I knew where they were headed.

I flew down the path, counting days in my head. How had we gotten it wrong? When did we lose track? And how much time did I have before the tide went slack? Not much, I realized. Roots grabbed at my feet; branches whipped against my face. I kept going. I had to get to Fisher.

I reached the clearing and threw open the door of the cabin, but he wasn't there. I scanned the room—one of the foraging baskets was missing.

I thought of Fisher, coming back angry and hurt, grabbing the basket and heading out, wanting to prove that he belonged here, too.

The lagoon, I thought. The last place I wanted him to be.

When I finally burst out of the woods, I saw the three of them standing on the beach. Fisher and his father faced one another like a pair of pillars holding up nothing. Henry stood to one side. I saw Fisher's hands, clenched by his hips. I caught a whiff of something rank, sharp and hungry.

"Stop," I yelled.

Henry spotted me, and his face flooded with relief.

"Emmeline," he called.

Fisher turned toward me, and his father's fist pulled back and cracked into his jaw.

AFTER

"That's enough," Henry said, with a firmness I'd never heard before. Even Martin stepped back. Fisher stayed on the ground where he'd fallen, staring at his father. The mark on Fisher's jaw was red and angry, but it was the look in his eyes that scared me.

Henry pointed to the channel. The first tips of the rocks were starting to appear through the water.

"We have to go," he said. "Now—or we're stuck here for a month."

It was too fast. Too much. Half my mind was still running down the path toward the lagoon.

"I'm not going," Fisher said, getting to his feet.

His father started toward him again. There was no way to win this, I saw that then. Martin would never leave without his son; he couldn't bear the insult of it. He'd beat Fisher into submission.

Or—and this was suddenly almost more horrifying—Martin would stay here himself. For a moment I had a vision of him touching the trees and our things in the cabin, his scent infiltrating everything. I couldn't stand it.

"Stop," I said again. "We'll go."

Martin paused. Fisher looked at me, my betrayal written all over his face.

What had I just done?

"Okay then." Henry saw the opening and moved quickly, leaving no room for discussion. "Martin, you're with me. Fisher, you take my boat through the channel."

I saw Martin bridle.

"Fisher knows the boat," Henry said to Martin. He turned to Fisher again. "After the channel, you follow me back to the cove, got it?"

Fisher didn't move.

"Now," Henry said. "Or not at all."

Fisher shot me one last look, and strode toward the small white boat.

"My father's bottle," I said suddenly to Henry. "It's still in the cabin."

"No time," Henry said.

If the journey out to the islands had seemed long a month ago, it was nothing compared to the ride back. Fisher and I barely made it through the channel, the rocks scraping against our hull as we exited. Once in open water, the only sounds were the roaring of the motor and the slap of the wake against our bow. The sky began to darken. Fisher stood at the wheel, silent, his grip stiff. I'd always thought he resembled his mother, but as he stood there, his shoulders rigid, his mouth hard and graceless, he looked like nothing so much as his father.

"Fisher," I said.

"Not now." He shook his head, and whether it was because of the waves or his father or me, I didn't know. I wondered if, this time, he would ever tell me.

Colette was waiting under the big light on the dock, her arm around Fisher's mother. Their faces went wide with relief, then fear. Colette practically leapt into our boat when we got close, gathering me into a hug.

"Darling girl," she said. "You scared us so."

Fisher's mother waited, her eyes locked on her son. He didn't look at her as Henry pulled up on the other side of the dock. Fisher got off our boat, stiff legged, his father right behind him.

"Keys," Martin said to his wife, holding out his hand. She put them in his palm. "Let's go," he said, starting up the dock toward their truck.

"There's dinner . . ." Colette said.

"No thank you."

And then they were gone.

"We can't just let them . . ." I said as the truck started up.

Colette just shook her head, exhaustion furrowing her face. "You think we haven't tried?"

Colette, Henry, and I sat at the dinner table. Food covered the plates in front of us, but it was as if we'd all forgotten what it was there for.

"It was my idea to go to the island," I said. I couldn't let Fisher take the blame.

"Today's been long enough," Colette said. "We'll talk about it tomorrow." And we would, I could tell.

But I knew in my gut that the day wasn't over yet. I had told myself I was saving Fisher by getting his father off the island, but I had only made it worse. They were home now, with no witnesses. None that counted, anyway.

I went to bed and sat there, dressed, waiting. It was three in the morning when Colette came in.

"It's Fisher," she said.

The hospital corridor stretched out in front of me, endless and blank, but the smells told me everything—blood and love and fear, and covering it all, the sharp, fake odor of bleach and cleansers, a mask that kept slipping.

Fisher's mother stood by the door to his room, her hands behind her back. Beyond her was a bed, and Fisher. His face was every color but his own. There was a cast on one arm, and where his hospital gown didn't quite cover his chest, I saw what looked like the edge of a boot mark.

I went to the bed, and touched his fingers. He opened his eyes, but the Fisher I found in them was so grown-up and complicated, I almost couldn't recognize him.

"I'm sorry," I whispered. "I'm sorry."

On the other side of the room, a nurse stood next to Colette and Henry. "I can't get her to let go of it," I heard her murmur.

When I turned, I saw the baseball bat in Fisher's mother's hand.

"She stopped it," the nurse said.

"Where's his father?" Colette asked.

"In the room down the hall. They'll both be fine."

"*Fine?*" Henry's incredulity chilled the room. "This will never be fine."

"I just patch 'em up," the nurse said, with the weariness of a late-night shift.

Down the hall a male voice blared out in anger. Fisher's hand curled tight next to mine.

I sat by Fisher's bed, his mother on the other side. She rarely left the room, and when she did, it was almost never in the direction of her husband's room down the hall.

She and I didn't say much over the top of that bed—*Can I get you some food? Should you get some rest?*—but I saw the way she watched Fisher, as if he were a bird that might fly away. Fisher himself rarely said anything, answering only the most necessary questions. I wished his mother would leave sometimes, so I could talk to him alone. There were so many things I needed to say, wanted to know. But it seemed every time she stepped out, a nurse came in, needing to take his blood pressure, temperature.

So instead, I tried to talk through my hands, my fingers against his or touching the unbruised part of his forearm. An unspoken message to a far-away place.

Where have you gone, Fisher?

On the second day, the local police came by the hospital; they decided it had been a bad fight, but a mutual one. There would be no charges. Fisher's eyes went dark at the news. Henry was furious, and followed the policemen out of the building. He took me down to the cafeteria for coffee when he got back.

"It's Martin's story against Fisher's," he told me. "The cop plays poker with Martin. Says he's a great guy. And Maridel . . . she still won't press charges."

"Why not? I don't understand."

"That makes two of us." His expression held an old and unspoken frustration.

Later, as I approached Fisher's room, I overheard him and his mother talking.

"A vow is a vow, Fisher." Her voice sounded two hundred years old.

"Jesus, Mom. Can you *hear* yourself?"

"It's hard for him, too."

There was something like a laugh, cut off by a grunt of pain. "Bullshit," he said.

Fisher's mother flew by me out the door. Fisher looked up and saw me standing there.

"You heard," he said. I nodded.

"I have to go," he said as I sat down next to him. "I can't stay here."

I remembered what he'd said on the island: *I want to kill my father.* His eyes held the horror of someone who'd tried.

"I'll go with you," I said. *Don't leave me.*

"You've got a good place here, Emmeline. People who love you. You can finish school." His words cracked with bitterness. I dug into them, searching for love.

"I don't care," I said, leaning forward.

He closed his eyes, tired.

"This is my fault," I said. "I'm sorry."

He shook his head, but he didn't open his eyes.

A doctor I hadn't seen before walked in the door. He checked the chart in his hand and then smiled brightly at Fisher.

"Good news, young man," he said. "You're progressing nicely. You'll be back home before you know it."

In the end, Fisher's release came unexpectedly, three days after his father's. Colette got a call from Fisher's mother early one morning, and we dashed over to the hospital. We opened the door to Fisher's room, false cheer on our faces.

But he was already gone. His mother stood by the bed, staring down at the indentation in the pillow.

I turned on her—she could have stopped this, too. But when she looked up, the pain I saw on her face shut my mouth.

There were notes on the bedside table, one for his mother, one for me. His mother's said simply, *Take care of yourself.* Mine said, *I'm sorry.* His name a scrawl across the bottom.

He'd vanished, left me behind with only a note. I couldn't believe it.

I sat down on the bed, the paper in my hand, my mind racing back through everything he'd said in the hospital, looking for clues. Hansel and Gretel had left breadcrumbs to follow. There must be something that could lead me to Fisher. If I could just talk to him, I could make things better, I thought.

But there was nothing.

~

I stalked the mailbox after that. I couldn't believe that note was the last I'd hear from Fisher. We'd been through too much together, meant too much to each other. Then I remembered his eyes, the way they'd looked that first night in the hospital. As if what was inside him was worse than anything that had been done to him. I wanted to tell him it didn't matter, that I knew who he really was—the boy on the island, whose fingers had slipped between the stalks of the sea plantains, touched the curls of my hair.

But I knew, too, that some things couldn't be fixed. Sometimes the water was too cold. Too deep.

Colette mentioned school, but I started throwing up at the thought, and we all decided it was the stomach flu. She and Henry watched me warily. It was as if everything was too big to talk about now.

~

Finally, after almost two weeks, a letter arrived.

Dear Emmeline, it said. *I'm okay. I got a job in a nursery. I'm working with plants and I found a place to live. It feels good to have my hands in the dirt.*

I am sorry I left the way I did. There's so much in my head right now. I can see you smiling, wanting to help, but you can't. You don't know what this is like.

I'll be fine. I'll write more soon.

I looked at the letter in my hand—*You don't know what this is like.*

Except I did. I'd stood on the bluff and seen my father looking up at me, seen the worst of myself in what I had done to him. I'd felt it crack my soul in two.

But I'd never told Fisher about that, had I? I'd held it back, my own precious secret. And now he was gone.

I turned the envelope over in my hands. It was slim, white. My name, c/o Secret Cove Resort. No return address, just a postmark from the city.

How would I ever find him? I raised the letter to my nose. It smelled of dirt and, faintly, of Fisher—but I needed far more than that.

I sat there, tapping that letter with my finger as if I could make it talk. It felt as if my whole life had been shaped by things people wouldn't say.

Enough, I said to myself. *Enough secrets.*

THE SEARCH

I went back to school the next day. As I opened the classroom door, I heard the whispers start, but they were different now. They didn't curl around me, looking for a crack to slip into and widen; they kept their distance.

"That island . . ."

"A whole month . . ."

"He almost died . . ."

Their voices were hushed, holding the story like it was something sparkling. Dangerous.

As I walked to my seat, Dylan stretched his legs across the aisle and looked up, his gaze locked on mine. The other kids watched. I stopped right in front of him, stared back.

Go ahead, I thought. *See what happens.*

I stood there until he pulled his legs under his chair.

With Fisher gone, I had no friends, but I was cloaked in a new island fairy tale now, one full of survival and bravery and, quite possibly, sex. The girls could hardly wait to find me in the cafeteria.

"What did you do out there?"

"Where did he go?"

The last question, quivering and eager: "Do you miss him?"

I never answered, but it didn't seem to matter. Maybe the story was better without the real details. Fairy tales often are.

But I was through with fiction. The only reason I'd willingly gone back to school was the computer. At lunch, I went to the library. The first thing I did was search for nurseries in the city. There were forty-nine. *Forty-nine.* A map popped up: bright red markers scattered across a grid of lines and colors that looked bigger than the ocean.

I remembered Jessie, our summer worker, strong and adventurous, talking about the city.

There are so many people, you can just get lost. In a good way.

I couldn't imagine a good way. And I knew that I couldn't just go, not into that seemingly endless grid. I needed something—a clue. But how to get it? My life was like a series of locked doors, and it didn't much care for giving me keys.

I changed course, shifted my research back to my father. I had the librarian teach me how to sort my searches by date, then I typed in *John Hartfell,* and clicked on the earliest hit.

THE POWER COUPLE OF SMELL
THE DAILY SUN
MARCH 12, 1999

The smell of your grandfather's pipe. Your first-grade teacher's perfume. One whiff transports you back in time. Now imagine being able to access those memories whenever you want them. Think a Polaroid camera for smells.

John Hartfell and Victoria Wingate exploded onto the olfactory scene last year with the Nightingale, a sleek, fit-in-your-hand device that captures the scents of our memories and preserves them forever. Overnight, Wingate and Hartfell revolutionized the way we think about smell, but as we found when we visited them in their modest home, paying attention to scent is nothing new to them.

They are the quintessential yin and yang of couples. John, the quiet scientist. Victoria, the vibrant businesswoman. They met at a fragrance company where John had the enviable job of traveling the world, finding new scents to use in everything from high-end perfumes to dish soap. Victoria was what is called a "nose," in charge of creating those fragrances.

"We like to say we had a very traditional relationship," Victoria says with a laugh. "He hunted and gathered. I cooked."

The idea for Nightingale came when the two were at a restaurant one night and a young man offered to take their picture with a Polaroid camera.

"It just struck me," Victoria says. "We want to capture our lives, and photos are wonderful, but what if we could do the same thing with scents?"

She stops, gazing off for a moment toward a world the rest of us can't see.

"Smells hold memories," she continues. "For just a moment they let you travel through time. We wanted to create something that would let you have that feeling, whenever you wanted.

"Once we had the idea, it was all up to John," she says, and gives him a loving smile. "He's the scientist."

Nightingale hit the market in time for Christmas, and turned Victoria and John's tiny company, Scentography, into a massive success story. Sales of Nightingale were triple the initial projections of 10,000 units in the first three months. Rumors of an IPO for the

*company later this year are already buzzing. If Nightingale continues
its astonishing flight, something tells us we'll be coming back to visit
this power couple for an article in our Houses of the Rich and Famous
issue.*

A photo had run alongside the article. The man was so young and clean-shaven it was hard to recognize my father in him. The woman beside him was stunningly beautiful, with long, dark curls and pale skin. Her smile was luminous; his was uncomfortable. I could just imagine how little my father would have liked all that attention.

As I looked closer, however, I noticed something else: a silver-gray scarf, tied in a loose, elegant knot around the woman's neck. I knew that scarf. I had burned it.

I sat there for a long time, and then I went back to the list and worked my way through the links. The story they told was not a good one. A flurry of breathless articles gave way to investigative reporting and angst-soaked accountings of marriage proposals and births and vacations lost forever. Apparently there was a price for memories, and lawyers were happy to name it. Victoria Wingate was mentioned in the articles, but more and more often as one of the duped, and vitriolic denunciations of John Hartfell began leaping off the screen. Then he went missing, and Victoria went on television, pleading for the return of her child. The press reported it all avidly.

But, as the reporters liked to say, John Hartfell had disappeared as completely as the scents his invention had promised to capture. The Nightingale machines were recalled, Scentography went bankrupt, and after a while the search for John Hartfell faltered, then seemed to stop.

I heard a bell ring and glanced up at the clock. Three P.M. I had been in the library all afternoon. No one had come to find me; the librarian sat at her desk, seemingly oblivious to my presence. As I left, however, she leaned forward on her elbows.

"Just this once," she said, and I wondered what she thought I'd been searching for.

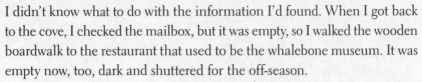

I didn't know what to do with the information I'd found. When I got back to the cove, I checked the mailbox, but it was empty, so I walked the wooden boardwalk to the restaurant that used to be the whalebone museum. It was empty now, too, dark and shuttered for the off-season.

I slipped in the side door and sat in one of the red leather booths. I closed my eyes, trying to remember how it had smelled that first day when I'd found the bones floating in the air, but all I got was the slippery odor of French fry oil, a lingering after-scent of fish. One story covering another.

I thought about the father I'd known—the way he'd cared for those bottles in the drawers as if they held the whole world. If he was a con man, as so many people seemed to believe, then why his love for the scent-papers? Why such personal agony when their smells began to disappear? And if his invention was a failure that took his life down with it, why didn't he hate that machine, destroy it, the way I had? He'd had as much, if not more, justification. None of it made any sense.

Then there was the other issue. Why had he never told me about Victoria Wingate, if he loved her as much as that article seemed to say?

I remembered when I was little and I'd asked my father why I didn't have a mother. *Because you have me,* he'd said. I hadn't asked again. Now I wanted to know.

The next time I could get to the computer, I did a search for Victoria Wingate. There was a blank period of five years or so after Scentography's bankruptcy, but then the hits began to accumulate again, often in connection with a new perfume.

It wasn't until 2010 that I found a full article devoted to her, however.

VICTORIA WINGATE ENTERS
NEW TERRITORY WITH INSPIRE, INC.
THE DAILY SUN
OCTOBER 28, 2010

Victoria Wingate is more than a classic success story. Ten years ago, her company, Scentography, collapsed amidst allegations of fraud. Wingate spent the next decade fighting her way back into a position as one of the fragrance industry's most respected noses.

Now, with her new venture, Inspire, Inc., she is bringing scent branding front and center to retail marketing, creating unique olfactory environments for stores, hotels, even restaurants.

"Smell is our most powerful sense. It taps directly into our emotions," she said in a recent interview. "Why not use it to subliminally enhance a customer's experience? At Scentography, we care right down to the last detail."

Studies have proven that smell is a powerful marketing tool. Want to make customers linger in a store? Adding clementine and vanilla to the air can make us underestimate how long we've been shopping by 26 percent. A survey of Las Vegas casinos revealed that infusing slot machine areas with an appealing fragrance increased the amount gamblers spent by an astonishing 45 percent.

Scent branding is estimated to be an over 300-million-dollar industry, and Wingate claims she has a list of well-known clients, although she cites privacy concerns when asked to name them. She asks for discretion as well when asked about her former business partner and husband, John Hartfell, who disappeared more than ten years ago with their infant daughter.

"I've had no choice but to move on," she says. "Inspire, Inc., is my way to focus on the future."

I sat, staring at the screen, trying to take in everything I'd read. There was only one thing that stuck, however.

She stopped looking for me, I thought. *She didn't even say my name.*

I thought of Fisher. Of my father. I knew what it was like to have someone you love disappear from your life. How could my mother have given up?

The bell rang and the librarian looked over.

"Time to go," she said.

I closed the page and turned off the computer. The screen went dark, and I could see myself in the reflection. Black curls, pale skin—my mother's daughter.

The difference between us was that I would never stop looking.

THE SHIRT

The next day was Saturday. It was early November, the weather turning cold and wet. When I went into the kitchen, I was surprised to find Fisher's mother sitting at the table drinking coffee with Colette, their heads close together. I hadn't seen Maridel since that last morning at the hospital.

It's your fault he's gone, I thought, bristling.

Colette turned to me. "There you are, Emmeline," she said. "Now that you're over your stomach flu, it's time for a deep clean of the cottages. They need new paint, and the curtains could use a wash. Maridel's going to come on weekends and help you." Her voice was loving, as always, but brooked no dissent. Apparently my punishment for stealing Henry's boat had only been delayed, not eradicated.

"Dodge and I are getting a bit old for that heavy-duty stuff," Colette added, reaching down to pat his head. He looked over at me. He'd been more watchful since I got back. He still came to my room at night, but instead of lying by the bed, he settled just inside the door, as if to block me from leaving.

"Is that okay with you?" Maridel asked. She looked tired and even thinner, if that were possible. I knew she still lived with her husband. I still didn't understand why, though, and I knew Fisher hadn't, either. So much was still hidden.

But as I observed Colette's raised and waiting eyebrows, the one thing that was obvious was that I would be working with Maridel, whether it was okay with me or not.

"Sure," I said.

Colette started us on the blue cottage. The last time I'd been inside had been the last day of summer, and I'd been trying hard not to think about Fisher. So much had happened since then, and yet, here I was again, cleaning the same cottage, still wondering if Fisher was okay. Some things never seemed to change.

It was cold, so Maridel and I moved briskly until the wall heater did its work. We headed toward the bed to take off its covers, and Maridel went instinctively to the side I'd always taken when I changed sheets with Fisher.

"Oh," she said, stepping back as we almost banged into one another. "I'm sorry."

She used to do this with him, too, I realized. For just a moment I thought of her, up there in that house, going from one corner of the bed to the next, by herself. I didn't know how she could stand it.

"That's okay," I said, and went to Fisher's side. We got the sheets and blankets off and took down the curtains before pushing all the furniture into the center of the room.

Henry came in, shaking off the rain. He brought us cans of friendly yellow paint, green masking tape, and two rollers on long handles.

"This will make Colette happy," he said, giving me a meaningful look as he headed for the door. I wasn't completely off the hook with him, either, it appeared.

While Maridel applied the tape to the trim, I got the rollers ready and covered the floor with a tarp. Fisher's mother was painstaking in her precision, often pulling up a piece of tape and reapplying it to make sure the coverage was perfect.

"That part will be behind the bed," I said at one point.

She jumped, startled, her fingers going quickly to touch the edge of the tape.

"Sorry," I said. "I just mean it won't show too much."

Maridel shook her head—I tried not to notice how much the movement reminded me of Fisher—and she continued her adjustments. Finally she finished, and we ran our rollers through the paint, pushing them up and down the walls. Maridel worked quickly, never stopping. At first I thought she must be stronger than she looked, but as the day wore on I realized that she simply didn't care about being tired. It was as if her body wasn't hers to take care of.

"Have you heard from Fisher?" I asked at last. I couldn't not ask—even though I knew Fisher would never send a letter his father might intercept.

Maridel nodded, however. "Through Colette." I hadn't known. "You got one, too?"

I nodded.

"Did he tell you where he was?" It was hard for her to ask, I could tell.

"No," I said. We looked at each other then, and I think we both realized that I wouldn't tell her, even if I did find out. Martin couldn't know.

We didn't say much else that first weekend. We seemed to be finding our way into communication, one informational question at a time. It reminded me of those days sitting on either side of Fisher's hospital bed.

Could you hand me that rag?

Are you ready for lunch?

Yet, the more I watched Fisher's mother, the louder the questions in my head, the ones I didn't say, became.

Why do you stay?

How could you let Fisher go?

If I was going to have to work with Maridel, I thought, maybe I could at least learn one true story. It wouldn't be simple; Maridel was as skittish as Fisher had been during that first big storm on the island. The events of the past weeks had only made it more difficult.

My father had taught me that the best way to get a wild animal to talk to you was to be quiet. So I forced myself to be patient. I let the hours unspool around us. At the end of the day, Maridel disappeared up the path like smoke, but I knew she'd be back. She'd promised Colette, and I knew how Maridel felt about promises.

I spent the next week of school lunches in the library, but didn't learn much more about my mother. Over the past five years, Inspire, Inc., had become a huge success. The list of clients—more public now—included hotels and stores, which promoted their connection to the company as a sign of their devotion to their customers, but there was nothing about Victoria Wingate's private life, and nothing about my father.

All my reading about fragrance got me thinking, however. For good or ill, scent had always been a huge part of my life—but I'd never thought of *using* it before, not in the ways these articles discussed. When they quoted Victoria, she made fragrance sound like a magic wand she could wield however she liked.

I wondered—if scents could make customers lose track of time, or gamble money they might not have, could you use them to get someone to tell you a secret?

When I got home that day, there was finally a letter from Fisher in the mailbox. *The nursery is fine. The guys I live with are okay. The city is big.*

The words were flat, informative, but just. The whole thing sounded like a report written by a reluctant student: "What I Did on My City Vacation." I wanted to hear from Fisher, but it broke my heart to have a letter that didn't say all the things I needed. *I love you. I miss you.* Each letter felt more distant, as if anything he had ever felt for me was slowly but surely fading. Was he writing just because he felt he had to? I had no way of knowing.

And still no return address. No way to write him back.

There wasn't anything I could do, which only made me more determined to learn Maridel's secret. I thought of taking it to Fisher, handing it to him like a gift.

See? I love you. I got this for you.

I knew I had one chance to get it right, and so I waited, watching. I could see Maridel relaxing over time, opening up, much the way Fisher had that first summer at the cove. When she arrived on Saturday mornings, Maridel's movements would be tense, tight, but over the course of the hours, she became more fluid. Her eyes stopped scanning; she didn't constantly redo her work. With each new weekend, her transition into our world happened more easily—and each afternoon, she seemed more reluctant to go back up the hill.

I waited for the perfect moment, and for another letter from Fisher, neither of which came. It had been more than two weeks since the last one.

Where are you, Fisher? I wondered. *Do you still love me? Did you ever?*

I thought of all the reasons he could want to forget me. Or maybe he was hurt, in pain, somewhere I'd never find him. I didn't know whether to be angry or sad or lost. The world was filled with things I didn't know.

The next Saturday, Colette said she wanted me and Maridel to scrub the red cottage—a toothbrush-in-the-crevices, make-the-inside-of-the-oven-shine kind of cleaning.

"It feels so good to get this done," Colette said as she sent us off.

"Easy for her to say," Maridel commented as we started down the board-walk. I saw a smile flicker on her lips. Her first.

It was time.

I still had the T-shirt I'd been wearing the last day on the island with Fisher, the one that held his scent. Back then, I hadn't known how that day would end, but after we'd returned to the cove, I'd hidden the shirt deep in the back of my dresser. Every once in a while I'd take it out and hold it up to my nose, be with Fisher for just a moment before I put it back.

Where are you, Fisher? I would ask his smell. *Write me. Please.*

On Sunday morning, I took out the T-shirt and put it on. The smell launched me back to the island, but I pulled a clean sweatshirt over it, mask-ing the scent.

Time to help me, Fisher.

I still ~~~

Maridel and I were working in the kitchen of the red cottage. I kept myself quiet, trying to match my movements to hers, the way Fisher would have. After an hour or so, my skin started heating up and the scent on the T-shirt began to warm, expand. Without looking at Fisher's mother, I pulled the sweatshirt off and let the smell of him slip out into the room.

I knew from personal experience how scents could come at you side-ways, sneaking in, setting your mind and heart wandering. It could take a while. As I watched, Maridel's face changed, opened. Her hand slowed in its circular cleaning motion. She looked up, out the window, toward the water. When she spoke, it was not to me, really—as if directing these words to the world outside somehow meant they were still a secret. Or as if, per-haps, she was trying to send them all the way to Fisher.

"My dad was a baseball player," she began, her sponge finding one spot, rubbing there. "He liked to hit things. We never had much, and if you asked for anything more, he'd kick you out of the house. He traveled with the team, so he wasn't always there, but it felt like every time he came home, my mom got pregnant. And if my mom wasn't available . . ." She did look at me then, a quick glance. "Well, he'd just choose somebody else."

I stood next to her, unmoving. A quiet well of water, waiting for the stones of her words.

"It was always my older sister," she said after a while, "until one night it wasn't. I'd just turned sixteen. I left before anybody got up the next morning. Hitchhiked out of the city. Martin was the one who picked me up— he'd come in to buy fishing gear. He was so kind. It just felt like fate. He asked me where I was going and I said, 'Somewhere nobody can find me,' and he told me he knew just the place." She laughed, more of a shrug than a sound. "You have to give it to Martin, he doesn't lie."

"But he . . ." I looked without meaning to at her arms. The bruises still showed up there sometimes.

"I know. He wasn't always like that, though."

"Why didn't you leave?"

"Where would I have gone?" She shook her head.

"You know," she said after a while, "Martin was the only person who ever told me I was beautiful. When we first met, he would just hold my face in his hands and look at me. I was the one who lied. I told him I could go out on his boat with him. Said we could be happy."

I wanted to argue with her, tell her that her only lies were to herself, but I couldn't speak. She glanced over at me. "Martin used to tell me how salmon always return to the same river to spawn. He said it's the smell that draws them upstream. Maybe we're more like fish than we think. All I know is that when I met Martin, he felt like home to me."

Again she laughed that strange laugh. "I guess that should've warned me, huh?"

I felt like I was drowning. I concentrated on Fisher's scent, though I could already feel it fading from the shirt.

"Why didn't you tell Fisher any of this?" I asked.

"To protect him." Her answer was quick, the words polished by years of thought.

"From what?" I thought of Fisher lying in that hospital bed, that boot print on his chest, the look in his eyes. She hadn't protected him from anything, as far as I could see.

"From me," she said.

I could only stare at her, dumbfounded. She struggled for words, as if logic shouldn't have to be articulated.

"When Fisher was born," she said at last, "and they wrapped him up and gave him to me, he was so perfect. So *clean*, you know? And I thought, if he didn't know where I came from, it couldn't touch him. Maybe I couldn't stop Martin, but I could keep that away from him."

"But he wanted to know. He asked you."

Maridel's face was sad, but set.

"You don't know what you'll do until you're there, Emmeline. And you're a long way from there."

She picked up the sponge, and started cleaning again.

THE CHOICE

Back when we were younger, Fisher had taught me how to read a face and spot a lie. Over time, I'd learned that lies have a scent, too. They always smell a little too sweet, like they need an extra boost of olfactory persuasion. Yet the whole time Fisher's mother had been talking that Sunday, I'd never smelled a lie, not once. What she said—her reasons for not leaving, for not telling Fisher—made no sense to me, and yet they did to her. She'd believed what she said. She was telling a truth, even if it was only hers. I could smell it.

I thought of Fisher's letters, and the articles that I'd found on the computer at school and printed out. If only those pages were like scent-papers, and could emit the smells of lies and truth along with their stories—then I would know, the way I had known with Fisher's mother. In the end, however, perhaps it wouldn't matter; perhaps those stories would be just like hers. A truth. Whether it would be the same as mine, I didn't know. I'd never know, I realized now, until I was there in the middle of them. Until I'd found Fisher. Found my mother.

And yet it was impossible to find Fisher without having a better idea of where he was. I kept hoping for another letter, a clue, an address. Weeks passed. Worry cinched my gut, raveled my thoughts. At night, I'd lie in bed, certain that he hated me, had forgotten me. In the morning, I would hate myself for doubting him. Every day the same cycle, over and over.

I promised myself that if I didn't get a letter by New Year's, I'd go to the city anyway. Track him down. Find my mother.

Autumn came and went. We cut down a Christmas tree. I helped Colette bake pies, and stirred the hot chocolate she liked to make from scratch. I checked the mailbox. I did my homework, pretending I would be there for graduation. I took Dodge for short walks, which were all his old legs could handle. I checked the mailbox. Maridel and I finished cleaning the cottages, but she kept coming to the cove, helping Colette with reservations. I checked the mailbox. By the last day of Christmas break, I'd gotten so antsy that Colette sent me outside to help Henry fix the railing around the restaurant deck.

It was freezing, the clouds low, with the kind of breeze that sneaks right through whatever you're wearing. I'm not even sure why we were working on the railing at that time of year, but it felt good to pound something. Henry mostly stood back and pointed; I hammered. I could feel the shock of it in my arms, loosening me.

"Watch your nail," he said. I'd sent one in crooked. He smiled and leaned in, caught the head with his hammer, and pulled it back out. "Try again."

We went on like that for a while. It was how we'd always worked together, not a lot of words. Colette was the one who talked. Maybe that's why I told Henry.

"I found out who I am," I said, not looking at him.

"Did you?" He didn't rush in with questions, and in the space he left I found a place for my words. I started to tell him what I'd read on the Internet, but when I got to the part about my father's machine, he put a hand on my arm.

"Do you think maybe Colette should hear this, too?" he asked, and I knew he was right.

We went back to the house, listening to our feet talking to the wooden boards as we walked. Colette was just finishing dinner preparations when we walked in.

"Good timing," she said, placing slices of slow-cooked pork roast on a serving plate. The aroma had turned the air around us golden.

"Emmeline has something she wants to tell us," Henry said. Colette put a bowl of mashed potatoes on the table and sat down, looking at me across the table.

"What is it?" she asked.

I took a breath, holding all the smells of that kitchen inside me, and then I told them—about my father and my mother, about Nightingale and the bottles my father kept in the drawers.

"I remember reading about that machine when it first came out," Colette said. "But then it was just gone. I always wondered what happened."

Henry was watching me, nodding slowly. "So that's why you wanted to go back for the bottle," he said. "The one you left behind on the island."

"Yes," I said. "I think maybe my father was making them to test the machine, to see how long the papers could last or something. That one was of the cabin. And us."

"Ah," Henry said.

"The stories on the Internet don't really add up, though," I said. "I want to know the truth."

"Of course you do," Colette said, her voice supportive, but I saw how she watched me, the same way she had when I'd first arrived, years ago. Like I was a tide that could leave as easily as it came.

You were a gift, she would say, *when I least expected it*.

We were done eating by that point. Dodge, who'd been begging bits of pork off my fingers for the past half hour, went and scratched at the front door. Henry came with me when I went to let him out. We stood on the porch, the winter night crisp around us.

"Did Colette ever tell you how we ended up here?" he asked me.

"She said you met in a park in New York City. You'd learned about a job here, and you asked her to come with you." Even after all these years, I still remembered the story.

"Did she tell you she said no?"

I looked at him, surprised. "No."

He laughed softly. "She did—said she couldn't go running all the way across the country with a guy she'd just met. I went anyway. I'd been here a week, feeling sorry for myself. Feeling like I deserved every bad thing that could come my way. And then one afternoon there she was, walking down that dirt road toward me. Said she didn't know what she'd been thinking, letting me get away." He smiled. "Best moment of my life."

Over the cove, the clouds parted just enough to let the moon shine through.

"It's a full one," Henry said, pointing. "There'll be a high tide tomorrow." I thought of the night Fisher and I had run away. I took Henry's arm and leaned close to the paint and sawdust smell of him.

"Henry," I said. "I didn't want to leave you and Colette, back when . . ."

"I know," he said, putting a callused hand on mine. "And you won't the next time, either. That's okay."

The next day there wasn't a cloud in the sky, and when I got home from school I learned that Henry had taken advantage of the weather to do his deliveries to the islands. Usually he was home by four, but by the time he got in it was well past dark, and Colette was getting ready to call the coast guard.

When at last we heard his motor, I went down the dock to meet him.

"Colette's having a fit," I said.

He chuckled. "Of course she is." He reached down into the boat and pulled out a cloth bag. "This is for you."

I took it with uncertain fingers. I could feel a weight, cylindrical and not too heavy. I pulled it out, and held it in disbelief. My bottle.

"Thank you," I said.

"I thought you might need it."

Up at the house the front door opened.

"You still in one piece, old man?" Colette called down.

Henry winked at me. "Can you put that bag somewhere less obvious? Colette said if I went through that channel again, she'd have my head."

That night, as Henry and Colette slept, I packed my things. This time, I wrote a note.

Going to find the truth. I'll call you, I promise. Love, Emmeline

I put the bottle in my pack for a second time. I leaned down and put my arms around Dodge, kissed him on the head.

"I'll come back," I said. He didn't open his eyes, but he shifted out of the way.

PART THREE

The City

ARRIVAL

There was only one bus per day, leaving town at 8 A.M., and my hands trembled as I counted out the money for a ticket. I'd left the house with 387 dollars, tips I'd saved over the years of cleaning cottages. I'd never had much need for money at the cove, but as the bus grumbled its way out of the station, the bills felt like a safety net made too small.

I curled into my window seat, my arms tight around my backpack, watching the trees go by, a wall of green broken only by flashes of clear-cut, or enclaves of houses, a small store or two. I'd studied the maps in Colette's atlas, but now those tiny paper kilometers turned into roads and mountains and the smells of the other passengers, their turkey sandwiches and burnt coffee, the leftover scents of cats and dogs and last night's dinner clinging to their clothes.

My body ached. It had been a long night, and a longer walk to get to the bus. I settled deeper in my seat, pretending its arms and back were the whorls of a shell, holding me safe. I fell asleep, barely registering the people exiting and entering, the way the smells were shifting, gaining edges.

I jerked awake to the sound of a blaring horn, and found myself in a forest of metal and glass.

Towers taller than trees grabbed at the sky. Cars swarmed around my bus, shrieking their way through intersections. People pressed by on the sidewalk, heads down into the phones in their raised hands as if they were praying. I saw a man who looked like a pile of leaves sitting on a box, playing a guitar. A dog no bigger than a squirrel scurried through black-clad legs. I could feel the smells, pulsing against the glass, trying to reach me.

I'd seen cities on TV, but never felt their physical force. How could you find anyone here? In my backpack I had two sets of clothes, a list of addresses, Fisher's T-shirt, and my father's green-wax bottle. Heroines in fairy tales set off with far less, but they had magic to help them. There was no magic in this place, only a smiling mermaid on a sign above a store.

I knew about mermaids.

The bus pulled over, and as the doors clattered open, the smells rushed in. Car exhaust and hot oil, cold coffee and old urine. The sharp stink of fear-sweat. The deep purple bruise of longing. Over it all, like a lowering fog, the reek of asphalt and plastic. I slid down in my seat, pulling my sweater up over my nose.

The bus pulled back into traffic once more, the doors closing. I shut my eyes, tried not to breathe. I imagined the aroma of warm yeast pillowing into bread, of dirt opening to the rain. I slipped my nose into the top of my backpack, tried to find the scent of Fisher's T-shirt, his skin.

After a while the bus stopped again, and this time the engine turned off. I opened my eyes and saw the driver looking my way.

"End of the line," he said.

What am I doing? I wondered.

The bus driver clicked his tongue impatiently.

Just go forward, Emmeline, I told myself.

I stood in front of the bus station, trying to get my bearings. Buildings rose up all around me. There was a hostel in the city, I knew; I had found it on the computer in the library. But the map I had seen on the screen made no sense here in the midst of this chaos.

"Do you know where you're going?" It was the bus driver.

"I'm trying to find this place," I said, holding out the piece of paper with the address.

The driver turned out to be sympathetic; he had a daughter about my age. He insisted on walking me to the hostel, giving me what he called an orientation along the way. He walked me through the forest of buildings, until they opened and I saw a body of water that could have held fifty, maybe a hundred Secret Coves.

"That's the harbor," the bus driver said, pointing. All along its edges were great buildings with towers and grand doors.

"Are those palaces?" I asked, and he laughed.

"Only for rich people."

The bus driver took me along a wooden walkway that ran between the wharf and a long row of buildings made of faded red brick. Our shoes made soft clomping sounds on the old wood that reminded me of home, and I pulled the music of it into me, a shield against all the other noises. We passed restaurants that looked out over the water, the people on the decks beautiful and laughing. My stomach woke at the smells of melting cheese and roasting garlic, cool lemons and warm chocolate, but my mind shut when I saw the prices on the chalked signs outside the doors. I wouldn't be eating at any of these places.

We turned back into the city, taking a complicated series of rights and lefts before heading down a narrow brick alley lined with tiny stores. Smells came out of all of them, dense, too sweet, too strong. A camera-carrying swarm of tourists came toward us, their voices clattering off the walls. We made our way through them, paddling against their tide.

How will I ever find you here, Fisher?

"There you are," the bus driver said as we emerged from the alley. I startled, thinking for a moment he meant Fisher, but then I saw he was pointing across the street to a narrow yellow building stuck like sandwich filling between a restaurant and a language school. "You gonna be okay?"

"Sure," I said, not believing it for a minute.

He patted me on the shoulder, and then he was gone.

Fingers shaking, I pushed the doorbell and was buzzed inside. I paid for a week's stay, giving the money to a young woman with too-black hair and ears pierced with what looked like fishing lures. She gave me a key and said, "Number ten."

Two flights of stairs and a long hall later, I found the room: three metal bunk beds and a single white sink, as spartan as everything outside was chaotic. The windows were tall, the floors made of scuffed wood. It might have been beautiful once, but it hadn't ever gotten one of Colette's deep cleans. All the same, it was cheap. If I was careful, I had enough money for almost two weeks.

Back in the hostel lobby, I spent a few precious quarters to call Henry and Colette from the pay phone.

"Where are you? Are you okay?" Colette sounded almost frantic.

"In the city," I said. "I'm fine. I'm staying in a hostel."

"You scared me."

"I know. I'm sorry."

"Do you want to come home? Henry can drive down and get you." In the background, I could hear the clink of Dodge's metal dog tag against the water bowl, and I thought for a moment I might break in two.

"No," I said. "Not yet." I would not give up on the first day.

We talked for a few more minutes, but all too soon the money ran out and I listened to the long flat buzz as the phone disconnected. A girl walking by looked up from the glowing screen of her cell phone.

"That thing still works?" she said as she passed.

I stood there, the phone receiver in my hand. All I wanted to do was go back to that plain, quiet room upstairs and hide. I wasn't sure what I'd thought would happen once I got to the city—maybe that I'd see the red of Fisher's hair blazing like a beacon across a crowded street. Or maybe I'd hoped an instinct born of love would guide my feet. But this city was like nothing I'd imagined. It made oceans feel small. Instinct drowned here. I needed a plan, something to hold on to.

I heard my father's voice in my head. *Assess the situation, Emmeline. Eliminate the variables. Determine the best course of action.*

I forced myself to go outside. Around the corner was a small grocery store, where I bought a jar of peanut butter, a loaf of bread, and a map of the city. Back at the hostel, I found a set of bus schedules. I took it all to my bunk, made a sandwich, and spread out the map. I noted each of the nurseries in green ink as my mouth worked on the sticky, dry bread. I didn't stop until I'd located all forty-nine.

The marks looked like a school of fish in a huge ocean. As I looked at them, the burst of energy that had taken me this far suddenly ran out. It was only eight o'clock, but I brushed my teeth in the sink and lay down on one of the beds, pulling the covers over my nose.

Sleep didn't come. I was alone in the room, and the emptiness of it reverberated around me. The only nights I'd ever spent by myself were the ones in the cabin after my father died. The memories shivered their way into me. I longed to have Fisher in my bed, or even Dodge by the door. I could hear noises in the hall, the rough laughter of young men, voices speaking in a language I didn't understand. Outside on the street, the traffic was a constant rumble. A man yelled, a harsh, howling sound. An ambulance screamed past, wailing into the night.

My roommates came in hours later, their voices strong and excited, like the summer workers at Secret Cove. They hushed into drunken giggles when they realized I was there. I rolled over, pulling my backpack close, my eyes shut tight, begging sleep to find me.

My days fell into a pattern of peanut butter sandwiches, buses, and dead ends. Every night I went back to the hostel and my revolving cast of room-mates, the room redolent with the smell of patchouli one night, limes and salt another. My dreams were filled with languages I learned to identify, but never understood. I listened to the laughter, the jokes, and the grand plans of my roommates, and I found myself jealous of the way this city was just a stop on their way, a place to collect memories or boyfriends before traveling on. I would lie in bed, trying to imagine myself discovering Fisher, surprising him with a kiss.

Found you, I'd say.

It never happened. All I got was hard bus seats and the blank faces of nursery owners. By the sixteenth nursery, I found myself having trouble describing Fisher; he was losing specificity amongst the hundreds of faces I saw every day.

Red hair, green eyes, I would say, forgetting the way he could raise his left eyebrow, just a fraction, when he wanted to send me a signal. The small white scar he'd gotten on his right thumb, collecting mussels in the lagoon. This city was too big, too fast, for such quiet details.

Did you lose me, too, Fisher?

At the end of the sixth day of searching, I went back to the hostel in the late afternoon. I was tired, but too restless to stay inside, so I went to the wharf, wanting to smell salt water. The scent of brine was lost, however, in the fog of cars and boats and seaplanes. Concrete sealed the ground, the smells of earth locked up tight beneath it. I continued on, ignoring my nose, just wanting to walk until my legs burned and I was somewhere, anywhere else.

When I looked up, I found myself at the edge of a rolling expanse of grass and trees. It wasn't a forest, but as I wandered deeper, following a concrete path that led in soft, sloping curves, I could feel the scents changing. Even though it was still winter, there was life here. I spotted a Douglas fir and went to it, putting my nose deep into the crags of its bark.

Hey, you, I whispered. I could feel my breath warming the trunk, surrounding my face. I made my way from one tree to the next, greeting each, inhaling spruce and cedar, cherry and apple, and some I didn't yet know.

When it started to get dark, I found the trail again and headed back to the hostel. I had more buses in my future, but I carried the scent of sap with me on my fingertips.

After that afternoon in the park, I redoubled my efforts to find Fisher. I told myself I couldn't afford to do otherwise, and it was the truth. I went from one dead end to the next. The world was concrete and jostling seats and buildings that all looked alike.

On the tenth morning, I went to the forty-seventh nursery, on the far outskirts of the city. I'd learned by this point not to talk to management—all the good stories came from the people with dirt on their hands. I found a young woman, her hair up under a baseball cap, wearing an apron with the nursery logo on it. We stood in the greenhouse, the air heavy with flowers that shouldn't have been blooming yet. *Spring is here*, they said, in stark contradiction to the weather outside.

"Is there a guy named Fisher working here?" I asked. By that point I could have said it in my sleep.

She shook her head, moved the watering hose from one pot to the next.

"Red hair?" I persisted. "Green eyes?"

"Oh," she said, "you mean Jack."

My heart leaped. *Of course*, I thought. *Of course he'd choose that name.*

"Is he here today?" I asked, my voice hitching with excitement.

"Oh. No. They fired him about three months ago. There was this thing with a girl . . ." She caught my expression. "Oh hell, I'm an idiot. He's a friend of yours?"

I nodded, but I wasn't listening anymore.

He found someone else.

I didn't know what to do with the thought. Fisher and I had never been like the other kids in school, who picked up and discarded partners as if they were shells on the beach. He and I were two halves of a whole—always had been, from the first moment we met. We could be separated, but never replaced. I had believed in that, in a way I had believed in nothing else since my father died. It had been my North Star for almost five years.

When Fisher left, I'd imagined so many scenarios, so many things that could have happened to him in the city, but never that one. Never the most obvious one in the world.

How stupid was I? Of course he'd found someone else. Someone who wouldn't betray him. I should have known.

"What happened?" I asked the girl in the baseball cap.

"Look, we aren't even supposed to talk about it. It was kind of a mess." She walked over to turn off the hose. I followed her.

"Do you know where he went?"

She twisted the spigot, then looked at my face and took pity on me. "I heard he didn't even pick up his last check."

I stood, surrounded by those deceitful flowers, and counted back in my head. Three months. When his letters had stopped.

I'd worried and waited and searched for a guy who didn't even want to be found. I had been wrong all along, sucked into a fairy tale. Again. In the end, I was just like the weeds in this nursery—something to be pulled and replaced by someone better, prettier.

I was half of nothing.

The hell with you, then, I thought, but the words were more liquid than steel. I wasn't even sure if I was saying them to Fisher or myself.

When I got back to my room, I shut the door behind me. I had only thirty dollars left, not even enough for the bus ride back to Secret Cove. Fisher was gone—he'd disappeared when things went bad, cut off his ties to his old life and started a new one, just like my father had.

Salmon always return to the same stream, Fisher's mother had said. I'd prided myself that I was different. That I had chosen better. But maybe none of us did.

I dumped my backpack on the wooden floor by my bed. It tipped over and the almost empty peanut butter jar rolled out, along with my map. The folds in the paper were ripped from wear, the forty-nine green marks smudged into camouflage. I stared at them for a moment.

Then I took out a red pen and found one more address. Circled it.

Inspire, Inc.

INSPIRE, INC.

Victoria's company was in a green glass building, set among its brick neighbors like a river running between mud banks. The receptionist at the front desk shot me a skeptical look when I entered, appraising me from top to bottom. I was suddenly acutely aware of what she must see. Old jeans, a faded red backpack with fraying straps. My hair hadn't been washed in a week because I couldn't afford the money for a shower. No one had noticed on the bus, but this was no bus.

The woman put her hand on her phone, but then a man in a stiff black suit came up to her desk. Her face opened like a flower, and I was forgotten.

Relieved, I slipped over to a backless leather couch, hidden from the woman by two willowy plants in tall black pots. From this position, I could observe both elevator and entrance. I wanted to see my mother before I told her who I was.

I'd arrived close to lunch. Well-dressed men and women streamed through the lobby. I watched them, and breathed in. The fragrance in the air around me was artificial, but beautifully crafted, a mix of cool greens—grass and water and something else.

Money, I thought, and almost laughed, for the first time since entering the city.

We care, the article had said, *right down to the last detail.*

An older man came through the revolving door. His jeans and simple shirt, the white hair pulled back in a short ponytail, were all in marked contrast to the sleekness of his surroundings. As he passed, I caught a whiff of what smelled like pipe smoke. It reminded me of the cabin so much it was all I could do not to follow him—but I stayed where I was and waited.

Now that I was here, I realized I wasn't sure what I thought, or hoped, would happen. I was searching for a woman who had gone on television and begged for my return. But I was also looking for a woman who'd stopped looking for me. I wasn't sure which one I would find. If she'd even want me.

After what I'd learned about Fisher, maybe my only real hope was that I'd have a chance to decide whether or not I wanted her.

For almost three hours, I watched the lobby. My stomach started to rumble. I had one last sandwich in my pack, but I didn't want to draw the receptionist's attention.

I was about to give up when the elevator doors opened once again and two women emerged. One was young, her white-blond hair cut in a clean line at her shoulders. The other was facing away from me, but I could see the graceful cut of her clothes, all black and white simplicity. Her hair was up, a few dark curls escaping. A fragrance came toward me, honey and amber.

Come find me, I heard it whisper.

I got up and followed them across the lobby, avoiding the gaze of the receptionist. At the revolving front door, the woman with the black curling hair turned to the blonde.

"Do you think you can handle it?" It was a question that only allowed one answer.

"Absolutely, Ms. Wingate. I appreciate your confidence in me."

Victoria placed her hand on the revolving door. "Good," she said. "I look forward to seeing what you come up with." She entered the swish and turn of the door, leaving the blonde in a wake of her perfume. I hurried after Victoria, shoving awkwardly through the stationary door to the right.

"Excuse me," I called.

Victoria turned, looking me up and down. "Yes?" she said, drawing out the vowel. Her fragrance surrounded me, making it hard to concentrate.

"My name is Emmeline," I said, barely getting the words out. "I think you might be my mother."

I heard the sharp intake of her breath. She shook her head, but whether it was in anger or disappointment, I couldn't tell. "My daughter's name is, *was*, Violet," she said. "If you're going to try something like this, you should get your facts straight."

Your birthday is the first day of spring, Emmeline. The smell of violets.

Oh Papa, I thought. *What did you do?*

She was turning away. She was going to leave; I could feel it. If she did, I'd never get any answers. I'd be half of nothing, yet again.

"My father was a scientist," I blurted out. "He hated winter and loved smells. He used to tell me stories about a man named Jack the Scent Hunter."

She stopped, her eyes sliding back to me. Looking at her was like gazing into one of those enchanted mirrors and seeing a beautiful, older, far more assured version of myself. I could see her making a similar assessment, her expression shifting from irritation to confusion.

"What did you say your name was?" she asked.

"Emmeline."

Her brow cleared in recognition. "Of course," she said. Her laugh was short and without humor. "His mother's name."

She looked behind me. "Where is your father?" she asked. "Where's John?"

I shook my head, unwilling to say it. For a moment something strange and private moved across her face. Then it cleared.

"You're here," she said quietly. "You're with me."

We stood there, facing one another as people passed us on the sidewalk. Victoria seemed unable to move, except for her eyes, which kept looking and looking at me.

A man jostled her, startling her into motion. She pulled out her phone, dialed. "Cancel my appointments for the rest of the day. Yes, I mean it."

She put away the phone. "Lunch?" she asked me. She sounded like Victoria Wingate again, smooth and confident. She sniffed once, almost imperceptibly, and glanced at my backpack. "I promise we can do better than peanut butter," she said, and then she smiled.

Victoria's car was low and silver, slipping effortlessly through the traffic. Her slender hands were firm on the wheel. Her perfume was so much a part of her it seemed to emanate from the very curls of her hair. I couldn't stop staring at her. How could someone this stunning be a mother, let alone mine? The mothers I'd seen on television, even the most beautiful guests at the cove—none of them looked like this. It wasn't just her skin or hair or eyes, because I had all of those, too. It was how she inhabited them. If I were a scent-paper, she was what it was like when it burned.

We pulled up in front of an old stone building. A long awning covered the walkway. A man in a green jacket came out and opened my door, then Victoria's. I was surprised when she tossed him the keys. She didn't seem to know him, but she also didn't seem worried when he drove her car away. I wondered if we'd get it back.

"This place is quiet, and the food is reasonable," Victoria said, ushering me through the door. The woman at the front greeted her by name, then looked skeptically at my clothes. Victoria said something in a low tone, and after a moment's murmured consultation, the woman seated us at a secluded table overlooking the garden, handing us each a menu as heavy as a book. A waiter was there instantly, setting down glasses of iced water. Half circles of lemons shimmered between the ice cubes like slices of sunshine. I looked up to thank him, but he was already gone.

"I helped them with their bar," Victoria said, leaning forward. "As it turns out, you can double the sales of rum drinks just by adding the scent of coconut to the air." She winked. I'd always thought winks were the

strangest of the facial expressions I'd encountered after I left the island.
One eye closed, as if in trust of shared understanding; the other open,
watching. For Dylan, a wink had been a weapon. With Victoria, it felt like
an invitation.

I tried to read the menu, but I kept getting distracted. The aromas from
the kitchen filled the room—melting butter, grilling meat, soft and sharp
spices. All of them better than any of the restaurant smells I'd had to pass
by during my time in the city. My mouth was watering, and my nose was
so focused that I could barely skim the first few items.

Sablefish with miso glaze

Duck, dry-aged and served with pureed butternut squash

Wagyu New York strip

I had no idea what these things were, except for duck, which I couldn't
help but feel sorry for. Dry-aged sounded like an especially bad death for
a waterfowl.

The waiter returned. "Shall I order for us?" Victoria asked. I nodded,
grateful. "Anything you don't eat? Allergies?"

I shook my head. Nobody had ever asked me that before. On the island, I'd eaten what I gathered. At the cove, I ate what came to the table.
Now I'd eat anything that didn't involve the jar in my backpack.

"We'll start with the clam chowder," Victoria said. "We can order more
later." The waiter nodded respectfully and disappeared again. "They make
it with fresh clams," she told me. "It's exceptional."

A young woman with a fancy braid in her hair brought us a basket of
French bread, still warm from the oven. I watched as Victoria spread one
slice with butter that melted as she applied it, releasing the faintest scent
of flowers.

"Here," she said, handing it to me. The crust gave way under my teeth
with a delicate crunch, the butter soft on my tongue. It tasted even better
than it smelled. After almost two weeks of hard mattresses and strangers
and failure, I wanted to crawl inside the comfort of this bread and stay
there forever.

Victoria lifted her water glass to her nose and took a quick, automatic inhalation before drinking. She caught me watching and gave a wry smile.

"I always check," she said. "But a fresh lemon makes a difference, don't you think? When it's been in the water too long, it smells like there's a basement lurking in there or something."

I hadn't ever had lemon in water; hadn't spent any time in a basement, either, but I knew what she meant, the way one small note could throw everything off. I'd thought only my father and I felt that way.

"Yes," I said, relieved and thrilled at the same time.

Victoria leaned forward, more intently. "Where did he take you?"

"An island." I thought of the archipelago, those dots and dashes of land, a code you could never unlock.

"What did it smell like?" she asked.

I'd expected a lot of questions, but not this one. As soon as she said it, though, I knew it was the only one that mattered. The only one that would tell you what a place, or your past, was actually like.

"Cedar and spruce and fir," I said. "Applewood smoke. Salt water. That metallic smell right before a storm." I was picking up speed. "Salmonberries, huckleberries, spruce on your fingertips. Wet dirt—oh, and morels." I stopped, embarrassed by my volubility.

"You *did* get my genes," she murmured.

"There were violets, too," I offered. "My father always said they were the scent of my birthday."

Victoria frowned. "Your name was Violet, but you were born on November twenty-second."

"What?" I didn't understand. My birthday was the first day of spring. That's who I was. *Green in the air*, my father would say.

"I'd remember," Victoria said dryly. "It was snowing."

I sat, stunned into silence. I didn't know this girl, this Violet born in a snowfall. But there was a precision, a factuality, to the date Victoria had given me that my father's version had always lacked. My father, the scientist—and the storyteller.

"Who else lived there?" Victoria asked after a while.

"No one."

"That must have been awful for you," she said.

The soup arrived, graceful round bowls filled with creamy white, the gray shells of the clams scattered across the top, opened as if in silent applause. The fragrance sent me back to the lagoon, the water fireworking out of holes in the sand as I raced across the beach.

Over there, Papa. There they are. Catch them.

What had been real about that life?

"Where are you staying?" Victoria asked, pulling my attention back to the table.

I pushed the memories away, and told her about the hostel. With each description, her perfect eyebrows raised higher.

"Well, that will never do," she said. "You're coming home with me. I've always kept an extra room. Just in case."

I breathed in the honey of her perfume, felt it wrap around me.

She kept a room for me, I thought.

THE STORE

Victoria's building was almost one hundred years old, four stories of creamy white stone with intricately carved pillars rising up along the walls, and delicate curves and notches etched beneath each window. It looked like a castle, dropped into the middle of the bustling city.

"This used to be a department store," Victoria said as she pushed open the heavy doors to reveal a gleaming, modern lobby. The floors were glossy tile; at the center was a glass table with a vase of tall, scentless flowers. Fake, I realized, but incredibly realistic. Everything was shining, flawless, nothing to catch your toes or thoughts. The contrast between outside and in was disconcerting, but Victoria didn't seem to find it so. She waved to a young woman sitting behind a sleek counter.

"Good afternoon, Ms. Wingate," the woman said, studiously avoiding looking at my clothes.

"How did it go, Becky?" Victoria asked.

The young woman's eyes grew large. "Incredible," she said, all attempts at professionalism gone. "We've got a date for Friday night. Thank you so much, Ms. Wingate."

"I'm so glad it worked." Victoria ushered me down the hall to the elevator. "Becky is our concierge," she said in a low voice as she pushed the button. "She was having some trouble catching a certain young man's eye, so I gave her a little olfactory assistance." She smiled.

My mind flew to Fisher. Would I have been able to keep him if I'd been able to use scents, not just smell them? Maybe that other girl had been smarter, known what to do. The thought grabbed my mind, dug in.

The elevator opened soundlessly. We entered into a fragrance of fir and citrus, so subtle it seemed to live in the wood paneling.

Victoria was watching me. "Do you like it?" she asked.

I nodded. I could feel it beginning to wash the smells of the city off me.

"It's one of mine—a scented transition between public and private lives. It helps remind people they're home."

"You made this? On purpose?"

She smiled. "Of course. That's what I do."

I looked around and saw a framed directory listing departments in old-style type: *menswear, ladies' clothing, perfume.* I pointed to the last item.

"How perfect for you," I said.

For just a second her eyes darkened, but then she smiled. "We're on the top floor. Department stores always put perfume by the entrance, to greet you—and make anything else you might buy feel less expensive. But yes, I like knowing it was here."

She'd said *we*, I noticed.

The elevator doors hushed apart, and we walked down a thickly carpeted hallway. Victoria unlocked a door, and it opened to a room with ceilings that soared up over our heads. The wood floors were dark and polished, the walls white as blank paper. The far wall was one giant window, divided by straight black lines and covered by white curtains so thin I could see a vague impression of the skyline beyond.

Victoria took off her shoes. "I like to protect the floors," she said.

She seemed smaller without the heels, but as she walked over to the windows, her feet owned every inch they touched. She pulled back the curtains, and the late-afternoon light poured in. Across the street, I saw a glass box of a building that reflected ours like a mirror. Somehow, the old and curving lines of Victoria's building seemed to make sense that way, seen from a distance, caught in time.

I stepped forward, and my tennis shoes squeaked against the floor. I hurriedly took them off, looking around for somewhere to hide them. They seemed so incongruous in that beautiful space.

Victoria saw me. "Make yourself at home," she said. "I'm going to change out of my work clothes."

I put my shoes in the closet next to Victoria's, then wandered into the living room and sat down on the black leather couch. It was all so different from the hostel, or the cove. No chattering roommates, no sound of fishing boats. Just a river of cars going by outside and the warm honey of Victoria's perfume.

On the table next to the couch I spotted a phone, and a flash of guilt ran through me. I hadn't called Colette and Henry since I'd found out the truth about Fisher. I'd told myself I didn't have the money to spare, but the reality was that every time I went near the phone, all I could think of was Henry telling me about Colette, following him across the country, and him, looking up to see her coming down that dirt road.

The best moment of my life.

I'd thought Fisher and I would be like that. I couldn't bear to admit to Henry and Colette that I'd failed.

But now I had something else to tell them, something I could be proud of. I'd found my mother—a beautiful, successful woman—and she'd taken me in. That was news to share.

I tiptoed down the hall, careful of the floors.

"Would you mind if I used the phone?" I said to the closed door at the end.

"Go right ahead," came the muffled reply.

Colette answered on the first ring. "There you are," she said. "Are you okay?"

"I found Victoria," I told her. "My mother."

"Oh," she said hesitantly, but then the warmth came back into her words. "How was it?"

The love in her voice took me back. In a flash, I was there in her kitchen, surrounded by the smells of bread dough and Dodge and the faint hint of lavender from her soap. I opened my mouth, ready to confide in her.

I lost Fisher. My name is Violet. I don't know what's true anymore.

But then I stopped myself. Colette had been a brave traveler. I might not get the love of my life, as she had, but I would not give up and go home yet. There were other things I could win here.

"I'm staying with Victoria for a while," I said. "But she has a phone, so I can call you."

"I've got the number right here on my cell," Colette said. It made me smile, hearing that familiar way she claimed any technology Henry would allow into the cove.

"So, what's she like?" Colette asked, and I brought my thoughts back to the city.

"Beautiful," I said. "Smart. We went to lunch at a fancy restaurant where the clams in the chowder were still in their shells."

"Huh," Colette said. "We generally do that work for our customers."

"I know," I said, and smiled again at the rough pride in her voice.

"Did you find Fisher?" she asked.

There was a moment of silence. "How's Dodge?" I asked.

She paused, as if deciding whether or not to let me off the hook. "Oh, well," she said eventually. "He's an old dog, but he's a good one. He misses you, you know?"

I swallowed. "Give him a kiss, okay?" I heard Victoria coming into the kitchen nearby. "I gotta go."

"Already?"

"Yeah—we just got here. I'll call soon. I love you."

As I hung up, Victoria came into the room, dressed in slim black slacks and a loose white shirt. Her hair was down around her shoulders. I thought of Dylan, pulling my curls—*Miss Piggy, are these your tails?* I was willing to bet nobody had ever done that to Victoria.

"You sounded so comfortable on the phone," she said. She was carrying two glasses of water, and she passed me one as she sat down. "I wasn't listening to your conversation; I just heard the way your voice sounded."

I nodded. "Colette and Henry are the ones who took me in after . . ."

She waited a moment. When I didn't continue, she leaned back and asked, "What was it like there?"

She reminded me of Fisher, the way she was able to read a person, a situation.

Don't think about him.

So I told her about the resort, about the guests and the scents they left behind. I told her about making cinnamon and cardamom rolls in the mornings, and helping Henry fix the boardinghouse. I didn't say anything about the whale building, or school, or Fisher.

"How long were you with them?" she asked.

I counted in my head. "Five years." Almost exactly, I realized.

"So much time," she said softly. She was looking out the window, and I couldn't see her face. "How did John . . . ?"

"Drowned." It was all I could say.

"Oh." She paused. Her index finger found its way through a curl, winding it tighter. "Did he ever tell you about me?"

"No," I said. *He never told me about anything.*

"How did you find me, then?" she asked, turning to me now.

"The machine—Nightingale. I looked up the name online, and it linked to you."

"Well," she said. "There's irony for you."

Cars buzzed by outside, making the windows hum. I could hear the occasional distant rebuke of a horn, the cry of a seagull. All I could smell, however, was her.

"He made it for me, you know." Her voice held a dreamy tone I remembered.

Once upon a time, Emmeline.

"He insisted we call it Nightingale," she continued, "although I told him it made no sense for a scent machine. Still, it sounded so romantic, like something out of *Romeo and Juliet*, so I said okay. The investors hated it, but we didn't care."

I remembered the story my father had torn from the book of fairy tales. I opened my mouth to tell her, but Victoria was still speaking, gazing past me now.

"It just about killed him when it turned out the machine didn't work," she said. "The backlash was horrible, and he was so sensitive to things like that, you know? He couldn't take it. He just . . . left." She rubbed her eyes, once, quickly. "All this time, I thought he was alive."

She shook her head and glanced at the clock. "We should get you settled in—let you take a nap. You've had a long day."

The wide bed in Victoria's extra room was covered with a comforter as soft and white as fog, and looked as if it had never been slept in. The carpet was beige, and thick beneath my feet. It reminded me of a fancy hotel, like the ones I'd seen in magazines guests left behind at the cove.

"Your bathroom is in there if you want to take a shower," Victoria said, motioning to a door on the far side of the room.

All I wanted to do was lie down. I was exhausted, mind and body, but I looked at the pure white sheets and decided it might be better for all of us if I did as she suggested. Besides, a shower that wasn't operated by coins, that wasn't a mere curtain away from strangers, felt like a luxury beyond belief.

I stood under the water for twenty minutes, letting it wash away the hostel, the nurseries, the past two weeks. I tried not to think about Fisher, or where I was. It was all too much, too new. Instead, I opened the bottles on the shower shelf, smelling rosemary and lemon, and then a flower so delicate it became the steam around me.

At last I dried off and lay down on the bed, my body falling deep into the mattress. Still, I couldn't sleep, no matter how tired I was. The texture of the sheets was so smooth, the fragrance too perfect, too clean. My thoughts skittered across them, unable to settle. Finally, I went over to my backpack and pulled out Fisher's T-shirt. The smell was almost gone, more peanut butter than Fisher by this point, but even if it was almost nothing, even if he was no longer mine, I wanted to feel his scent around me. I took the shirt back to bed with me. I wouldn't think about him, I promised myself. I would just breathe.

It wasn't until I was almost asleep that the back of my mind found Victoria's words again.

All this time, I thought he was alive.

Just for a moment, I wondered what she'd thought about me.

The aroma of coffee woke me. Throughout my years with Colette and Henry, that scent had been my alarm clock, pulling me out of bed. Even when I was too young to drink it, it was the way the day started.

When I entered Victoria's kitchen, she was standing at the counter, working an espresso machine. I'd only seen them in pictures, and the fragrance was astonishing, as deep and rich and complicated as the dirt on the island. Victoria put a pitcher under a thin metal pipe and turned a knob. There was a hissing sound, and I could smell milk heating, expanding.

"Hello, sleepyhead," she called over the noise. "Ever had a latte?"

I shook my head.

"Here," she said, holding out the cup.

It was as luxurious as the bed I'd slept in, silky and warm. I thought of Colette's coffee—the *let's-get-going* feel of it. The way Henry would carry his thermos all day, drinking it even after it got cold. I took another sip and breathed in the smells of freshly ground beans and hot milk and just a touch of cinnamon. Beyond them, hovering in the air around me, was another scent. *Spruce*, I thought. I must have still had some on the sweatshirt I'd pulled from my pack that morning. I relaxed into the familiarity of it.

"What do you say to coming with me to work today?" Victoria asked as she sat down across from me. "I have a hunch you might enjoy it."

I looked down at my clothes.

"We can find something better than that," she said with a laugh. "Let's see if I have something that'll fit you. Bring your coffee."

When she opened the door to her bedroom I stopped, stunned. On the far side of the room, surrounding the double doors of the closet, a grid-work of shelves lined the wall from floor to ceiling. In each of the square openings was a small bottle, all different shapes, made of blue, green, yellow, and clear glass.

"My scent collection," Victoria said. "I started it when I was just about your age."

I walked over, put a finger on the faceted edge of one of the bottles, saw the liquid within. No scent-papers here.

"They're beautiful," I murmured.

"Normally I keep the curtains closed to protect the perfumes, but I love to wake up to the light on them. It's quite a show in the morning. Now," she said, opening the closet, "let's find you something more fun than a sweatshirt."

I sat on the bed as she brought out one thing after another, passing through the wall of scent bottles each time. I could almost feel them watching, leaning toward her. Loving her.

No closed drawers this time, I thought. *No secrets*.

It turned out Victoria and I were almost the same size. The jeans she gave me were elegant, dark blue, and tighter than any I'd ever worn, but when I looked in the mirror I was surprised to see the line of my legs, the slim curve of my hips. She handed me a loose sweater, white and soft as baby chickens.

"We won't make you go full business mode," she said. "We'll call it take-your-daughter-to-work day."

Victoria drove with one hand on the wheel, using the other to gesture. Her voice raced along with the engine. Her hair was straight today, and her scent was lighter, more air than honey.

"You may have noticed," she said with a wry smile, "that not everything smells good in a city. My job is to make things smell better—because when they do, people spend more money. They don't know that's why, of course. They think they're buying a shirt because it fits them, or a couch because it's comfortable. But we know better. We make them *want* it."

She plucked her travel mug from the cup holder and took a quick sip as she changed lanes.

"We're just doing what nature already does, honestly. A flower has a scent for one reason—to attract whatever will pollinate it. Animals use odors to communicate all the time. The difference is, they pay attention to those messages. People don't." She put the mug back, and sent me a considering look. "I'm thinking you might be different."

I was. *Dirt Sniffer. Miss Piggy.*

"We speak a language other people don't even know exists," Victoria said. "I go into a hotel and figure out what scents will make someone feel at home, or *not* at home—make them feel younger, more confident, sexier. It depends on what the hotel wants."

She was engrossed in her topic, her eyes bright.

"You have to match the fragrance to the place, or it doesn't work. Put roses in the men's clothing department and you're in for all kinds of trouble. There are big stores in New York City that have a different scent for each department—*that's* how careful we get in this business."

We pulled into an underground parking lot and took an elevator up into the store. As the door opened, a fragrance like the soft pink of a sunrise met me. I looked about and saw snow-white chairs and couches as big as beds, glass vases and silver picture frames. Confident, well-dressed women swirled about, considering a candle here, a pillow there. I knew at once I didn't belong in a place like this, even in Victoria's clothes.

"I need to talk to the manager," Victoria said. "I'm going to check the sales records and see how we're doing. While I'm gone, you explore. Let me know what you think."

I wandered about, trying to get my bearings. I went by a metal umbrella stand that reminded me of Henry's fishing bucket, but the price was more than a week's stay at the hostel. There was a wall of framed mirrors, all different sizes and shapes, but my reflection in Victoria's clothes didn't make sense in any of them. I turned my back to them, and it was then that I spotted the table toward the back of the store. It looked just like the one we'd had at the cabin, unfinished, its legs thick and straight, its top a solid plank of wood. I went over to it as if pulled on a tide, closing my eyes and running my fingers over its rough surface. I inhaled, hoping for an undercurrent of wood smoke or bread yeast. But there was nothing—just life, wiped clean, like the sheets on my bed the night before.

"You don't like the smell?" I opened my eyes. Victoria was standing on the other side of the table, her expression inquisitive.

"It's fine," I said.

"It's okay. I want to know what you think."

"It's just . . ." I paused. "It doesn't smell like home." My words sounded feeble, even to me.

"Ah." She nodded. "How would you fix that?"

The thought had never occurred to me. Home smelled like home because of what was there. You didn't *make* things smell like home.

"Home isn't perfect," I said finally.

Victoria's head tilted. "Oh, but it can be," she said with a slow, delighted smile. "In fact, that's our job." She came around the table, put one hand on my elbow. Her voice was low. "Sales are good, but I'd like them to be higher. We've got every scent in the world at our disposal. What would you do?"

It was a test; I knew that. Still, it was one I desperately wanted to pass. For Victoria, my sense of smell didn't make me weird—and if I proved I knew what I was doing, it could make me special. Maybe it would make her love me, want to keep me.

I scanned the room, my nose alert. On all sides, customers idly picked up one item after another. I could hear Fisher's voice in my head: *People guard their faces. They forget about their hands.*

Don't think about Fisher, I told myself.

But I looked at their hands anyway. I watched as one woman's fingers ran over the softness of a blanket; another's passed along the curving lines of a silver candle holder. They were curious, but nothing more.

The gauzy pink fragrance lay in the air. I watched it drape itself around the woman's shoulders like a shawl. Comforting, effortless.

"You're making it too easy," I said.

Victoria cocked her head, intrigued. "What would you do instead?"

I thought about the island, how I used to push my face into the moss at the base of the trees to be part of its smell. About Fisher, the way the best of his scent waited in the warm spot just behind his ear.

"Hide it," I said. "The fragrance."

"Where?"

I looked around. "In the pillows—and the blankets. In the candles, too, just a little bit, so you have to lean in to find it."

"Give them the thrill of the hunt, and they'll want to take a trophy home." Victoria's eyes went bright. "What an amazing daughter I have." She put her hand on my shoulder, and I warmed to its touch.

TRAINING

I spent the rest of the day watching my mother move through her world like a breeze over tall grass. Everything in her path turned to motion, admiration. She was as different from me as anything I could imagine. When we walked into Inspire, Inc., however, the receptionist did a double take.

"Miranda," Victoria said to her, "this is my daughter, Vi . . . Emmeline."

Miranda nodded. "The resemblance is striking, Ms. Wingate," she said. She'd seen me less than twenty-four hours before and hadn't noticed it then, I thought. What a difference a day and some clothes made.

"We should get going," Victoria said. She walked me through the building, showing me sparkling-clean rooms filled with people in starched white coats and endless shelves of small bottles. When I got close I could hear the scents, murmuring and clamoring inside. It was all I could do not to open the bottles and let the stories out.

"You hear them?" Victoria asked in a low voice.

"Yes," I said. I wondered if the people working so studiously around us did, too. Maybe this whole building was filled with people like me. Then again, maybe not—Victoria had whispered, after all. That thought, and the small private circle it made of the two of us, made me shiver with delight.

That evening, back at the apartment, Victoria and I made a large salad for dinner.

"I have to eat out so often. It's hard to keep your figure," she explained as she chopped tomatoes, her fingertips close to the sharp edge of the knife. "And trust me, you have to keep your figure. A woman can't leave anything to chance in this world."

I wished someone had told me that before I lost Fisher.

I looked at my mother, her creamy skin, her strength and effortless confidence. I thought of the scent in the elevator, all the fragrances I'd smelled at Inspire, Inc., the way each one had colored my mood, changed my thoughts. Maybe that's what happened when you left nothing to chance.

We sat down at the dining room table. She chewed delicately while she considered me.

"Did you have a good day?" she asked.

"Yes," I said fervently. The side of her mouth twitched in amusement.

"What would you think about training to be a nose?"

I hadn't expected that. Before I'd met her, I considered Victoria a source of information. In the face of the assured, elegant reality of her, I'd figured that she'd soon tire of having me around, and send me back to Colette and Henry. As recently as last night, that scenario would not have made me sad. I loved Colette and Henry, and there were far worse things I could do with my life than help them run the resort.

But after today and all I'd seen, things—and I—felt different. Victoria's offer sparkled in front of me like light on water. I could do something, be somebody. Maybe Fisher would hear about it.

"You could stay here," she added. "Live with me."

Maybe I would have a mother.

"I'd like that," I said to Victoria.

"Good." She smiled. "Of course, you still have to get your high school diploma."

My fork skittered against my plate. That was the last thing I wanted to think about.

"I'm not kidding," Victoria said. "It doesn't have to happen right now, but it's not negotiable. No daughter of mine will put herself at a disadvantage."

Her ferocity was beautiful. *No daughter of mine.* I could feel the words claim me, warm and possessive. She wanted me, even if Fisher didn't.

"So, do we have a deal?" she asked.

I imagined days spent swimming in smells, with no need to hide who I was. I could be myself. I could be like her.

"Yes," I said.

"Wonderful," Victoria said, taking a sip from her wineglass. "I have just the person to teach you. She's a real up-and-comer; she'll be perfect."

Later that evening, I called the cove and told Colette I was going to stay. The story spilled out of me and she listened quietly. When I was done, she said she was glad for me, but in the slight hesitation in her voice I could hear the reflection of my own words—shiny and a little too fast. Armed with excitement. I imagined them banging around the kitchen, bouncing off the pots and pans.

"I'll call again soon," I said, and got off the phone as quickly as I could.

The next morning, my teacher was waiting for us in a small, white room on the third floor of Inspire, Inc. It was the young woman I'd seen talking with Victoria that first day in the lobby; I recognized her white-blond hair. She had on a formfitting black skirt and blouse, the one accent a gray-blue scarf tied in a complicated knot around her neck. She wore no perfume, but I detected a hint of ginger nonetheless.

"Claudia is a wonder," Victoria said. "She'll take good care of you."

Claudia smiled. "Of course, Ms. Wingate. I'd be honored to teach your daughter."

Victoria gave her an approving look, then turned to me. "I'll see you at the end of the day, Emmeline. We can have dinner together."

The door clicked shut behind her, and Claudia's smile disappeared. She walked over to the table, her heels clacking against the hard floor, and motioned for me to sit facing her. When I'd done so, she leaned forward. Her eyes were the same cold blue as her scarf.

"I trained in Paris for three years," she said, each word clipped. "I worked my ass off to get hired here. I was just given my first big assignment two days ago. I was going to make bespoke fragrances for *seven* different houses for a *major* actress."

She paused, expectant.

"That's amazing," I said. It was all you could ever say to girls like this. I'd learned that much in school.

"Now I'm training you," Claudia said. "The boss's daughter, who's probably never been inside a lab in her life." For just an instant, I saw the right corner of her upper lip curl. "Victoria says you were raised on one of those little islands up north?"

I nodded, and she lifted her hands in disbelief. "Okay, then; I guess we better get started. We've got a long way to go."

She reached under the table and brought up a box.

"You probably think all you need is a good nose to make it in this business," she said. "The truth is, a professional perfumer's mind is a giant database. You have to be able to retain literally thousands of scents in your memory. Do you think you can do that?"

I nodded. Scents I could hold on to; it was everything else that left me.

"Let's see if you're right." Claudia opened the box and handed me a bottle. I unscrewed the top, and breathed in.

Once upon a time, Emmeline, Jack went to an island covered with trees whose flowers glowed like tiny lamps . . .

"Nutmeg." Claudia grabbed the bottle and screwed the cap back on. The story was still filtering through me when a new scent exploded forth.

"Orris root," Claudia said, tapping the new bottle on the table. "Am I going too fast for you?"

"No," I lied.

"Good."

Linden blossom. Tonka bean. Benzoin. The smells came at me, little glass missiles fired across the table in rapid succession.

"The point is speed and precision," Claudia said. She pushed a stack of papers toward me, the pages divided into rows and columns. "Put each scent in a category. Fresh, floral, woody, spicy, animal, marine, fruity. You need to recognize them instantly, without thinking."

The bottles started again, and the world turned into charts and rows, filled with an onslaught of strange names. *Litsea cubeba. Frangipani. Neroli. Tagette. Orange* broke into pieces, became *pettigrain, bergamot, tangerine, mandarin, bitter, sweet,* and *blood. Pepper* was *black, green,* or *pink. Mint* was *winter, spear,* or *pepper.* Hour after hour. Box after box. Every once in a while, Claudia slipped in a repeat, just to see if I could catch it.

"This one?" she asked.

"Labdanum." I remembered it from hours before, the feel of it like the touch of a hand on your lower back.

Claudia blinked, the barrage of scents hesitating.

"Huh," she muttered.

When the scents started to flow again, they came even faster.

At the end of the day, head pounding, I went back to Victoria's apartment and took a shower, using the hottest water I could stand. The steam swirled up into my nose, blissfully neutral, clean.

"How did it go?" Victoria asked when I came into the living room.

"Fine," I said. "Good."

I meant it, I realized, almost to my surprise. As much as I disliked Claudia, the intensity had been as exhilarating as it had been exhausting. By the end of the day, I'd reached the point where I could sense the category of a scent almost before the bottle was open. *Fresh* was quick and cool, never warm. *Floral* was soft and seductive, the kind that kept its clothes on, showing only an ankle or a shoulder. *Spicy* bit your nose, woke you up. *Woody* sent me to the island so fast I couldn't stop the tears from filling my eyes. I couldn't wait to start combining them, creating something new.

Victoria was right—this was a language, my language, and I wanted to write.

Claudia was determined to overwhelm me, that was obvious, but the effect she had was the opposite. My mind had never felt so alive. I plunged into the work, stayed as many hours as she demanded. Weeks passed and I didn't even notice. I was doing the thing I was made for. And caught up in the scents, it was easier to try and forget Fisher, wherever he was. Whoever he was with.

Victoria and I fell into a companionable schedule. She worked as late as I did, and often later. On the evenings when I was alone, I'd walk back to Victoria's apartment, taking the route along the wharf, letting the sound of my feet on the boardwalk settle my mind. On those nights when Victoria didn't have a business dinner, we ate together, shopping for groceries on the way home. She introduced me to spices and ingredients I'd never encountered, textures that were new to my tongue. Maybe it was the feeling of Victoria's attention, the way she watched each and every reaction I had, but even after a day of smelling bottle after bottle, there was something thrilling about holding these new smells in my hands, tasting the samples in the tiny paper cups. Everything that was tired in me woke up anew.

Back at the apartment we'd eat while the rest of the world was already half-asleep. Victoria said I was grown up enough to drink a glass of wine, and we'd sit there and talk about fragrances and the business. There were times when I missed Dodge and Colette and Henry, the smells of fish and fog and the marinade of life that slips into the walls of old houses. But more and more, the girl who'd curled up in front of the fireplace, a wet dog be-side her, was beginning to feel like a different Emmeline. A child.

One evening, Victoria and I had finished dinner and were sitting on the couch in the living room. I had a cream-colored throw blanket around my shoulders; it was soft, made of cashmere. We'd had salmon for dinner, so fresh I could swear I even smelled a bit of salt water and cedar in the air. Victoria's honey-and-amber perfume was there, too.

"You don't wear that perfume very often," I noted.

She smiled. "A signature scent is a brand," she said. "It works fabulously for helping people make emotional connections with places, but if a per-son wears the same perfume all the time, you risk muddying the memo-ries." She leaned back in her chair, contemplative. "I remember when I was younger, I learned about this artist named Andy Warhol—he would wear a fragrance for a while, and then put it in his museum, as he called it. Whenever he wanted to go back to a particular time, he'd just open that bottle."

"Like your collection?" I asked.

"Yes," she said. "Except I make my own fragrances." The pride in her voice was unmistakable. She looked over at me. "You will, too."

It was as close as Victoria ever got to an embrace, and I held her words close.

"Do you ever think of scents as colors?" I asked impulsively. It was the kind of question that would have had the girls in school rolling their eyes.

Victoria nodded, however. "Absolutely. And sounds. Some of them even seem like people."

"Yes," I said. "Exactly." We sat there for a few minutes in easy silence.

"Were scents always like that for you?" I asked eventually.

She considered her wineglass. "My mother worked the perfume counter at our local department store," she said. "She'd bring home bottles and line them up on her dresser. I didn't have a lot of friends at school—we didn't have much money, and in school, differences matter, you know?"

I did.

Victoria took a sip of wine. "Anyway, I'd go into my mom's room and smell her different perfumes before she got home from work. I'd give them my own names. Sometimes I'd even carry one around in my pocket for a while."

She smiled, a sad one. "I've heard it said that great perfumers don't have a lot of friends; they have a lot of ingredients."

The thought of Fisher picked the lock of my memories and sauntered out. It did this more often than I wanted. This time, there was another girl with him. Prettier, smarter. There were no smudges of dirt or life on her face; she carried no baggage.

Why don't you want me, Fisher?

I looked at my mother. "I know just what you mean," I said.

"When can I learn to mix scents?" I asked Claudia the next morning. She'd been grilling me for more than two months by that point, throwing an ever-changing combination of old and new scents at me with machine-like rapidity. I hadn't missed one in more than a week. My conversation with Victoria had made me want to surprise my mother, show her I could do more.

"You're not ready," Claudia said, taking her seat. Her boredom was like a third person in the room. "Get out your charts."

"Try me," I said.

Claudia paused in irritation, but in the end her desire to prove she knew more than me won out.

"Fine," she said, and then launched in, the words rote, mechanical, coming as fast as the bottles had. "Every perfume is made of top, middle, and base notes. Top notes are light, middle notes last longer, base notes last longest. A good perfume has all three, but they have to be in the proper proportions."

The sentences washed over me in a wave of technicalities, but I could *feel* what she was talking about. It had happened with every scent-paper I'd smelled, the fragrance shifting, telling a story that deepened even as it disappeared. Even nature was that way, if you thought about it—the bright green of the trees giving way to the dark and complicated dirt beneath, the ocean holding the scent of death under all that life. What Claudia was talking about so arrogantly was simply the world I had grown up in.

"I can do it," I said.

"It's a precise *science*, Emmeline. It's not for children."

"I can do it," I repeated, stronger this time.

Her eyes woke, tightened. "Is that so? All right then, let's educate you, if that's what you want."

She opened a bottle; the scent was tart, quick, and the tiniest bit sweet, like the sparkle of rain on a blade of grass.

"White grapefruit," I said automatically.

"Top note," Claudia said, trimming the edges of her *t*s.

Another bottle—lavender. Softer, kinder. Colette's soap, the scent hidden in her clothes.

"Middle," Claudia said. "You following this?" Her dark eyebrows were raised, two slim curves providing their own parenthetical commentary.

"I get it," I said. The *t*s on my own words were sharp now.

"Good. So, ready for the big boys?"

"Sure."

She dug around in the box at her feet for a moment, and brought out a bottle. "Here's a good one." She passed it across the table. It was filled with a dark paste, rather than liquid. I unscrewed the cap. The smell rolled toward me, and I reared back. I could almost hear growling, the pop of a bone socket.

"Civet," Claudia said, unfazed. "It takes a strong stomach to smell an animalic base note straight, don't you think? But a drop or two, down there in the bottom of a perfume? It sends that *other* message. Death and sex— that's what perfume's all about. You'll understand when you're older."

I stared back at her. I knew about death. I knew about sex. I didn't need her to tell me.

She held out another bottle, her expression bland. "Jasmine."

I was cautious this time, barely sniffing the contents, but the smell was a relief—sweet, white, and creamy, almost euphoric. I felt as if I were floating in it.

Just as I was about to put the bottle down, though, I caught a whiff of something else in the background, something narcotic and sticky. I inhaled more deeply, trying to pin it down.

"You like it," Claudia said. For the first time, she seemed pleased with me. "Do you know what that is, that note you're searching for?"

I shook my head. It was right there, but in that cool, blank room, I couldn't quite name it.

"It's shit," Claudia said. She smiled, slow and lazy. "Technically, the molecule's called indole, but a rose by any other name . . ."

Something in me tightened.

Want to smell my shit, Miss Piggy?

I looked over at Claudia. I hated her right then, in a way I had never hated anyone, even the kids at my school. This cold, sleek girl wanted to break me, just like they had. Back then my skills had worked against me; they'd made me a freak. Here they were finally in my favor.

Claudia thought she knew smells—but all she knew was names, rows, charts.

You have *no idea what I can do,* I thought.

THE ISLAND

I was glad Victoria was working late that night; I needed the walk home. The chill in the air, as well as anger, kept me walking quickly through the dark evening. My feet took the usual route along the wharf, my thoughts completely focused on the events of the afternoon, on the scent I could make.

My mind roamed through possibilities, then landed on the pink sunrise scent in the first store Victoria had taken me to. She'd told me recently that hiding it was having an effect on sales. But I could do more; I knew I could.

Suddenly, water crashed down in front of me, splashing my shoes, my pants. Broken ice cubes danced on the pavement around me.

"Shit!" I exclaimed, jumping back.

I looked up. On the back balcony of one of the faded brick buildings that lined the wharf stood a young man in a half apron, an overturned white service bucket in his hand, water still dripping. The light from the open door behind him spilled out, illuminating pale skin. Red hair. The shoulders were broader, the hair longer, but I would have known him anywhere.

Fisher.

Without thinking, I stepped back farther into the shadows. It wasn't necessary, though; he hadn't even looked down. He lit a cigarette, staring out at the dark water.

Now I watched him from below. How many times had I walked this route home? How could I not have felt that he was nearby? And yet, he didn't seem to sense me, either, standing right there, looking at him. The old Emmeline and Fisher would have known.

Up above me, a woman's voice called out and Fisher looked up, stubbed out his cigarette, and went inside.

A cigarette. Since when did he smoke?

Who are you now, Fisher?

I made my way around the building and found the front entrance. The glowing neon green sign above the doorway made me pause—*The Island*.

Maybe you haven't forgotten everything, I thought, unsure if I was happy or angry or both.

I could hear the tumbling waves of voices inside, the music low and bluesy. I opened the heavy door and slipped in. The room was dark and smelled of beer and bourbon. The occasional table candle illuminated old brick walls, the few overhead lights gleaming off a long expanse of mahogany that ran the length of the room.

Fisher was behind the bar, his back to me as I entered. I slipped into the darkness of the alcove by the door, watching him. The place was crowded, and he worked without stopping, never looking past the next order. His movements were quick and certain; when he finished pouring a beer he pushed it across the bar hard enough that it slid, requiring the recipient to put out a hand, absorb the movement. When he used the shaker, the ice cracked against the metal. If you didn't know him, you might think it was confidence. You might not sense what was smoldering underneath.

He turned his back to the crowd, reaching up for a bottle on a high shelf, the movement suddenly, achingly familiar. I had seen that same motion so many times while we were cleaning the cabins. I used to secretly watch the way his muscles moved under his pale skin, as I did now. He turned back again and poured a stream of clear liquid, ending with a sharp twist of his wrist. I could see the length of his neck, the lines of his jawbone. I could feel the curves of them under my fingers. The longing I felt then made me furious. How could he work here, surrounded by smells and men destined to bring out the worst in him?

At the end of the bar, the busboy had stopped to talk to a young woman. Their faces were lit, happy. The glow seemed to catch Fisher's attention.

"You going to work or not?" he asked, shooting the words down the length of the bar. I remembered us, standing in the clearing, the ax in Fisher's hand, the way he had teased me.

You going to help with this, or not? There had been such joy in his face.

But this wasn't that Fisher. This was how his father would have said it— digging in, searching for the weak spot. Making himself feel better at the expense of someone else.

Salmon always return to the same stream.

Fisher, too, it seemed.

But I didn't have to. I refused to be Maridel, ignoring what was right in front of my eyes, forgiving everything.

I yanked open the door of The Island and thrust my way out into the street. I didn't want to watch anymore.

After that, creating a new fragrance was all I could, or would, think about. I went to Inspire, Inc., each day on a mission. Every scent in Claudia's bottles was a possible component, a potential magic key. *What smell would make women want to buy things they didn't actually need?* I was so caught up in the combinations and implications that my reaction times slowed, faltered.

"Emmeline." Claudia snapped her fingers. "Pay attention."

But I was, more than she knew.

It was the scent of cardamom that finally did it. As Claudia opened the bottle, the smell seemed to yearn toward me. I inhaled and was back in Colette's kitchen. Fisher and I were making coffee for the summer guests, the rolls turning golden in the oven. The longing in me blew past all my defenses.

I reached out and took the bottle from Claudia's hand, held it to my nose.

"Don't you know what it is?" she asked, shaking her head at my stupidity.

But I didn't care what she thought. I wanted that scent. It didn't matter that the coffee, the yeast, the melting sugar weren't actually in it. I wanted the memory it evoked, and as I inhaled more deeply, I could feel it wanting me, too. Wanting the warmth of my skin. When Claudia wasn't looking, I tipped the bottle, letting the opening touch the inside of my wrist. A drop of liquid sank into me.

And that's when it hit me. I'd been going at this puzzle all wrong. I'd been following Claudia's approach, treating the scents like component parts instead of the living things I knew they were. I'd been trying to come up with a fragrance that was a perfectly polished equation, but the fragrances I knew were never like that. They mingled and danced and whispered. Their scents slipped into yours, and each of you changed the other, became something new. We didn't use each other. We needed each other.

And that need could make you do almost anything. I'd seen that.

Now I wondered—what if I left something out of the fragrance on purpose, something so elemental, so necessary, that a person's own body would strive to fill that absence? And what if that missing thing could make a person need to buy the things around them?

"Emmeline?" It was Claudia, her impatience overflowing.

"Cardamom," I said, and dove back into my thoughts.

I could do it. I knew I could. This was something I understood, something Claudia could never imagine. I couldn't wait to see the expression on her face.

⌒

The missing element couldn't be in the top notes. I figured that out quickly enough. Top notes were the ones that caught your attention, the glittering invitations that led you deeper into a fragrance.

It couldn't be a middle note, either—those warm, round things, full and loving. Taking them out would induce the soft purple of wanting, but that was still too passive. *Need* lived in base notes. It was the difference between appetite and craving, a bruised heart and a broken one. Base notes were just that, base—subterranean and simmering, dirt and blood, grief and desire and memory.

As I stepped into the elevator of Inspire, Inc., at the end of the day, I was thinking about the store: its snowy white couches that had never known dog hair; its tall vases waiting to be filled with flowers by husbands who would never actually remember an anniversary, a birthday.

"Dammit." A woman in a suit pumped the lobby button with a well-manicured finger, checking the time on her watch.

"Day care?" said the woman next to her.

"Yeah. If I'm late one more time, they're going to kick us out."

The two women exchanged glances.

"I had a talk with Tim," the second woman said as the elevator started its ponderous way toward the ground floor. "Told him he needed to help more at home."

"How did that go?"

"He said he'd just washed his car."

"Christ."

"I just want . . ."

"I know."

The elevator opened and the two women quickly exited. I followed them onto the sidewalk, hearing a different conversation in my head.

Home isn't perfect.

Oh, but it can be.

I'd known perfect. Against my will, my mind went back to my time on the island with Fisher. Lying in bed, our smells blending in the sheets. His hand on the small of my back as I cooked.

A man bumped into me, jostling my thoughts to pieces. I blinked, looking around at the people thronging the sidewalk. The suits and strollers, the frustrations and exhaustion of day's end. In the middle of it all, half a block ahead, a couple waited for the light. There was nothing exceptional about them. He wore jeans and an old sweatshirt. Her hair was an uncombed cloud around her head. But they were looking into each other's eyes as if nothing around them existed, or needed to. I felt something go through me, sharp as a spike.

And just like that, I knew the base note I needed to leave out.

I turned around, and flew back up in the elevator to the third floor. Even before I entered my classroom, I could hear the scents whispering, moving in their glass containers. I went through the boxes, pulling out bottles almost without seeing them. I placed them in the beautiful leather messenger bag Victoria had bought me. I could hear them clinking softly as I walked down the hall and I tried not to remember the last time I'd heard that sound, or what had happened.

This is different, I told myself.

I got the bottles back to Victoria's apartment, sequestering myself in the bathroom and closing the door behind me. I laid out my supplies on the white tile floor, took a breath, and began mixing. The scents were talking now, full of ideas. They leapt from the bottles, eager to blend.

Come play, they said, and I did.

At one point, Victoria came and knocked on the door.

"What are you doing in there? I can smell it all the way out in the living room."

I straightened up, feeling a sudden ache in my shoulders. How long had I been working?

"It's a surprise," I said.

"Smells like a good one."

I pushed the hair back from my face, breathed in the developing fragrance on my fingertips. I was so close.

"Can we go to that store tomorrow?" I said. "The first one you and I went to?"

"Why?"

"I want to show you something."

In the mixing bottle, the scents swirled.

Inspire, Inc., used a machine that dispersed fragrances in a mist so fine it was effectively invisible. The smells spilled into the imaginations of customers, hitched rides on their clothes and the products nestled in their shopping bags. A perfect branding delivery service.

I breathed in the store's scent, that pale pink sunrise of a thing. *Just you wait,* I thought.

"Ready?" I asked Victoria, the mixing bottle raised in my hand above the machine.

She hesitated, looking out toward the sales room.

"I know what I'm doing," I said. "I'm your daughter."

Victoria smiled then, and stepped back. "It's all yours."

I tipped the liquid into the container.

"Okay," she said. "Let's go see what happens."

The fragrance started off bright and happy, fresh-cut grass and sunshine, iced hibiscus tea, the best of a Sunday afternoon. Lavender and rose released their sweetness into the air so serenely you knew there was not a weed within ten yards of them. The scents filtered out through the store, and as Victoria and I watched, the customers began putting down their phones, looking about with greater interest, smiling at one another.

"Well, you've certainly made them friendly," Victoria said.

I just smiled.

The fragrance began to deepen. Vanilla, the clarion call of mothers in aprons and after-school cookies warm from the oven. The women's expressions softened.

Your life can be like this, the fragrance said. *Your children will love you.*

Then, slowly, lazily, in came the scent of jasmine.

Victoria tilted her head. "Hello, troublemaker," she said.

It floated out across the room, heavy and sensual, the essence of beautiful, younger women. Women who birthed children and wore bikinis within a month, or worse yet, never had children at all, their stomachs taut, their breasts ripe. Women who drew the wandering eyes of husbands.

Then, even as the customers began shifting away from each other with polite, nervous smiles, there came another scent, lurking inside the jasmine, where it always waited—a touch of indole. A trail that led you downward, into the dirt.

But not enough—the fragrance was still too sweet. It hovered in the store, off-kilter.

"Hmm," Victoria said, her eyebrows pulling together.

"Wait," I said.

The want of balance was like an ache in the air. The fragrance reached out, searching, begging for completion. It didn't want sweet. It didn't want nice.

And then, out of the skin, the sweat, the very heat of the women's thoughts, came the missing base note. Keen edged as a knife, it rose to meet the sweetness.

Jealousy.

As we watched, one of the women picked up a cashmere throw and clutched it to her chest. Another sat down on a leather couch, her arms spread out like a claim jumper. *Mine.*

"Brilliant," Victoria said, stifling a laugh. "Absolutely brilliant."

THE MALL

Claudia started speaking even before the door was fully open.

"You're late," she snapped. "I'm not paid to—"

She froze like a squirrel when she saw Victoria.

"Ms. Wingate," she said, her fingers going to the perfect knot of her scarf. "What a pleasure to have you stop by."

"Hello, Claudia." Victoria's voice was as cool and relentless as an incoming tide. "I wanted to thank you for your efforts, but I think we're all done here."

Claudia sighed. "Ms. Wingate, I want you to know I did everything I could, but she just doesn't get it."

"That's where you're wrong." Victoria considered the charts spread across the table. "What's the first rule in this business, Claudia?"

"Learn your customer."

"Indeed," Victoria said. "And if you'd followed that one simple rule, you would have understood that this girl knows fragrances better than you ever will. I'll be taking over her training. I'm sure there's something you can do in the lab."

Claudia glanced at me, her face pale, and I raised an eyebrow.

It was the most fun I'd ever had in that room.

Victoria said we should celebrate my new fragrance by taking the rest of the day off. She wanted to buy me some clothes. I had more than enough, I told her, but she was insistent.

"Coco Chanel used to say, 'Dress shabbily and they remember the dress. Dress impeccably and they remember the woman.'" We were walking across the parking lot toward a magnificent shopping mall. "You want to be remembered, don't you?"

My mind flicked back to Fisher, and I nodded without thinking.

"Chanel was a genius," Victoria said, shaking her head in admiration. "She started with nothing but grit and brains, and she fought her way to the top."

The doors of the department store opened with a sigh, and the smells clamored toward me. Even after three months in the city, the sheer cacophony was overwhelming. I wanted to bolt, but I clenched my teeth and followed Victoria, who wandered through the smells the way others might peruse flowers in a garden. I could almost see her mind, picking and gathering, pruning and arranging, as if all the scents were there for her to do with them as she pleased.

In the end, despite her comments about the importance of clothes, I noticed she paid far more attention to the customers' fragrances. As we headed toward the escalator, she tilted her chin in the direction of one of the shoppers, breathing in.

"Cinnabar—orange blossom, clove, lily, a touch of patchouli." She ticked the ingredients off. "That woman picked her perfume in college in 1978, and she's worn it ever since." She looked over at me and smiled. "She thinks it *defines* her. She's right. And that one." She nodded toward a woman standing by the leather boots in the shoe department. "Roses and gin, one of those boutique perfumes. She likes the joke of it, but she's more traditional than she'll ever admit. I bet she has plenty of fantasies she never acts on."

It was like the game I used to play, back when I read the bedsheets in the cottages at the cove, tried to figure out who the guests were, what they wanted.

As we started up the escalator, a woman in her midsixties passed us going down, trailing a wake of fresh oranges behind her.

"Did you know," Victoria said over her shoulder, "that if you put men in a room with just the faintest smell of grapefruit, they tend to think the women around them are six or seven years younger than they actually are?"

I watched the straight line of Victoria's back ascend the escalator in front of me, and breathed in her scent of the day. It reminded me of the fragrance in the lobby at Inspire, Inc., cool and clean, with just a touch of money.

We were on our way out of the department store, bags in hand, a lunch of fresh crab salad in our stomachs, when Victoria took a detour.

"Let's try something fun," she said, steering me toward the makeup counter. I shied back. "Don't worry," she said, and sat me down on one of the tall stools. A ridiculously thin young woman glided toward us.

"Can I help you?" she asked.

"Let's see what you can do," Victoria said. The woman became a flurry of action, opening bottles and tins, pulling out brushes in multiple sizes. The world narrowed to powders and liquids and colors, greens and peach, black and smoke.

"Close your eyes," she said, and I did, hoping I wouldn't ever have to open them and see what she was doing. I thought of the girls at school, their bright blue eye shadow, the blush that looked like finger paint. I sat, frozen, as brushes and pencils marked my face, pushed against my eyelids, my lips.

"Blot," the woman said, putting a Kleenex against my mouth; when I did nothing, confused, she said, more insistently, "Press down." I did.

After what felt like forever, the movement stopped.

"There you are," she said. "Perfect. You can open your eyes."

I did, slowly, and almost jumped back. The face in the mirror was nothing like mine. If Victoria was an elegant, refined version of me, this was the opposite end of the spectrum. My eyes were huge, garish things, sur-rounded by what appeared to be a bed of wet moss. My mouth was so red it looked like I'd been eating raw meat.

"No," I said.

Victoria came around from behind me and looked.

"Oh my." She deftly moved the woman aside. "Just a moment, Emmeline," she said. "Close your eyes again."

I felt fingertips this time, hers, moving across my face. Along my cheekbones, across my lips, my eyes, but gently, like a benediction, a promise. I was held, shaped, loved by those fingers. I could feel it on my skin, in my blood. I wished it would never stop.

"That's better," Victoria said a few minutes later. "You can look now."

I opened my eyes. After the last time, I wasn't sure what to expect. But the face I saw this time was beautiful, luminous. My eyes were big, but soft, haunting. My cheekbones were defined and full of stories. My lips didn't scream for attention; they were available, but still mine. A secret, barely whispered; the prologue to a book you could get lost in. I'd say it didn't look like me, but it did—a me I'd never thought I'd reach.

"Wow," I breathed.

Victoria smiled, pleased with her work. She turned to the makeup saleswoman. "It's all about subtlety," she explained. "The best seduction is the one you never see coming."

I couldn't stop looking at myself. *If only Fisher could see me*, I thought. *He'd want me now.*

No matter what I'd seen in the bar, no matter how much I tried not to, I still thought of him far too much, spent too many hours not writing letters to him in my head, not wondering who the new girlfriend was, not holding on to his shirt when I slept. I missed him in my bones and my lungs and my skin. He was like the scents in the bottles, murmuring, waiting, eager for me to crack the seal.

He doesn't want you, I told myself.

You are beautiful, the face in the mirror said.

Victoria handed me a small turquoise bag. Inside, the small bottles seemed to sparkle.

"A little magic for you," she said, and we walked out into the mall. I saw a young man's head turn to follow me; another one smiled a hello as I approached.

"This is your power," Victoria told me. "You get to choose what you do with it."

We wandered down the row of stores, commenting on the window displays, the smells, but not entering. Toward the middle of the mall, we approached a shop that was emitting a bruising bass beat. The light inside was low and murky, the customers close to my age, with tight faces and meticulously ragged clothes.

"We're trying to land this chain," Victoria said. "What do you think of it?"

"It's like a cave," I said. I could just imagine men with rough hair and faces standing by a campfire, the night shadowy and dangerous around them.

She laughed softly. "Exactly. So what kind of fragrance would you design for it?"

Her eyes were bright; we were playing a game. I cocked my head in response. "I'm not sure," I said. Looking at the casual nonchalance of these kids, I could feel my newly found confidence starting to ebb.

Victoria leaned close to my ear so I could hear her.

"What's the first rule of our business?" she asked. It didn't feel like the same question she'd asked Claudia. This time it felt like a secret handshake.

"Learn your customer," I said.

"Exactly. Figure out their story, and once you do, they're yours."

We stood there together, and I watched the kids picking up T-shirts with ads promoting rock concerts that happened before they were born, in cities they would never visit. One girl elbowed her friend, pointing to a shirt that read *Get Off My Back*. She made a crude motion with her hand and they both giggled. Two strangers with equally flawless bodies tried to share

a three-way mirror, careful not to look at one another as they turned this
way and that in identical jeans.

They're no more comfortable than I am, I realized, shocked.

The scent-story came into my mind easily then—notes of old leather
and clove, a puff of cigarette smoke. An invitation from the cool kids, a
nod of approval pulling customers in, and then, beneath, a bit of talcum
powder.

You're still a baby, it would whisper. *Everyone knows.*

I knew without thinking what that would pull out of these kids. *Fear*—
sharp as sweat, an olfactory balance to the softness of the powder. With it
would come a desire for armor, fashionable protection—a half-ripped shirt,
jeans that said, *Yes, I do fit in.*

I could do this in my sleep.

The fragrance landed us the account. It worked so well that Victoria
joked the store would have to provide bigger bags for all the purchases, and
after that she brought me along whenever she courted a new client. I'd carry
a notebook and look demure—her assistant, jotting notes.

"You're my secret weapon," she told me. She set me up with my own
lab, a small, bright room, its glass shelves packed with every scent I could
ever want. For a week or two she stuck around, offering suggestions, showing me techniques, but it wasn't long before she threw up her hands in
mock surrender.

"You don't need me," she said. "It's all yours."

I dove in, exhilarated as a dolphin with a whole ocean in front of it. I
made moods, worlds, memories of things that had never happened. I designed the flowery scents of romance for a jewelry store, but left out a missing note of lust. The sale of engagement rings skyrocketed. I concocted a
fragrance for the waiting area of a restaurant, so light and virtuous that the
orders for high-end steak went through the roof. Just for fun, I released odors
of metal and electronics outside a bookstore, and watched people race in-

side and put their faces deep inside pages, searching for the rustle of paper, the welcoming scent of ink.

With the right ingredients, I could make people do anything.

At the end of every day, Victoria would stick her head in the door.

"Come on, worker bee. Time to get some fresh air in that brain."

I would show her what I'd been doing, and then we'd head home, walking down the halls of Inspire, Inc., while people nodded and smiled in our direction. Their attention was for both of us now. Word was getting around the company about my scents.

Back at the apartment, the messages from Colette were stacking up, the light blinking on the machine. I'd called her regularly at first, regaling her with stories of my fragrances and what they'd accomplished.

"Really?" Colette would say, but her voice came from a distance that had nothing to do with miles, and my calls diminished as the months passed. It felt as if every time I talked with her, I was reminded of Emmeline-from-the-cove. Scared. Unsophisticated. Unable to hold on to her boyfriend. And beneath it all was the uncomfortable question: How did Colette view the current iteration? Each of our conversations seemed to have its own missing base note.

Pride.

But I didn't want to think about that. I liked this new Emmeline. I liked the way that men looked at her, the praise she'd earned for her talent. The envy, even.

"Are you going to check those messages?" Victoria asked one evening. "They aren't for me; I don't use that line for anything but avoiding solicitors."

"I will," I said. "Later." But each new message made it harder to listen to the others.

One morning in September, Victoria looked up from her coffee and said, "*The Daily Sun* wants to do an interview with you. It seems they've heard we've got a *wunderkind* at Inspire, Inc."

"A what?"

"A prodigy."

I fingered the handle of my mug. "I don't know."

"It's time to let my secret weapon out of the box," Victoria said. "Let the whole world know how good you are."

I had an image of magazines fluttering through the city like birds. Maybe Fisher would see it, I thought. Maybe Colette and Henry would read it and be proud of me. I remembered discovering the article about my mother and father on the Internet. The photo, the way I'd been drawn into it, into them.

Would you come find me, Fisher, if you knew where I was? If you saw how I look now?

It had been almost a year since I'd seen him. I told myself every night that I didn't want him anymore—but people lie. My father was right about that.

"Okay," I said.

"Great. It's set for two this afternoon," Victoria said. "Let's find you a good outfit."

THERE'S A NEW NOSE IN TOWN
THE DAILY SUN
OCTOBER 2016

In a small lab on the fifth floor of Inspire, Inc., works a young woman with an astonishing story. Eighteen years ago, Violet Hartfell went missing, kidnapped as a baby by a father driven mad by failure. He hid away with her on a remote island, utterly cut off from civilization.

He forced his young child to hunt and gather food, convincing her there was nothing beyond the island they called home.

That girl, now called Emmeline, survived the ordeal. In a dramatic turn of events, she was recently reunited with her mother, Victoria Wingate.

"I knew she was special from the moment I saw her again," Wingate says. "She reads smells the way others read words. She's an amazing olfactory storyteller."

Wingate is the founder of Inspire, Inc., a company that creates olfactory environments. If you've ever walked into a store and were tempted to buy for no reason you could pinpoint, or walked into a hotel and suddenly felt as if you were on vacation, you've probably encountered the work of Inspire, Inc.

Emmeline now works to contribute to her mother's legacy. In just a few months, she has created fragrances so successful that they are rapidly becoming the gold standard for olfactory branding, increasing sales for companies by a seemingly effortless 20 percent or more.

Numbers don't seem to mean much to young Emmeline, who looks not a minute older than her almost nineteen years. She is shy, and seems more comfortable with scents than conversation. Ask her about fragrance, however, and she opens up.

"They're alive," she says, pointing to the bottles that line the walls of her laboratory. "They tell me things."

"Emmeline was like a savant when she first arrived," says Claudia Monroe, who trained her. "Like she'd been raised by olfactory wolves or something. She had this incredible raw talent. It was a joy to polish it."

For now, Emmeline seems content to stay hidden away in her laboratory, churning out her magical creations. She has all the air in the world to work with. We can hardly wait to see what comes next.

RENE

I put the article down, my hands shaking. *Forced to hunt and gather food? Survived the ordeal?* They'd made it sound as if I grew up wearing sealskins. I'd talked with the woman for more than two hours. I hadn't said a thing about the island, or my father. I'd talked about the sense of smell, about how scents weren't real anymore, about how Dodge paid more attention to the world around him than most humans.

None of that was in there.

I stuck my head out my office door. I wanted to find my mother, but instead I saw Claudia, heading down the hall, a cardboard box in her hands. Fury rolled through me.

"Olfactory wolves?" I said as she came closer. "Really?"

"Don't worry, princess," she said. "Your mother just fired me." She lifted the box in her hands. I saw a framed photo inside, Claudia and a boy, maybe her brother. For a moment I felt sorry for her.

"She's using you, you know," Claudia said. "Like she did me."

"She wouldn't," I said. I was her daughter. Her secret weapon.

Claudia shook her head, disgusted. "You're just a customer, Emmeline. We all are."

Figure out their story, and they're all yours. I remembered Victoria leaning in close in that hot, loud store, telling me a secret. I remembered the glow of her approval for my first fragrance. Claudia had received none of that.

"You're jealous," I said, but she just shrugged, as if nothing could matter less to her, and went down the hall, the open flaps of the box bouncing with her steps.

"Don't worry," Victoria told me when I found her in her office. "It's actually great press."

"But it's not true."

"Sales did go up," she noted. "They got that part right."

I shook my head, miserable.

"Come on, Emmeline." Her voice was friendly, persuasive. "It's just a story—and a hell of one, really. People will pay attention. Chanel always said, 'In order to be irreplaceable, one must always be different.' Take advantage of this."

"What if I don't want to?"

Victoria met my gaze, and shook her head. "Sometimes," she said, "you remind me of your grandmother."

There was a disappointment, a bitterness in her voice that brought me up short. All I knew of Victoria's mother was that she had worked in a department store. I'd never even seen a photo of her.

"How?" I asked. Whatever it was, I didn't want to be like that.

Victoria shrugged. "My mother had a great nose," she said, "but she never took it beyond the perfume counter. That work doesn't pay much, so she had boyfriends, one after another. She wasted her talent figuring out which fragrance would catch them. Tabu for the man who already had the white picket fence at home. Arpege for the widower whose wife had loved flowers. And my mother didn't just wear the fragrances, she *became* them." Victoria's voice had shifted as she talked, changing from sultry to saccharine, ending with everyday disdain. "The irony was, the men never did marry her. Do you see what I'm saying?"

"No," I said. I was lost in the story.

"It's simple, Emmeline. Nobody respects you if all you care about is what they think. I learned that lesson early on."

But it wasn't as simple as just not caring. I went back down a hallway lined with curious faces, and shut the door of my office. I thought of Fisher finding that article, of Colette reading it. They'd think I'd said those things.

When Victoria came by at the end of the day, I told her I was working on something, and I'd see her at home. Her brow furrowed, but she left me alone. I stayed in my office, surrounded by scents, listening to them whisper. The susurration of saffron. The sweet reassurance of benzoin. The way sandalwood always seemed to be asking a question, and vetiver always seemed to have an answer. Of all the things I'd heard that day, those were the only ones that made sense. I settled into my chair and closed my eyes, shutting out the rest of the world.

I awoke with a start from a dream about the cabin. It was as tangible as the chair I was sitting in; I could still smell the pipe smoke. I breathed in, trying to calm myself, but the scent remained, stubborn, beckoning. I paused, sniffing hesitantly.

The smell persisted.

I rose and crossed to the door, poking my head out. There was no one there, just the wake of an aroma. Still half lost in my dream, I followed the scent along one hall, and another, then down a flight of stairs. The building was empty, and my steps sounded huge in the quiet, but the trail was there, leading me all the way to the far corner of the fourth floor, where a door was cracked open, light trickling out.

With trembling hands I pushed on the door. A man with a short white ponytail sat at a long metal table, a ring of glass bottles around him. He looked up as I entered.

"I'm sorry." I fumbled. "The smell . . ."

His bushy eyebrows rose over his gray eyes. I didn't know if it was the scent, or how different he was from everyone who worked around me, but I recognized him. I'd seen him in the lobby that first day when I came to find Victoria. He worked here. It surprised me; he didn't seem to fit in with Inspire, Inc. Then again, maybe I didn't, either.

"You don't like the scent of pipe tobacco?" he asked.

"No," I said. "I mean, yes, I do. It reminds me of a place I used to live." He waited, inclining his head toward me. "The smell lived in the walls," I said, and cringed, thinking of the article, and my stupid, naïve words— *They're alive. They tell me things.*

But the man just smiled in a way that filled his eyes. He held out his hand. "I'm Rene."

I took it. "Emmeline," I said.

"Do you know what I'm working on here, Emmeline?" he asked.

I shook my head.

"I'm re-creating scents that are disappearing," he said. "Pipe smoke. Typewriter ribbons. Those tiny wild strawberries that grow in the forest. It's a pet project I work on in the evenings. I just can't bear for them to be gone, you know?"

I nodded. I did know.

He reached out, taking a bottle from the ring in front of him. "This one is my favorite," he said, undoing the cap.

"What's that?"

He held it out like a gift. "Smell for yourself."

I took in the scent—not with the small, clinical sniffs Claudia had taught me, but as my father had. I closed my eyes, and let the picture fill my mind. The smell of dry earth, opening to the rain in the spring. It unlocked me like a key.

Once upon a time, Emmeline.

"*Petrichor*," Rene said. "The word comes from *petra*, which means stones, and *ichor*, the ethereal blood of the Greek gods. Plants release an oil that stops their seeds from germinating when it would be too difficult to survive. The oil soaks into the pores of the stones, and is set free with water. They say it's the smell of waiting, paid off."

I wiped my eyes with my thumb, trying to hide my reaction.

"You know," Rene said, "you remind me of someone."

I looked up. "My mother, probably—Victoria Wingate. People say I look like her."

"Yes," he said. "You do, but that's not who I was thinking of."

"Who then?"

"Your father, John." The affection in his voice was clear.

My voice tightened to a croak. "You knew him?"

Rene nodded. "We worked together, a long time ago. Your father believed scents were alive, just as you do. It's what made him so good at what he did. It was his gift."

I saw the yearning in my father's face as he breathed in the burning scent-papers. His hand, reaching out to grab the blue-wax bottle as he fell through the sky.

"Not always," I said.

"Nothing can be always. That's the first thing a smell teaches you." He looked at me, considering. "Did he ever tell you about how he got started with scents?"

"No." Another secret.

"It was his mother. She died when he was young—twelve, I think."

"What happened?" I asked, holding my breath. *Please*, I thought, *don't let it be drowning.*

"She got cancer," Rene said. "And apparently she waited too long to go to the doctor—she didn't want to say anything. She was in the hospital for weeks, though, before she passed. John said she hated the smells there, so he'd smuggle in new ones." Rene gave me a sad smile. "He said he brought about half the spice bottles from the kitchen. He'd sit on her bed while she made up stories about each one, and her brave Jack who hunted for smells."

Once upon a time, Emmeline, there was a beautiful queen who was trapped in a great white castle. None of the knights could save her . . .

"Oh," I said quietly.

Open the back of your mind, I could hear my father saying. *Listen to the story.*

The truth had been there all along, I realized—hidden in his fairy tales like the scent-papers inside the bottles.

My brain was pounding; I needed time to figure out what it all meant. "I have to go," I said, getting to my feet.

Rene nodded. "Come visit me again sometime."

I headed for the door, then turned. "Thank you," I said.

His eyes met mine. "He was a good man, Emmeline. Don't let anybody tell you otherwise."

I rode the bus to Victoria's apartment, avoiding the walk along the wharf. The bus had the same hard seats, the same tired people as the one I'd taken that first day when I'd come to Inspire, Inc. Nothing had changed except me. I sat there amidst the tag end of everyone's day, remembering the Emmeline in the old sweatshirt who'd come here searching for her boyfriend, her past.

I had lost Fisher, but when I met Victoria, I thought I'd found a future. A new life. A better Emmeline. I'd gone forward into Victoria's world, shedding the rest like my old clothes. Now the conversation with Rene, the smells of pipe smoke and petrichor, were like fists knocking at a door I'd closed.

Let me in.

I'd known Rene for all of half an hour, but I trusted him. What he'd said made sense in a way that felt elemental and true. He'd given me back something I thought I'd lost, or maybe never had.

In my mind, my father had always been my father—he'd never been a child. Now, for the first time, I could imagine him as one. Young and scared, left alone. I knew what it felt like to lose a parent, the way it became a hole you fell into and never came out of.

Oh, Papa, I thought. *What else don't I know?*

It was late when I got home; I could hear Victoria in the shower down the hall. I started toward the kitchen, but as I walked through the living room, I saw the light blinking on the message machine, and a longing for home swept through me. Colette and Henry wouldn't have seen the magazine yet; they didn't have a subscription, and it would be a while before someone gave them a copy—if they saw it at all. I picked up the phone, dialing through to the voicemail. I was hungry for the comfort of their voices, even if it was only a recording.

The first messages were much like the last ones I'd listened to. Colette relating snippets of life, a funny comment about a summer guest. Keeping in touch, no matter how far I'd gone away. But as I made my way through the fourth, then fifth, then sixth message, I could hear them changing.

Give us a call, darling.

We need to talk to you.

And then Henry's voice. *It's Dodge, Emmeline. I'm sorry . . .*

THE PARK

I dropped the phone back onto the receiver and stood there, unable to move, to breathe.

I'll come back, I'd promised Dodge—but I hadn't, and now he was gone. I remembered him waiting outside on the front porch until I was no longer scared, the way he'd helped me understand my new world. He'd been the only being on earth who knew every one of my stories, even the worst ones, the ones I'd whispered into his fur so no one else could hear. I could still feel the curve of his head in my cupped palm.

I'd found my bright new life here and barely looked back. I'd left him behind—just like I'd left Cleo alone the night the bear came. The pain of it buckled me.

Down the hall, Victoria's shower stopped, and I realized I couldn't stand the idea of talking to her, to anyone. I darted into my room, shutting the door behind me. When she knocked a few minutes later, I turned on my own shower so I wouldn't have to answer. I sat under the falling water and sobbed into my hands, ugly gasps of air—until the water went cold, then freezing, and the bright sting of it sucked the heat from my skin and the thoughts from my brain.

Eventually, I got out, shivering, and climbed into bed. My body shook itself back to warmth, but I still couldn't sleep. I watched the bright red hours tick by on the clock until finally I yanked off the comforter, dropped it on the floor by the bed, and curled up inside it.

"You okay?" Victoria said in the morning. She was standing at the counter, her back to me, the smell of hot milk and cinnamon in the air.

"Sure," I said. I couldn't tell her. In the past twenty-four hours, my whole world had been overturned, again, and I didn't know who I was. I felt as if I'd lost not only my dog but myself—both the girl I used to be and the carefully constructed version of these past few months. So many pieces, lying on the ground.

My mother handed me a latte, and took in my still-blotchy face. No amount of cold water or makeup had helped.

"You got in late last night," she commented.

I looked around her perfect apartment. It was strange to even think of Dodge here. All I could imagine were his nails scratching across the polished wood floor, his fur collecting on the rugs, his food and water dishes cluttering the kitchen. I had luxuriated in the elegance of this place, the effortless feeling of organization and control. Now I just wanted the heat of Dodge's breath across my bare feet and the mess he brought into my life.

I looked at Victoria. I couldn't even begin to explain that to her.

"I'm fine," I said. "I just worked too late."

I went to Inspire, Inc.; I didn't have an excuse that wouldn't invite questions. Besides, I thought, work might help—when I made fragrances, I was in charge, a feeling that was in short supply right then. If people were talking about the article as I walked through the halls of Inspire, Inc., I didn't notice. All I wanted was the familiar feel of the bottles, the scents whispering in my head.

I got to my office and sat in my chair, trying to focus. My latest project was for a car manufacturer. The leather smell of new cars hadn't been real for years; it was just a scent sprayed on the undersides of the seats before delivery. This manufacturer wanted another fragrance, a signature scent that would play off the anticipated smell and promise of something new and exciting. Expensive.

I made myself think about cars—the shine, the metal, the glass and not-leather, the couples with children running around their legs. Did I want smells of home? Of escape? I listened, waiting for the story. Something to make the customers open their wallets, buy.

But there was nothing. Just a dull buzz, opaque as fog. I looked at the bottles, willing them to speak, but they just sat there. Shaking my head to clear it, I started pulling bottles from the shelves and opening them. I could still *smell* each scent; I knew their properties and could have put them in the proper place on any of Claudia's charts, but the magic, the voices, were gone.

Was this what it was like for other people? I wondered. How could they stand it?

Maybe I just needed to get started, and the scents would come along with me. I began combining accurate proportions of top, middle, and base notes, but it was like fitting square blocks into square holes, no more or better than that. I mixed one fragrance after another, my efforts speeding up, becoming frantic. Each one emerged dull and dishonest. A thing, not a story.

I worked for hours, but it never got better. I made passable fragrances—but I could still smell enough to know the difference.

Finally, I stood. I had to get out of there. I needed green. I needed trees.

⁓

I hadn't been back to the park since I'd met Victoria. Months had gone by while I worked in my little white office, and I'd barely noticed. The closest

I'd come to nature was my walks along the wharf, and I hadn't done that since I'd spotted Fisher on the balcony of The Island.

It took almost half an hour of searching and backtracking before I turned a corner and saw that great green meadow in front of me. I could sense the air beginning to lift and move in the open space—and yet, this time something felt different. I looked at the trees and what I saw now was their meticulous, even spacing. I saw the concrete, not dirt, of the gently curving paths; the signs that told you where to go, how to be, the name of each tree and bush.

When I'd been in the park before, I'd been happy to find anything that felt like home, but this time it all reminded me of the grocery store Victoria liked, the one with the hothouse tomatoes whose stickers read *limited edition*, and the mason jars decorated with red-checked ribbons, each one containing a single cup of organic oatmeal. Like a memento, or a proxy. The real thing had dirt on its vegetables, underbrush between its trees that tangled and whispered against your pant legs as you pushed through. It had dogs that swam in salt water, and brought the smells home whether you liked them or not.

What was I doing in this city? I'd been leaping from one thing to the next, chasing Fisher, following my mother, filling my loneliness with her assurances that I was special. And I *had* been; I'd made masterpieces—but they'd been crafted for her approval, and they'd manipulated other people in the process. In the end, I'd been no more faithful to the scents I'd loved than I'd been to my dog, and now I'd lost them all.

The fairy tales my father read me had made sense when I was young. Within their pages, the lines of the world were simple. Stepmothers and queens and little crooked men were evil. Children triumphed, and there was invigorating clarity to the way things ended.

But how did it work when you were the one who'd left others behind in the woods? When you crafted the potions? Did it matter that you didn't mean to? That you were sorry?

I'd been walking the concrete path as I'd been thinking, and I found myself next to an old kiosk, left over from when the park had had a small enclosure of animals—a few to ride, some to watch from the other side of fences. There was still a pair of swans in the pond, holdovers that had claimed the water as their own even after the ponies and chickens and the baby bear were considered too expensive to keep.

The kiosk had the lovely, mournful quality of a building that's half given over to nature. A series of faded promotional posters in glass frames still clustered around the darkened ticket window. I went over to get a closer look. The artwork was from another time, fantastical and friendly. The ponies were cheerful, with feather headdresses; the bear posed on a striped ball, although I doubted that trick had ever actually happened.

As I turned to walk away, I saw a movement in the reflection of the ticket window. I thought it was my mother—the pale skin and dark curls, the chin making a quick lift of dismissal, as I'd seen hers do so many times when a fragrance, or an employee, or a head of lettuce did not meet her approval. But it wasn't my mother's chin this time; it was mine.

I'd spent so many months wishing to be her. And now—when I was no longer sure I wanted to be—I was.

It made me think of that evening I'd seen Fisher on the balcony of The Island, cigarette in hand, staring out at the water. A living incarnation of his father. I'd shied away from who I thought he'd become. Never given him a chance to explain.

But now I had to ask myself—was I any different from him? If I could not even recognize my own reflection, what did that say?

I headed back out of the park, toward the wharf. I needed to see Fisher. I knew I was risking hurt, but I didn't care. I'd already lost Dodge, and it appeared I was in good danger of losing myself. I wasn't going to make the same mistake three times.

It was almost five o'clock when I left the big green meadow behind and reentered the bustle of the city. I walked past the buildings rising high above me, the cars flying by on the streets. When I got to the wharf and felt the wood of the walkway beneath my feet, I breathed a sigh of relief. It wasn't home, but it was something.

I wasn't sure what I would do when I got to the bar. Fisher might not even still work there; it had been months, after all. And if he was there—if he was suddenly in front of me in flesh and blood—what would I say? I'd spent so much time preparing retorts, pondering scenarios of what might have happened, what might happen.

I had no idea where we would fit in the midst of all that. So when I arrived at The Island I slipped inside the heavy wooden door and stood out of sight. Again.

He was there behind the bar, just as he had been the last time. That restless, simmering energy was still the same, although his hair had been recently cut, I noticed. When he reached down to get something, I made my way quietly along the back of the room. I found a chair in a dark corner and sat watching him, my focus intent, refusing to wonder whose fingers had touched the waves of that red hair. A sturdy waitress with a flat American accent and tattoos sprawled across her hands placed a glass of water in front of me, took one look at my face, and left me alone.

The place was as crowded as it had been before, but now I spent more time looking around me. Customers lined the mahogany bar—an odd mix of boat builders, construction workers, and hip young software engineers washed up like flotsam, jostling at the edges of their territories, staking claims of space. It made me nervous, but Fisher didn't seem to care. His hands moved, fast and hard, among the bottles, but then, just as I was thinking I might have been wrong to come back, I saw him pause, just for a moment, to watch the light catching on a stream of clear, sparkling liquid as it poured into a glass. My Fisher was still there, I told myself. I settled in to wait.

A few minutes later, the front door opened and an older man, tight and wiry, walked in, accompanied by a large black dog, which seemed as calm in demeanor as the man was sharp. I was surprised, not only because the two didn't resemble each other, the way dogs and owners often do, but because I didn't think animals were allowed inside bars. No one said anything, however, and the dog wandered through the tables like a familiar shadow. It was the same size as Dodge, even if the coloring was different, and I longed for the feel of its fur between my fingers. It was all I could do not to reach out.

The dog raised its nose, tested the air, and then came over and sat down next to me.

"Who are you?" I asked, letting my open palm run along its backbone. The dog looked up and put its chin on my knee, its eyes brown and waiting. I could feel the tears starting in mine.

"You like him?"

The man's voice was loud and amused, as much for the room as for me. I glanced up and saw his face, too close. His eyes were the dark blue of a bruise, his mouth pulled into a smile. Behind him, I noticed a movement and saw Fisher, his eyes growing wide as he caught sight of me.

"He's a good dog," I said to the man, shifting back in my chair.

"I'm a good trainer," the man said. His smile grew wider. "I could train you." He laughed, inviting the bar to join in, but Fisher had appeared beside him.

"Knock it off, Frank," he said. He looked at me once, quick.

"Emmeline," he said, and for a moment the longing was there in his voice. I wanted to grab it, and him, and run away. But I wasn't the only one who heard it.

Frank raised an eyebrow and stepped a bit closer to me. "Come on, Fisher, I'm just talking to the girl. She likes my *dog* . . ." He was grinning now, an ugly thing.

Fisher's fist rose fast, but the man caught it in his hand. They stood there, their arms a tight bridge over me, their faces contorted. The room waited; I could feel the warmth of the dog's breath against my leg.

With a flurry of movement, an older woman with bottle-orange hair stepped up and slapped their hands down, the shock of it more effective than force.

"What have I told you about this, Fisher?" she said.

"Wait," I said, trying to stand, but there was no room.

The woman looked me over. "And you are . . . ?"

"Leave her alone, Izzy," Fisher said, turning on the woman.

"Really, Fisher?" She gave a disgusted shake of her head. "You're gonna pull that shit on me? Okay, you *and* the girlfriend—out. I'll take the bar tonight."

The dog's owner gave a small, victorious smile. One of the dockworkers leaned back from the bar. "Aw, come on, Izzy. Give the boy a break."

She ignored him and flicked a dishtowel toward the bar, never taking her eyes off Fisher. "I don't care how good you are—this is the last damn time this happens. Don't come back until you can control yourself."

Fisher seized my hand and headed for the door. As we left, I looked back and saw the dog's big, dark eyes watching me.

THE BOAT

As soon as we got outside, I yanked my hand from Fisher's and stomped down the wooden stairs toward the water.

"Hold up!" Fisher said, catching up with me as I reached the docks. I turned on him.

"You said you didn't want to be your father," I said, breathing hard. "I waited for you. I looked for you. And I find you *here*, in a bar? Getting in a fight?"

Fisher's face flushed. "I was protecting you."

And now he sounds like his mother, I thought.

"That turned out well," I said, my bitterness sharp and undisguised.

He stared at me, his eyes running across my face, taking in my fury, the makeup on my face. "You've changed," he said.

"No choice." I shot the words home like the bolt of a lock. Fisher pulled back as if I'd punched him. I knew I had no right to be so cruel—I was hardly blameless. I had set so much of this in motion.

Fisher's shoulders slumped. "I'm sorry," he said.

The words fell on the dock in front of me and broke, the sound jagged and sad. And just like that, I could see my twelve-year-old self again, riding my wave of righteous indignation toward my father.

You lied, Papa. There are no mermaids.

I remembered how that wave had crashed on all of us. My father, Cleo, me. I'd been so focused on the ride, I hadn't even tried to stop it. And here I was now, doing the same thing again.

Fisher stood in front of me, waiting.

"What do you want me to do?" he asked.

I took a long, shuddering inhalation, slowing my momentum. I could smell our scents reaching out toward each other, searching, slipping underneath our words, caring not at all about the ways humans tried to hurt one another. I waited for a moment, letting the air move around me—and then I knew. The question I hadn't asked my father, the one that might have changed everything.

"Tell me why," I said.

Everything grew still. Then Fisher spoke, slowly, gradually, as if easing himself down from a high ledge. "Okay. Can we go someplace else, though? There's something I'd like to show you."

When I nodded, he took us toward a wide channel that headed out of the harbor. A footpath ran along one side, and we followed it, away from the center of the city. We didn't speak. Everything still felt raw; we needed time to let our old and new selves find their positions in the space between us. I listened to the sound of his footsteps, their familiar, steady rhythm, and I wondered how much of my Fisher was still left inside the man next to me. As his arms moved with his stride, I felt the heat of his skin come close, then swoop away. I wanted to take his hand, but then wondered who else had.

Just as I was starting to question how much farther we would go, the path opened into a wide street that ran between a row of elegant houses and a dark green slope of grass that rolled down to the channel. Out on the water, I could see a cluster of ramshackle boats—an antiquated tug, some battered fishing trawlers, a couple of bedraggled yachts, and half a

dozen sailboats, their masts like a row of fingers obscenely gesturing at the
houses up the hill. A part of me drew back at the sight. But there was another part of me that remembered how it felt to be different, set apart.

Fisher, of course, led me toward the boats.

When we reached the edge of the water, he whistled and a man popped
his head out of the closest sailboat. A black flag hung limply from the mast,
and what looked like wet laundry was draped along the railing.

"Ferry?" Fisher called out. The man clambered down a ladder into a
dinghy and headed toward us, oars slapping at the water.

"Will we all fit in that thing?" I asked.

"Don't worry," Fisher assured me. The dinghy scraped against the shore.
"This is Jim. He's our ferryman."

Jim clambered out of the boat. His hair was ragged and his arms were
like wire. He reminded me of the men who stood on the corner by Inspire,
Inc., sometimes. Victoria refused to give them money. *You need to make
your own way in life*, she always told me as we passed. *You can't rely on anybody else.*

Now Jim turned to Fisher. "Did you bring any beer?"

"Couldn't. I got kicked out," Fisher said. "Next time."

"Man, you know that's not how it works." Closer up, Jim's face was as
craggy as cedar bark. He looked at me, head cocked, and then said, "I'll
give you a pass this time because I like her curls."

I braced for Fisher's reaction, but he just smiled. "Thanks, old man,"
he said.

I looked over at the dinghy, which was as battered as its owner. "Seri-
ously, it's fine," Fisher said to me, and Jim held out his hand.

"Mademoiselle," he said, motioning to the back bench.

Fisher took the oars. As we approached the boats, I saw they were in
even worse condition than I'd thought, rust running down the sides, blue
tarps forming temporary roofs, windows sealed up with cardboard. Two of
the sailboats appeared to have sails, but something told me none of the
vessels had pulled up their anchors recently.

It took Fisher no more than ten good strokes of the oars to get us out there. When we arrived, Jim secured the dinghy, and we all climbed the shaky metal ladder onto his boat.

"Welcome to the Desolates," Jim said, and I heard the note of proud defiance in his voice.

From this vantage point, I could see the boats were arranged around a floating deck made of pallets and plywood. Four mismatched plastic chairs surrounded a barbecue grill, a five-gallon jug of water, and a single terra-cotta pot with a pink geranium in it. Still life, courtesy of a yard sale.

"Thanks, Jim." Fisher smiled at him and took my hand, gently this time. "We go here," he said, leading the way along Jim's deck and across a wide plank onto an old tugboat. Its once-white paint and the wood of its trim were so faded that they'd blended together into an indeterminate gray. If that vessel was a log, it would have been sprouting new trees by now.

"You live here?" I asked.

"No choice," he said, echoing my words with a sideways smile.

He was different here. Something calmer, less obvious had replaced the roughness I'd seen in the bar, the despair he'd shown on the dock. Even as the boat rocked in the current, his feet seemed steadier.

Fisher opened the cabin door and ducked inside. I followed him, cautious, then stopped in stunned silence. Looking at the interior of the boat was like gazing at clockwork, each thing in its own, well-loved place. The wood and metal gleamed; every surface was clean. There were books, lined up along a shelf, five bottles of spices, a pot and a pan, each hanging on its own hook. Behind the kitchen I could see a cubbyhole of a room with a bed, neatly made with a plaid blanket.

"Wow," I said, forgetting my doubts, my anger, falling back into the way he and I used to be, two children creating worlds of their own.

Fisher grinned. "I did it myself."

"It's beautiful," I said. "But how does this all work?" I motioned to the boats around us, and the opulent houses beyond. I didn't see how the two could coexist.

"We're outside the city limits," he said. "A couple years ago, rich people started abandoning their old boats here, and some folks thought it was a shame to let them go to waste. We're kind of like hermit crabs." He smiled. "Everybody wants to kick us out, but so far they can't figure out whose jurisdiction we're in. Thank God for bureaucracy."

He leaned toward a cabinet. "Can I get you something to drink? I've got water, and water."

We went back outside and sat on the dilapidated deck, leaning against the wall of the cabin, looking out at the canal. For a long time, we were quiet. The sky still held the light of late summer, and I could hear rustling from the boats around us, men's voices, the sounds of cooking and settling in. In the houses that lined the channel, illuminated windows held small moments, like the open doors of an Advent calendar. A woman walking back and forth, a baby in her arms. A couple sitting at a table. A boy playing with a dog. All those stories, all those lives, each one an entire world to the person living it, and yet I knew none of them. Maybe that's how it always is, I thought—we all just go along, catching glimpses of one another, thinking we know everything.

"Okay," I said, turning to Fisher. "Tell me."

He took a slow sip of water, put the bottle down. "I don't know," he said. I waited, and he shrugged. "Everything started out well enough, I guess. I got the job in the nursery, found a room in a shared house. It wasn't great, but I could afford it."

I considered the boats around us, their slow but certain future at the bottom of the water. What could *wasn't great* mean?

"Why did you stop writing me?" I asked, and steeled myself for the answer.

Fisher just sighed. "I thought everything would be different. You know, away from my father. It turned out I didn't know as much as I thought. I know about growing vegetables—but that nursery was all about fancy names and colors and *landscaping*." His voice shifted to disdain. "It sucks to go to a place where you don't know what you're doing, day after day. Nothing I did was right. And the manager hated me from the start—said he didn't have time to babysit."

"What about the girl?" I asked, breaking in.

"What girl?" He looked at me, puzzled.

"The one who got you fired."

He almost laughed. "So you do care," he said. "Jesus, Emmeline. She was just somebody who worked there. The manager was hitting on her. I told him to leave her alone. That was all the excuse he needed to get rid of me."

I had been wrong for so many months. So much time spent imagining, hating, longing.

"Why didn't you tell me?" I asked.

"I got fired, Emmeline. I screwed up at the only thing I thought I knew how to do. How was I supposed to tell you that?"

"I would have understood."

"Says the girl wearing a two-hundred-dollar pair of jeans."

I felt a sudden rush of shame, sitting on that boat, knowing where I lived. What I did.

"I'd say you've got a story or two to tell me yourself," he added.

"My jeans don't get you off the hook," I said, though I realized that, as always, Fisher had seen more than I wanted him to.

He shook his head. "I didn't want you to know, okay? And then later, it was just easier to be here—to be who I am here—if I could pretend you didn't exist."

I had a sudden vision of the blinking red light on Victoria's answering machine. The messages piling up. The push and pull of my old and new selves.

"So, what happened?" I asked.

"I couldn't pay my rent, so I got kicked out of there, too. I just kept walking around the city, thinking about all the things my dad used to say about me. Thinking he was probably right. I couldn't go home like that." He laughed, but it was more of a chuff. "I mean, I couldn't go home, in any case. But then I saw that bar, and I went in." He shrugged. "Turns out, I'm pretty good with alcohol. I started out bussing, and then Izzy trained me to be a bartender."

He looked around. "A guy told me about this place, said there was an available boat. I know how it looks, but you'd be amazed. Jim used to be an aerospace engineer. Lost his wife to cancer and just fell apart. Jamie," he nodded toward the old fishing trawler, "ran away from home, just like me. Wants to be a musician. He's always talking about living *intentionally* and trying to get us to eat vegan."

"But you're getting paid now, right?" I asked.

As soon as I said it, I wanted to grab back the words. Fisher's face darkened.

"I happen to like it here—and I can feed a lot of these guys on what I make. Seems like a better use of my money."

A boat motored through the canal in front of us, new and glaringly white, slowing as the people on board pointed and stared at the enclave of moldering boats. A woman pulled out a phone and aimed it at us. Took one photo, then another. I felt Fisher tense beside me.

"You know what you learn bartending?" he said. "People never order what they really want. That lady there," he pointed straight at the woman, who was taking another photo, this time horizontally. "She'd order a glass of chardonnay, but she'd guzzle a shot of scotch if you gave it to her."

He stood up. "We're not a damn tourist attraction!" he yelled. The woman's hand dropped and the boat sped away.

I hugged my knees with my arms. Fisher glanced over, flushed, and sat back down.

"Sorry," he said.

The wake of the departing boat rocked us toward and away from one another.

"You should have told me," I said.

"Really? Don't you think that's a little hypocritical?" His voice had an edge to it. "Look," he said, "I was wrong not to write you, and I've told you everything you wanted to know because I *am* sorry. But that's an awful lot of stones you're throwing from your big glass house, Emmeline. You shut me out first."

My mind filled with the image of him standing on the trail at the turn-off to the bluff. The confusion and pain on his face. The way he'd turned around and left.

"I've told you everything," he said. "Again. Will you ever do that for me?"

I still wasn't ready, even though telling Fisher my secrets had been the reason I'd come to the city in the first place.

But he was right, I knew that. I also knew this was the last time he'd ask. He might not leave me completely, but in all the ways that mattered, he'd be gone. I'd lost almost everything I loved because of secrets—Cleo, my father, the island, Dodge, the stories in the smells. I was about to lose more, and I was sick of it.

Fisher reached out his hand and took mine. "Tell me, Em," he said.

No, I thought. *No, no, no.*

I took a breath. The water stilled around us.

"I killed my father," I said.

COCKTAILS

Fisher and I talked and talked, while the sky went black and fell asleep. I went back to the beginning of everything, told him about my father's machine and the scent-papers, the bear and Cleo, even about pitching the bottles off the bluff.

"They were yours?" he said. "The ones that washed up on the beaches?"

I nodded.

"That one I found," he marveled. "It came from you."

"Yeah," I said. "I thought I was doing the right thing. I thought he'd be willing to leave the island if they were gone."

And still I went deeper, digging out words so old I could taste the rust. I told him about finding the blue-wax bottle, and my father falling into the sea. About waiting on the beach. Burning the scent-papers in the cabin.

When my words finally slowed, we sat for a while in silence. I wondered what to do with the extra space I could suddenly feel inside my chest.

"Why did you leave me, Fisher?" I asked.

"How could I stay there?" he said, staring at the houses across the canals, the perfect lives they promised. "The longer I was in that house, the more I became like him. I couldn't risk that. I couldn't let it come near you."

And that was when I finally told him what his mother had said, as she stood by the window in the red cottage at the cove.

When I finished, he put his arm around me, his cheek against my hair. "It seems like all we do is re-create our parents' mistakes," he said.

"So what if we both just stopped?" I asked.

I could feel the nod of his head, but what he said was "It's not that easy, Em."

"Okay," I said. "Then we start with the small stuff." I leaned across him and took the pack of cigarettes from his shirt pocket, crumpling them in my hand.

He pulled back and looked at me, and then I could see the start of a grin.

"Does this mean we get to get rid of your jeans, too?" he asked.

It was after 3 A.M. when I said I really had to get home. Fisher rowed us back to the shore, each stroke a ruffled break in the silence. He tied up the dinghy under the dock and we set off down the path, a wideness in the dark lit only by stars.

When we arrived at Victoria's white building, with its carved detailing and big glass doors, Fisher stared openly.

"You live here?" he asked, and I remembered how this place had felt the first time I'd seen it. Like a castle.

"That's a story for another night," I said.

He laughed under his breath. "I don't think they'd even let me in the front door."

I hugged him. "I'll find you tomorrow," I said as I fished my key out of my pocket. "Good luck with Izzy."

"She'll take me back," he said with a wry smile. "She likes to yell like I like to fight."

"Fisher . . ."

"I won't," he said. "I promise."

I let myself into the apartment as quietly as I could, but it didn't matter. Victoria was sitting on the couch, an unopened book in her lap.

"Where have you been?" she asked, rising. "I was worried."

I looked at her tangled hair, her exhausted expression, and I wanted to tell her what had happened. But then I imagined how it all would look through her eyes—Fisher ready to fight in the bar, Jim ferrying us over to those wrecked boats. I wasn't ready to mix those worlds.

"At work," I said. "I got caught up."

She came closer, and I saw her inhale, once, through her nose. Her eyebrows drew together, but all she said was, "Okay. Go get some sleep."

The next day, I didn't even try to make progress on the car fragrance. I sat in my office, thinking about how Fisher had listened to my secrets the night before, catching my words and folding them into himself, even as I told him the worst of me.

"*I don't know what to do about Colette and Henry,*" I'd said at one point. "*I haven't even called them back yet. How can I talk to them after what I've done?*"

"*How did you manage to talk to me?*" he'd asked.

He was right. I picked up my office phone and dialed. Henry answered. I could hear Colette in the background, the metallic clang of a cookie sheet landing on top of the stove.

"Henry," I said.

"Emmeline. There you are." His voice was the same as always, the low lapping of the tide against pilings.

"I'm sorry," I said. "I've been horrible."

"Dodge never had much need for apologies," Henry said. "Neither do we."

"How did he . . . ?"

"In his sleep. We buried him on the hill behind the vegetable garden."
I heard Colette rush up and take the phone.

"How are you?" she asked. "When are you coming home?"

"I don't know yet," I said. "I found Fisher, though. Can you tell his mom?"

"That's a relief. Of course we will."

"How is she?" I asked.

"We keep her here as much as we can. It's time Henry and I found a few people to take over this place." The hint was hardly casual.

"You're going to be there forever," I said.

"Just sayin'." It was something the summer teenagers always said. I used to tease her when she'd use their phrases. Now it made me want to cry and smile, hearing the way she always knew how to bring me home to her.

At three o'clock I slipped out of my office and left the building, heading for The Island. The place hadn't started to fill up yet. There were just a couple guys drinking beer at the far end of the bar, and Fisher, polishing glasses behind it.

"She took me back," he said, "but I've got to clean fifty more of these as penance. Want to help?" He tossed me a bar towel. I settled myself on a stool and started working. Izzy walked through; I raised the towel in response to her unasked question.

She turned to Fisher with a roll of her eyes. "I'm not paying her, for the record."

Fisher laughed.

Over the next few hours, the place filled until the crowd at the bar was three deep. Izzy came to help Fisher, bottles flashing, beer taps flipping up and down. At one point a middle-aged woman pushed her way through the crush of customers until she was standing right next to my stool. She wore a sweatshirt with a pirate on it, and white tennis shoes. A tourist—although how she had ended up at this bar was hard to fathom.

"When am I gonna get a drink?" she complained. Her voice had all the grace of a power saw, and I saw Fisher's shoulders tighten.

"In a minute," he said, raising a bottle of scotch and pouring a shot from twelve inches up.

"I've been here for twenty minutes and I haven't even gotten to order." She said it loud enough to carry over the rest of the bar noise. "This is bullshit." The room quieted.

Fisher's face reddened; I could feel the heat starting in him. At the other end of the bar, Izzy glared in our direction and dumped ice in a margarita glass.

Fisher turned and faced the angry woman, automatically scanning her expression, her posture, reading her the way the best fishermen do the water. Reading her the way he did everyone, everything.

Ever since we were both young children, I thought, our parents had taught us—whether intentionally or not—to observe the world around us, down to the minutest detail. We had learned, knowing with the instinct of children that it meant our survival. We had both developed skills that few could match.

Since coming to the city, however, we'd used those skills differently— to predict weakness, to win. It brought out the worst in us, as well as those around us. It was time to alter that equation.

"He can guess your drink," I said to the woman in the sweatshirt. I could feel the energy in the room crack open in curiosity.

"What?" she asked.

"If you don't like it, you don't have to pay."

Fisher shot me a look; I gave him an apologetic shrug, but the woman leaned across the bar toward him.

"All right," she said, her voice loud as a gaggle of geese. "Go for it. Guess my drink."

The crowd shuffled, necks craning for a better view. Fisher handed the shot of scotch to a bearded man, then paused to consider the woman again. He took longer than he needed; I could tell by the ready twitch in his right index finger that he'd known what he'd make from the moment he first saw her, but finally he nodded and started pulling down bottles, keeping the labels hidden. He took out a cocktail glass with an open, shallow bowl, his hands moving smoothly from one bottle to the next, the contents of the glass shifting from clear to pale yellow to a warm, dark amber. With a deft twist he dropped a slip of orange peel on top and slid it across to the woman.

She let out a snort. "I drink beer."

"Yup," Fisher said. "Miller Lite, I'd guess."

Surprise washed the triumph off her face. "Yeah."

"Try this instead."

She sniffed it; I could smell its fragrance, sharp and smooth, citrus and herbs and something almost metallic. The woman took a sip and glanced up, cocking her head at Fisher.

"What is it?" she asked.

"Death and Taxes," he said.

She took a bigger sip and grinned. "Well, shit. Guess I have to pay."

After that, it became a parlor trick—everyone wanted Fisher to guess his or her drink. People didn't mind waiting when there was entertainment to be had. Construction workers chatted with girls in yoga pants; the regulars exchanged names with people they'd sat next to for years. Sometimes the new drink was just a slight left turn—rye instead of bourbon, the extra flowers softening the hard exterior of a glowering man. Sometimes the drink was something entirely different—an umbrella drinker, as Fisher would call them, switching over to a straight botanical gin.

"I don't know how you're doing this," Izzy said to Fisher at the end of one evening, "but keep going."

He did, night after night. For a full week, I cut out of work as soon as I could to get to the bar. I loved watching Fisher change the atmosphere around him. Everyone else thought it was magic, but I knew better. In the end, it wasn't the flavors or the alcohol that made people relax—it was the experience of being seen and understood. And Fisher opened up right along with them. He was finding himself again, and I could sit there all night, watching.

Each morning I would go back to Inspire, Inc., and try to think about car dealerships, and each morning it grew harder. I'd told Fisher about Victoria and my work; I even told him about the trouble I was having with the fragrances, in the hope that confessing might help. But it hadn't. The scents remained quiet in their testing bottles, devoid of the alchemy that made new fragrances possible. I could almost avoid thinking about it while I was with Fisher, but when I was in my lab, it was there in front of me at every moment. The scents had become the olfactory equivalent of white noise—a freeway in the distance, the hum of a refrigerator. No surprises; no communication.

I'm sorry, I told them. *I'm sorry. What do you need from me?* But I think I already knew.

Victoria had taken to dropping by my office a couple times a day. I wondered how many more times she came when I wasn't there. I felt badly for not telling her what was going on, but I couldn't, for so many reasons. I was still trying to figure out how the person I became around Fisher fit into my life with her. But even more than that, I was afraid of what she might think of me, what they all might think of me, if they knew my talent had disappeared.

"How's it coming?" she asked one afternoon as she poked her head in my office door. "I've been getting calls from the car people. They want to know when the fragrance will be done."

"I'm working on it," I said.

Victoria considered the shelves of unopened bottles; my face, devoid of makeup.

"I trust you," she said, and left.

I spent the next hour shoving scents together, but each fragrance came out flat as a billboard and twice as obvious.

Bring me a scent that will break down the walls, I thought, but none came. Eventually I gave up and headed for The Island.

It was a Friday night, the busiest of the week. Word had gotten out about Fisher, and a semicircle five deep had formed at his end of the bar. There was laughter, even cheers as Fisher got one customer after another to change his or her order.

"Who knew?" a fisherman said, holding up a martini glass filled with bright yellow liquid.

"Lemon Drop," Fisher murmured to me. "Kills the smell of fish. And the guy could use a little more sugar in his life."

A man shoved his way up to the bar, towing a blonde in a low-cut shirt. I recognized the dog owner from my first night. As far as I knew, he hadn't been in since, and this time, there was no dog. Just the blonde, who was leaning against him in a way that seemed to have more to do with her spike heels than affection.

"Frank," Fisher said, the word both a question and a greeting.

"Guess hers," Frank said, motioning toward the blonde.

Fisher looked from Frank to the woman and back, and then got out a rocks glass. He made a show of angling his body so no one could see what he was pouring; when he turned back, the glass was full of a clear liquid. He handed it to the woman with a gallant flourish.

"For you," he said.

"Ah," Frank said, addressing the crowd. "The straight stuff. I'm gonna have a good night, boys."

The woman took a sip and looked at Fisher, puzzled. She leaned forward. "But this is just . . ." I heard her whisper to him.

"Did you get what you wanted?" he asked, loud enough for the crowd to hear, and I watched the comprehension wash over her face.

"You're a genius," she said.

"Free refills for the pretty lady, all night long," Fisher called out, to a round of cheers.

"Thanks, Fisher," Frank said, grinning. He took the woman's elbow and pulled her through the crowd to a table.

"He'll be pissed when he figures it out," I said to Fisher in a low voice.

"He'd never let anybody know he couldn't bag a sober woman," Fisher said with a shrug.

Across the room, the front door opened, letting in a spill of cool air. Fisher looked up, then caught my eye and jerked his chin toward the newcomer.

"Narcissist's Martini," he said.

I had to boost myself up on my stool to see who he was talking about. A woman, in a slim white suit, standing like a lily in a field of beans.

Victoria.

THE DINNER

As usual, the crowd parted before my mother. She made her way to my side, and the man on the stool next to me stood up and offered her his seat. As she sat down, I smelled the honey-and-amber perfume she'd been wearing the first day we met. A wave of guilt washed over me. She'd taken me in, asked so few questions. Opened her home to me.

"So this is where you've been coming," she said now. She looked around the bar, leaned closer. "I have to admit, I'm curious why."

"I'm sorry," I said. "I should've told you." I nodded toward Fisher, who was watching us with obvious interest. "Fisher's a friend, from the cove."

Victoria looked from me to Fisher and back again. It reminded me of when she tested a new fragrance, going from one version to another.

"Have you two known each other a long time?" she asked.

"Since I started school," I said. "I wouldn't have made it through without him." Suddenly, now that she was here, I wanted her to like him, to understand how important he was to me. "He's the reason I came to the city in the first place . . ."

I felt Victoria go still beside me.

"Really?" she said. There was a crack, deep down below the question mark. A small sound, barely audible, but I heard it.

"I mean, I came to find you, too," I said. I was fumbling now, making a mess of it. A small pool of quiet rippled out into the crowd around us. Victoria's expression went smooth, polished.

"Well," she said. "I'm just glad he got you here." She leaned across the bar, extending a hand. "I'm Victoria Wingate. Emmeline's mother."

Fisher looked at me once, quickly. I could feel Victoria watching us.

"Nice to meet you," Fisher said to her, swiping his wet hand across the apron around his waist, then shaking hers. "Sorry," he said, "busy night."

"Not a problem." She took a napkin from the stack next to me and gently wiped the moisture from her long, beautiful fingers. It felt as if the whole bar was watching her, entranced.

"What's *her* drink?" one of the regulars called out. The group around him nodded, eager. Victoria tilted her head in question.

"He can guess what people really want," I said in a low tone. "He's amazing at reading people." I was still selling; I could hear it.

"Really?" Victoria said. This time it was only half a question. Her back straightened, the slightest shift of movement.

"It's just a party trick," Fisher said, offhand, but he was watching her more closely now.

"Do it!" the crowd started chanting. "Do it!"

"All right," Victoria said, sending out a gracious smile around her. "Let's see what you can do, Fisher."

The crowd cheered, and Fisher gave a shallow bow. He hesitated for one more moment, looking from Victoria to me. He always paused at this point, ramping up the effect, but this time it felt different, as if he really was making a decision.

"Well?" Victoria said. Teasing, almost.

Fisher straightened then, and moved into action. He put ice in a metal shaker, then poured Plymouth gin in a clear, continuous stream. He put on the lid and gave the cylinder ten quick shakes at shoulder height. With a small flourish, he produced a chilled cocktail glass, opened the lid of the shaker, and let the liquid tumble out through the strainer and down the angled sides of the glass. It was a poem—or maybe a declaration—of a drink.

"Here you go," he said, offering it to Victoria.

She took a sip, considering the taste with her eyes closed, her face a striking combination of beauty and concentration. The voices around us hushed in expectation.

Then she shook her head. "Beautifully done, Fisher, but I'm afraid it's not my thing." She looked up at him and their eyes met. "I'll have a glass of Viognier, please, if you have it."

The crowd whooped. "You got him!" yelled one of the boat builders. "That's a first."

Fisher's face colored. But then he turned to the crowd and inclined his head in defeat. "What can I say? The woman knows her mind."

The rest of our time at The Island was uneventful. Fisher was busy with other customers. Victoria's wine disappeared and she declined a refill, leaving us with no particular reason to stay. I had some explanations to give, I knew, and no way left to avoid them.

We rode the elevator up to the top floor, the fragrance of citrus and fir surrounding us. "I'm sorry," I said again. "I should have told you where I was going."

"All women are allowed to have a few secrets," she said, and I breathed a sigh of relief. I was confused about many things right then, but one thing I knew—she was the only parent I had left.

We walked down the hall, and she put her key in the lock.

"Have you eaten?" she asked. She took my coat and hung it in the closet. "I bought a beautiful chèvre at the farmer's market."

"No salad?" I asked, an apology dressed in shared memory. She smiled.

"It looked too good to pass up," she said.

She went into the kitchen. I could hear her opening cupboards, the crinkle of plastic as she pulled crackers out of a box. She returned to the living room, setting down a tray containing a round serving plate and two glasses of wine. She handed me one with a small smile.

"So tell me all about him," she said as she sat down, pulled her legs up underneath her.

"We met in school," I said.

She nodded. "But who is he, really? I mean, what makes him a boy you'd follow all the way to the city?" Her eyes held that same curiosity I remembered from that first time we'd gone to the pink sunrise store, and she'd asked me what I thought about the scent. It made me realize how much I wanted to tell someone about Fisher, how much I wanted to let a beautiful secret out into the world for once.

"You saw how he is," I said. "He sees everything. His father was tough— is tough, that's why he's here—but he's better than that. He's special."

"Are you sure?"

"Yes," I said, and I could hear how much I meant it.

She looked at me, nodded. "That's how I felt about your father, too."

She shifted position on the couch and gave me a knowing smile. "So, can I assume Fisher is the reason you're so late with my car manufacturer fragrance?"

"No," I said, caught off guard. "He isn't. I just . . ." I shook my head, unable to explain.

She spread cheese on a water cracker, giving me time.

"We all get blocked now and then," she said when I didn't continue. She handed me the cracker. "You've been working so hard. It makes sense."

Why was she being so nice? I'd lied to her, put her in a bad position with the car people. I'd seen how she'd punished employees for far less. Maybe it *was* because I was her daughter. Maybe she really did love me.

"Yes," I said, grateful for the understanding.

An hour later, the plate of crackers and cheese was empty, as was my glass of wine. We'd found our way into a discussion of car manufacturers after all, and I'd told her the ideas I was working on before everything fell apart.

"You see?" Victoria said. "You've got more than you give yourself credit for."

I didn't tell her that the concepts I was giving her were so old they tasted like dust in my mouth. Maybe she already suspected as much—generally when Victoria was listening to my ideas, I could almost see her writing notes in her head. Now she was just listening, until I finally ran out of things to say.

"You know," she said, "I'd really like to get to know Fisher better. Let me take the two of you out to dinner."

"I don't know," I said. "He works most nights." I looked around me at Victoria's gloriously tall windows, the gleaming wood floors. I thought of the contrast with Fisher's boat, with its peeling paint and cans of food.

"Come on," Victoria said. "I know just the place."

Maybe if I tried hard enough, I thought, I could bring Fisher and my mother together, balance two disparate scents into a new fragrance. It's what I did. At least, what I used to do.

"Okay," I said. "Let me talk to Fisher."

"Why would she want to do that?" Fisher asked, the next day at the bar. "She doesn't like me."

"Fisher," I said. "She just wants to get to know you."

"I was right about her drink, you know," he said, lining up the bottles on the shelves with their labels out, getting ready for the evening crowd.

I avoided his comment. "She's been great about all this."

"Of course she has. She's your mother." It didn't sound quite so nice when he said it.

"Please," I said.

He picked up a glass, checked it for water spots. "Okay," he said finally, shaking his head. "But I'm telling you, it's not a good idea."

The restaurant Victoria chose was hip and new, with metal chairs and concrete floors, white linen tablecloths and single, out-of-season peonies in slim glass vases. The menus were tall, the paper thick, the writing rolling across the page like waves. When the waiter came, Victoria ordered a crab salad. I asked for the salmon with Béarnaise sauce.

"I'll have the burger," Fisher said, handing the menu to the waiter, who hid a smile.

"I haven't been to this place in ages," Victoria said, gazing about. "I heard they have a new chef. He's supposed to be wonderful."

She talked for a while about other restaurants in the city, and the challenges of creating fragrances for settings that so actively generated their own smells. Next to me, I could see Fisher watching the drinks coming out on small round trays. He looked as if he was trying to guess the intended customers. Every so often, Victoria would glance over at him.

A couple walked in, the young woman rail thin, with artfully torn jeans. I could smell her perfume, sultry and deep, too loud for such a small space.

"Poison," Victoria said, shooting me a knowing smile.

"What?" Fisher said, turning.

"It's a fragrance, circa 1985," she explained. "It got completely cheapened later, but the vintage stuff is still striking." She paused, sniffing lightly, ticking off scents on her fingers. "Plum, coriander, and opoponax."

"What?"

"It's a myrrh."

Fisher shook his head. "You've lost me, I'm afraid."

She nodded, pulling lightly on one long curl of hair, observing him. "You do know this is what Emmeline does? She's brilliant. She's going to do fantastic things, given the right environment."

I saw Fisher bristle slightly at those last words. "She's always been brilliant," he said.

Not anymore, I thought. I was about as uncomfortable among the scent bottles these days as Fisher must have been in this restaurant.

I watched the two of them, Fisher in what I knew was his only clean long-sleeved shirt, Victoria in a green silk sheath of a dress. Their conversation was a volley of top notes, but I could sense something moving underneath. I felt my foot start to jiggle. I reached for my water glass and took a sip, the ice clicking against my teeth. I wished it was wine, but I was still too young to be served in a restaurant. The one good thing about my November birthday, I thought, was that I would be nineteen five months earlier, legal to drink here.

The waiter returned with our order and set the plates noiselessly in front of us. Victoria's salad was an artwork of green and white. My salmon was the size of a clamshell, drizzled with a creamy golden sauce; five dots of pureed green surrounded it like an appreciative audience. Fisher's hamburger took up most of his plate.

"Ketchup?" Fisher asked the waiter, who nodded. He returned with a small glass bowl and an even smaller spoon. Fisher took off the top of the bun and added the ketchup, one scooplet after another, like Gulliver attempting to use the Lilliputians' tools. Victoria waited patiently, her fork raised. When he was done, he picked up the burger with both hands and took a bite.

"Good chef," he commented.

"Yes," Victoria said.

We ate in silence for a moment.

"Where are you living these days, Fisher?" Victoria asked. I stiffened, just barely, but both of them saw it.

"A boat," Fisher said, the burger still held aloft. I saw ketchup emerging at the far edge of the bun.

"A houseboat?" Victoria asked. A drip of red landed on the rim of Fisher's round white plate.

"Kind of," I said, stepping in.

Victoria's eyes studiously avoided the upraised hamburger across from her. "There are some wonderful houseboats out in the West Bay, but I've heard it gets expensive. Do you have roommates?" She selected a piece of crab from her salad. "It must be hard on a bartender's wages."

Fisher stopped chewing.

"There's Jim," I offered. "He's older."

Fisher put down his hamburger and licked off the grease that had trickled into the curve between his right index finger and his thumb. "I live in the Desolates," he said. His voice was matter-of-fact, a dare.

"The Desolates?" Victoria asked.

"That's what people around here call them. You know, those boats just outside the city limits?"

"You mean where the homeless men live?" Victoria put down her fork. "Did you take Emmeline there?"

"They're just people," Fisher said.

"Who live in places that aren't theirs," Victoria noted. For every degree of heat that his voice gained, hers dropped two.

"Places that were abandoned by people rich enough to throw a boat away," Fisher said. "But you're right; it's hard to afford rent around here when you're the one serving others." His gaze went to the waiter, who was trying to maneuver his way around Victoria's water glass to refill her wine.

"I know about serving others." Victoria raised her wineglass toward the waiter. "My mother worked in a department store."

"Good for her," Fisher said.

"Not really." She looked at him. "I know exactly what it takes to succeed, Fisher," she said. "Everything I own I got for myself. You might want to try that."

Years ago in school, our history teacher had taught us about knights throwing down gauntlets. I had thought that gauntlets were like gloves—soft. But the original ones were made of metal. Hard as words.

Fisher stood, more in reaction than intention, his chair rasping across the concrete floor. The waiter quickly approached. He'd been hovering nearby—listening, probably.

"Everything all right?" he asked. He turned to Fisher. "Can I get you something, sir? A box?" He motioned toward the food.

Fisher drew himself up, turned to Victoria. "Sure," he said. "I know someone who appreciates leftovers." The waiter scooped up the plate.

"I'll see you later," Fisher said to me. He leaned down and kissed me, right in front of everybody, and then followed the waiter to the back of the restaurant. I just sat there, stuck in my chair by all those eyes upon me.

The waiter came back into the dining room. Victoria made a motion, and he brought me a glass of wine without any questions. I downed it like a sailor and felt it rush to my head. Victoria watched, saying nothing.

"Why did you do that?" I asked after a while. She knew I didn't mean the wine.

She wiped the corner of her mouth with her napkin. "You don't really know a fragrance until you get to the base notes. And I'll tell you this— I've been challenged plenty of times in my life, and I never gave up the table. Your sweetheart, apparently, does."

"That's not who he is." She, who read her customers so well, was wrong about him. The kiss he'd given me had been a promise, not a challenge. He'd left to keep his pact with me not to fight.

"Are you sure?" Victoria said. "I thought you said you came to the city to find him. You've been here for what—almost eight months? Why is that just happening now?"

I wanted to defend Fisher, to tell her that things had been hard for him, but doing so would mean letting her know he'd failed. I stayed quiet, trying to figure out what this whole evening meant going forward.

"Men will always betray you, Emmeline," Victoria said, shaking her head.

"They aren't all the same."

"You think?" she said. "Because that's certainly been my experience." She pushed her plate aside.

"What about my father?" I asked, leaning toward her. "You said you loved each other."

"Exactly. And look what that got me. When things went bad, he ran away and left me to clean up his mess. Men are selfish. They may or may not mean to be, but they are."

I tried to reconcile what she'd said with what I knew of my father. She was right in some respects, I had to admit. He'd left me, too, even before he drowned—disappeared into those scent-papers that he'd loved more than me. And he'd lied about so much. My name. My birthday. He'd taken me away from any chance at a normal life, brought me up in a way that suited him.

But even as I thought these things, I had a vision of him on that first day of spring, walking up to the cabin with Cleo on a leash, bringing me a new friend—even though I was his only one.

He was a good man, Emmeline, Rene had told me. *Don't let anybody tell you different.*

His voice competed with Victoria's in my head: *He ran away and left me.*

But then something about my mother's words struck me: she'd never mentioned me. Once again, I was a footnote, skimmed over in the story of her reinvention.

I stood up.

"Where are you going?" Victoria asked, her voice low.

I could see a white office, full of the scent of petrichor, and a figure surrounded by bottles.

"There's someone I need to find," I said.

At the door, I looked back and saw Victoria, taking a bite of her salad, as if the staring eyes around her existed not at all.

THE STORY

The world had grown thick with mist while we were inside the restaurant. The lines of the buildings had lost their precision, the sidewalks turned dark and glossy. The moisture found my face and then my curls, but I ignored the chill and set off. I wanted answers.

Something told me Rene might still be in his office. His rumpled clothing and the stacks of old coffee cups on his worktable had suggested late nights and a social life lived more among fragrances than people. When I pushed open his door, I saw that I'd been right. He looked up, seeming almost confused to find himself somewhere real and solid. The room was suffused with the aroma of hot chocolate—not the watery, instant kind, like they sold in the cafeteria at school, but the real thing, like Colette made, a bar of chocolate grated into shavings and melted into fresh milk. I looked for a hot plate, a pan, but there were only small glass bottles.

Rene took in the dripping mess of my hair with a quizzical tilt of his head. He cast about, then seized a brown paper towel and handed it to me. It was stiff and scratchy and did almost no good, but I smiled at the gesture anyway.

While I did as much as I could with the towel, Rene's hands continued to play among his scent bottles, moving them about like chess pieces, like friends. I wondered what they were saying to him. I would have given anything right then to be able to hear their stories.

I put down the paper towel. "Will you tell me about my parents?" I said. "I'd like to know the truth."

Rene gazed about as if trying to figure out what exactly to tell me. "You know," he said after a while, "I think one of the most fascinating things about perfumes is how they change with each person's skin chemistry. I've always thought of them as verbs, not nouns. Truth, I've found, is much the same."

"I want to know," I said stubbornly.

He nodded, picked up one of the bottles, and peered into it.

"I met your father fresh out of graduate school," he said, almost as if talking to the scent inside. "He was a scientist—could talk to smells more easily than people. I think he liked smells better, too. We got along well."

His smile was directed toward the past, but I understood what he was feeling.

"Your mother worked at the same company," he continued, turning his gaze to me. "They had her making fragrances for dryer sheets and hand soap. A complete waste of her talent, if you ask me. She wanted to try something new, to prove herself, and I told her about a scent John had just discovered on one of his travels. I introduced the two of them, but I wasn't matchmaking. They were not an obvious combination."

I nodded in agreement.

"I should have seen it, though," he added ruefully. "In the end, I don't think I've ever met two people with more restless minds, or a stronger fear of being deserted. They made a powerful—if unstable—combination. I do think they loved each other, as much as they were able."

"And Nightingale?" I asked.

"Your mother's idea. She started talking about Polaroid cameras, asking why we couldn't do the same with scents—capture and re-create them in one machine. That kind of challenge was perfect for John, simple and complicated at the same time. He worked at it for years. He could have played with it forever."

I thought of my father sitting at the table in our cabin, taking the machine apart, night after night. I bit off the words before they left my mouth: *He did.*

"But you see," Rene said, "that's where your parents were different. I remember your father warning Victoria, telling her about how when photos were first invented, they used to fade. He was worried the same thing might happen with his machine. He wanted more testing—but she couldn't wait. She kept dropping hints into the right ears, and before long she had investors signed up. When John found out, he was devastated. It was like she'd sold him instead of the machine."

I thought of the look on my father's face when he found out I'd broken my promise and gone to the lagoon. His trust, cracked into pieces. The second time, I realized now. First his wife, then his daughter.

Rene continued. "Your father threatened to tell the investors the machine hadn't been fully tested yet, but Victoria said it would ruin them both. So he took one of the prototypes and left—said he was going to do his own testing, as far from her as he could get. The price for his silence was that the machine would be called Nightingale."

I thought of the fairy tale, with its broken machine. *He'd known,* I thought. And if Rene was right, then all those articles about my father—even the story Victoria had told me herself—were wrong. It wasn't his ego that had brought them down. It was my mother's.

"What about me?" I asked.

Rene shook his head. "Victoria found out she was pregnant after he left, but nobody knew where he was. I finally tracked him down in Sri Lanka, and he got back right before you were born. She almost didn't let him see you. She said you were hers, not his."

Then why didn't she keep looking for me? I was so deep in my own thoughts that I almost didn't catch his next words.

"The first time I saw him holding you, I could tell," Rene said. "You were his missing note."

"What?"

"The thing that made him whole. It wasn't Victoria who did that—it was you."

Victoria's bitterness came back to me: *Men will always betray you.* Whatever Rene had seen in my father then, she'd seen it, too—felt the loss of being replaced. I knew what that was like. All the same, I could never have done to Fisher what she did to my father.

And I had been a child—a baby, blameless—but still I'd reaped what my parents had sown.

Rene and I were quiet. His hands went back to moving among the bottles, arranging and rearranging their order, formulating fragrances without ever opening a stopper.

"She's not going to like that you've told me," I said.

"Probably not," he said, and gave me a crooked smile. "But I'm not so sure I belong here these days, anyway. A scientist friend got in touch recently—he's researching the influence of scents on people with Alzheimer's. Sounds far more interesting."

I shook my head, trying to clear my thoughts. "If you knew all this," I said, "why work for her?"

"I love scents," Rene said with a shrug. "And your mother has one of the most brilliant minds for them I've ever met."

"Is that enough?"

"If you want to work with genius, you usually aren't signing up for easy." Rene started putting away the bottles, tidying his notes into stacks.

"You know," he said after a while, "that machine of your father's was incredible. Those scent-papers captured everything you could possibly smell in one particular place at one point in time. It wouldn't be the same an hour, even a minute later. Nobody chose what went in, or didn't. It was life, held in your hand. A whole moment."

"Except they didn't last."

"But they were beautiful."

I sat there, my mind curling into the memory of my father as he broke open a red-wax seal and let out the world inside.

"He made a scent-paper of you, you know," Rene said. "That first time he saw you. He made sure to put it in a bottle right away. Even gave it its own color of wax so he'd never open it by mistake. Don't ever think you weren't loved, Emmeline."

"What color?" I asked.

"What?"

"The wax."

He shrugged. "I can't remember. Blue, maybe?"

I saw the bottle, flying through the air, falling toward the water, and in the almost silent whoosh of it, I could hear the cracking of my heart.

Fisher was behind the bar when I walked into The Island. I went straight to him and wrapped my arms around his waist, shoving my nose into the crook of his neck and disappearing into his scent. We didn't move for a full minute.

Izzy came up behind us.

"Sweet as this is," she said, "we happen to be running a bar here."

I looked up. Her face softened.

"Would you do me a favor and get this guy out of here?" she said, jabbing a thumb at Fisher. "He's not even on the clock tonight."

We went back to the boats and crawled into Fisher's cubbyhole bed. He wrapped the plaid blanket around us, and in the darkness I told him what I'd learned.

"She let your father take the fall for Nightingale?" he asked.

"More than that, I think. Somebody had to point the finger at him."

"Jesus," he said, "that's cold."

When I told him about the blue-wax bottle, I heard his breath catch. The silence that followed seemed to last for days.

"What do you want to do?" he asked, finally.

"I don't know," I said. "I can't live with her now. Mostly I just want to go home."

"Forever?" he asked.

"I'm not sure. For a while?"

"I'll go with you."

"No—you can't. What about your dad?"

"Don't worry. I won't go back to that house. He can't make me now." His hands rested open against my skin, and I leaned into the reassuring calm of them. "Besides," he said, "it's time I saw my mom."

For hours, we lay there in that snug little bed and made plans. I'd go back to Victoria's, get my things, and stay on the boat with Fisher until we could catch a bus to the cove. After that, who knew? Izzy wanted to move Fisher into a position with more responsibility. Rene's talk of Alzheimer's research had opened up possibilities in my mind.

And then there was the cove, the resort, the island. I could feel the pull of them, growing stronger with each rock of the boat.

We talked until we fell asleep, midsentence, and woke in the morning with our arms still around each other.

I waited until I was sure Victoria had left for the office; I wasn't ready to see her. I didn't know when I would be, honestly. Fisher had offered to come with me, but I told him this was mine to do.

When I entered the lobby, Becky the concierge was at her desk. I tried to slip past, but she spotted me and gave a small wave as she leaned forward to pick up the phone.

I got to the apartment without further incident and let myself in, feeling more like a burglar than an occupant. It was just as beautiful as the first time I'd seen it, no matter what I'd learned since. I looked about for proof of my mother's treachery, but what I saw was the kitchen where we'd cooked together, the couch where we'd sat and talked late into the night.

Do you ever think of scents as colors?

Absolutely.

She'd understood a part of me that no one had since my father died. Not even Fisher. She'd opened my mind, taught me things.

She hurt your father, I told myself.

So had I, though. I saw that blue-wax bottle in the air, the way he'd instinctively reached for the memory of that baby—the one who hadn't betrayed him yet.

Just go forward, Emmeline. I started down the hall, but at its far end, I saw the partially open door of Victoria's bedroom. She always kept the door closed. She said it made things neater, kept out the dust. After that first day, I'd rarely entered her room.

Now I went to the door and poked my head in. The bed looked as if someone had been sleeping on top of the covers. A dresser drawer was half-open. Small things, unless you knew Victoria's penchant for order.

The wall of squares with their bottles of scents, however, was as precise as always. Victoria had forgotten to close the curtains, and the liquid in the bottles shone in the light, drawing my eye. I remembered her talking about Andy Warhol's museum of scents. How he used the fragrances to help him recall times in his life. How each one held memories, things that had happened.

People lie, Emmeline, my father had said. *But smells never do.* I walked across the room and faced the wall of squares.

"Tell me a story," I said. "Please."

THE WALL

Stories always begin at the top of the page.

I dragged over a wing-backed chair and scrambled onto it, reaching up to the top left square and pulling down a clear glass bottle, nearly full of a dark golden liquid. Its lines were simple but elegant, the stopper heavy, rectangular. On the side that had been facing the wall, I saw a label, yellowed and curling at the edges. The words were spare; straight black lines on white, no frills or flips.

No. 5. Chanel.

I returned to the floor and removed the stopper, inhaling top notes of bergamot, with a sultry middle of jasmine and orris root sliding into base notes of amber and vanilla. It was gorgeous, generous, set off by a series of synthetic, surreal scents, bright as searchlights, precise as expertly manicured fingernails tapping against a table.

Who are you? I asked it, but it said nothing. It wanted to mingle with skin, but not mine.

I set the bottle on the dresser and turned back to the wall, scanning for more hidden labels, but there were none. There had to be another way to crack this code.

My father's wall of drawers had been a timeline, divided into red-wax bottles at the top and green ones below, a clinical partitioning of the out-side and inside world. Before and after the island. His travels, our life. On that wall, the green-wax bottles had started roughly halfway down.

Maybe the same logic would apply here. I went to the center of my mother's collection and chose a bottle of pale pink liquid. The perfume in-side was lush, brilliant in its complexity, but again, it told me nothing. I un-stoppered four or five nearby bottles, looking for a hint, a clue. A trace of myself, in any form, in my mother's memories.

I was close to giving up when I opened a small vial of sepia-colored liq-uid and felt a memory lurch up from my mind to meet it. I was in the cabin, my father's machine in pieces on the floor, the long gray scarf burning in the woodstove. I could see it curl, twisting in the flames, its treacherous scent infiltrating the fading remains of my father's smell.

Here it was again. Indolent and spicy, full of longing. I pushed the stop-per back in, but the scent had already slipped out, wandering around the room, lazily circling the ordinary bottles on the dresser, exploring the bed. *That feels good*—its voice was low and scratchy as the swish of branches across a roof, round as resin spilling from trees.

I want more, it said.

Focus, I told myself. *Your father must have taken that scarf when he left Victoria. You have a time marker now. Use it.*

Trembling, I opened the bottle that preceded it in the row, then the one before that. I found four scents based on the same essential fragrance, each with a subtle difference—a series of threads in an exquisite, invisible net, I realized. I lined them up and started with the oldest one, smelling them in order, noting the variations. The first contained a hint of musk, that basic, animal fire to stoke the passions. The next held the cool drift of water lilies, tangling around me, whispering promises.

I love you.

In the third one, so subtle I almost missed it, I detected that crisp note from the scent in the lobby of Inspire, Inc. *Money*. It vanished in the fra-grance after that, replaced by the animal scents again, but stronger, more insistent this time. An olfactory urge to procreate.

It was my parents' history, told through scents—orchestrated, controlled, one perfume after another. She'd done this.

Once upon a time, Emmeline, there was a beautiful sorceress who lived in a mansion made of scents . . .

Truth hidden in fairy tales. He'd told me that story, too.

I reached for the next bottle. I expected a variation, another piece of the narrative, but what came out was completely different. The fragrance was soft, floral—sweet orange and sunshine, with just a touch of violet leaf—and it hit me in a wash of pain. I felt fear spiking up through me, a desperate need to survive. Then comfort. I gasped, shoving the scent away. It was horrible. It was wonderful. More than any of the others, it was familiar.

It was me.

I pulled the bottle closer, sniffing, and then I could see it—the cool, sterile room. The white walls. A doctor, and there, in the corner, my father. I searched the memory, trying to locate a warm, animal smell, my mother's skin, but there was nothing. Even for my birth, that most intimate mother-child experience, Victoria had put a fragrance between us. Held herself apart, pulling strings. Crafted the moment.

My whole body was shaking. I set the bottle in its square, and checked the remaining ones with renewed vigor. I found the lobby fragrance for Inspire, Inc. The citrus and pine of the elevator, the soft pink sunrise—and then, sure as rain, I found the one I had composed for that same store, held in a gracefully curved blue-glass vial. After that came a series of plain mixing bottles, like the ones we used in the lab.

They were small things, those last ones, each about half-full of liquid. I think I knew, even before smelling them, what they would be.

I opened the first, and my past smoked up to me—applewood. I kept going. Spruce. Cedar. Cinnamon. Sea salt. A single note in each bottle. All the smells of my childhood that I had told Victoria about, scents that somehow, inexplicably, had found their way here, into this clean, white space, hidden in a blanket, the food, my clothes. They'd made me feel safe. Each time I'd smelled them, I'd allowed myself to believe in a rational explanation for their presence. Now I sat there on the floor, surrounded by lies.

She'd used me, too, I thought, just like she had my father. Spun her scents to get what she wanted—my father's machine, my fragrances for her company. I should have known. My father's stories had told me. Claudia had warned me. Even Victoria had let me know.

A woman can't leave anything to chance.

I hadn't listened.

"What are you doing?"

Victoria was standing in the doorway. She scanned the room, taking in the bottles spread around me, the Chanel No. 5 on the dresser.

I stood up, holding up one of the small, plain bottles. "How could you do this?" I asked.

Her pale skin went a shade whiter.

"I wanted you to feel at home," she said. Her voice was careful, gentle, but she didn't even bother to pretend that she didn't know what I was talking about.

Home isn't perfect.

Oh, but it can be.

"I'm not a customer," I said. Victoria's eyes widened.

"No. You're my daughter." She took a step forward. "I'm your mother."

That first day I'd met Victoria, I'd hardly dared hope that that extraordinary woman would ever claim me as her daughter. Now I blazed out at her.

"Do you even know what being a mother means? You've manufactured everything. Nothing here is real."

I could see red rise across Victoria's face, as if I'd slapped her. Then she laughed once, a hard sound.

"All right, *Emmeline*," she said, and I could hear the irony of my other name underneath it. *You're not just one thing, either,* it said. She picked up the Chanel bottle, hefting it derisively. "You want to know about a *real* mother? How about this? The only time my mother ever stuck up for herself was when she kicked me out."

I paused, taken aback. "What?"

Victoria's hand closed tight around the bottle, raised it up. "This was the perfume that was going to catch *the* guy—but she had it wrong. Again. She always concentrated too much on the top notes. Missed what was going on underneath." Victoria gazed at the amber-gold liquid. "Inside every fragrance Coco Chanel made, every little black dress or suit she designed, there's a base note of steel. *That's* what the guy wanted—the strength, not the flowers. I understood Chanel, and he knew it. My mother saw that much, at least. She didn't want competition, so she threw me out. I was eighteen."

She looked at me, defiant, beautiful.

"So I took the bottle," she said, "and I took him. He got me to Paris, and I got my training."

She put the bottle down on the dresser with a sharp click. "Now, wasn't that pretty? Nobody wants the real story, Emmeline. Nobody. I did what I did for you."

And just like that, we're back to lies, I thought, anger rising up again, washing away my sympathy. "If I was so important, why didn't you look for me?"

She stared at me. "I did."

"How long?"

"Jesus, Emmeline." She pushed her hand through her hair. "Your father killed my company. Do you have any idea what that's like? The lawsuits? The debt? I didn't have the luxury of sitting around for the rest of my life mourning a daughter I couldn't find."

The words hurt, but even as I tried not to hear them, I knew she was speaking the truth.

"Why didn't you tell me any of this?" I asked.

Victoria sighed, exasperated. "Because people want their bodies to smell like oceans they'll never have time to visit. They wear a perfume that promises sex, when all they really want is someone to snuggle on the couch with in baggy pajamas. We'll all choose a good story over the truth any day."

"Not me," I said. I was sick of stories that weren't real. Sick of clues

instead of answers. Tired of love that was hidden like a base note you'd
never live long enough to smell.

"Just wait until you're a parent, Emmeline. What'll you tell *your*
daughter?"

Your daughter. Those last two words shifted my world. Time slowed,
changing direction, becoming a thing that moved forward, not just something to stare at over your shoulder. *My daughter.*

"I'll tell her everything," I said.

"And when she hates you for it?" Victoria asked. "What'll you do then?"

"I will love her," I said. A promise.

I met Victoria's gaze and held it. In her eyes, I saw something I never
would have expected—desperation. She wasn't afraid of being left, I understood then. She was afraid of losing me.

It struck me then—in all those months I'd lived in my mother's home,
we had never had a guest. I'd never seen her go to lunch or dinner with
someone who wasn't a client, never heard her voice rise in the joy of friendship on the phone. There wasn't a single personal photograph on the
walls. I assumed her mother was dead, but for all I knew, she might not
be. Victoria lived on more of an island than I ever had. And she had let
me in. Perhaps her reasons were twisted into the only kind of love that
made sense to her, but I was there, all the same.

Now she turned away, her shoulders straightening, her hand going to
her hair, rearranging herself back into Victoria Wingate. Watching her, I
realized that there was only one language she truly understood, one way I
could reach her. I needed a whole truth, a pure and complicated moment
of my life, a memory where nobody chose what went in and what didn't.

And I had one left.

THE BOTTLE

In the back of my dresser, I found my father's last bottle. I pulled it out and held it in my hands, the scent-paper rolled up inside, the green-wax seal starting to crack with age. The last bit of us.

Come find me, I heard it whisper.

How many times had I held that bottle over the past six years, longing to go back to our life again? How many times had I stopped myself, kept the seal unbroken?

I remembered my father, burning that first faded scent-paper, sending it back to the sky—the way the fragrance had come out of the smoke like a gift we had not thought to ask for and knew we would not get again. How precious that had made it. How much, just for that moment, we paid attention. Perhaps that had been the lesson all along, the message the scent-papers had been whispering as they lay in those drawers in the walls. I wondered what would have happened if we'd listened to them then. If we'd let them out, let them live.

Still, I hesitated now. If I opened the bottle in my hand, the scent inside would mingle with this place. Both would change, become part of one another.

But then I understood that that, too, was what I wanted.

Carefully, I broke the seal, listening to the swish of glass against glass as I pulled out the stopper, the rustle as the scent-paper unfurled in my hand.

I walked to the kitchen, and lifted down the white ceramic bowl that Victoria and I used for salads. I put the paper inside, lit a match, and touched it to one of the corners. It began to glow, then burn.

Victoria came into the kitchen.

"I smelled smoke," she said, and I pointed to the bowl. She caught sight of the scent-paper, and she let out a laugh brittle with irony.

"That's about all those are good for anymore."

"Just wait," I said. She raised an eyebrow but stayed where she was.

In the white bowl, the paper caught fire, burning like a desperate flower, blooming and dying at the same time. Its scents came on tendrils of smoke, wrapping themselves around me.

We missed you.

I inhaled, and Victoria's kitchen disappeared around me. It was early morning in the cabin, winter; I could smell the woodstove working to keep the frost at bay. My father had fed the sourdough starter, and the tang of it played off the warm scent of coffee grounds. I could smell my own warmth in the air, rising from the blankets I'd tossed aside.

I remembered that morning. It was the first time I ever saw the machine. I must have been three, maybe four years old. I'd woken up and seen my father, standing in the middle of the room, a box in his hands, bright and shiny and magical. I remembered racing across the floor, my bare feet tingling from the chill.

What is it, Papa? It's wonderful. I want to know.

And he'd put the shiny box aside and lifted me up high and said, *You are the most wonderful thing in the world, little lark.*

The last of the paper crumbled to ash. I stood there, trying to remember what had happened next—but I couldn't. Did my father show me the machine, or did we go outside and chop wood?

You'd think I'd remember, but I didn't. What I remembered was how it felt to be held in his arms. To be loved that way, before everything else happened.

And in that moment, I felt whole.

"Oh," I heard Victoria say, and when I turned to her, her eyes were filled with tears.

EPILOGUE

I wish I could tell you everything changed after that, my little fish, that your grandmother started baking cookies and bought a house with a garden that you could play in, but you'll soon discover that life is never that simple.

I left the city a few days after I burned the last scent paper. Fisher and I went to the bus station and bought our tickets to Secret Cove. I could feel its tidal pull, and when the bus arrived, I went toward it with anticipation.

"Emmeline?"

I hadn't seen my mother since that day in her condo; we had both needed some time to get used to our new visions of each other. But there she was in her elegant suit, the same outfit she'd been wearing on the day we met, right down to the earrings and swept-up hair.

"Victoria," I said. Fisher took my backpack and stepped away, but not too far.

"I wanted to say good-bye," she said.

"It's not forever." Although if I was being honest, I wasn't sure.

The bus driver opened the door and started taking tickets.

"I need to go," I said.

She nodded and stepped forward. Before I knew what was happening, she put her arms around me. I gasped with the shock of it, and with the air I

breathed in came the aromas of morning coffee and rosemary shampoo. I
waited, wondering what perfume she'd created for this occasion, but all I
could smell was a hint of sweat. A touch of fear. And then—the scent of my
mother's skin.

I closed my eyes.

Breathe in, Emmeline, I heard my father say.

I opened my mind and took in the fragrance of my mother. I took in the
scents of the other travelers and Fisher and the city and the sky, and I held
them all inside me, pure and complicated and alive. It was the truest perfume
I had ever made.

Perhaps, my little fish, you will create great fragrances one day, just
like your mother, and your grandmother. You will play among the sparkling
top notes, the hints of citrus and the salt mist of waves. You will sink into the
flowers and spices of the middle notes. But never forget the base notes, for no
fragrance is ever balanced without a touch of musk, or smoke, or sadness. Base
notes can come from dark places, but they can create beauty all the same.
They are reminders of what we will do to live, and what we can give each
other. My parents taught me that.

ACKNOWLEDGMENTS

The Scent Keeper began with an image in my mind of a young girl in a cabin made of drawers—but it was real people and places that helped bring her to life. So here are my thank-yous, although they could never be inclusive enough.

I was lucky to have an extraordinary support system while writing this book. The Seattle7Writers take what could be a lonely discipline and give it a true feeling of camaraderie. My writing group members—Marjorie Osterhout, Thea Cooper, Jennie Shortridge, Randy Sue Coburn, and Tara Austen Weaver—have been a lifeline throughout this process. Your insights and wordsmithing genius mean everything to me.

Early readers are an author's safety net. Deedee Rechtin, Nina Meierding, Holly Smith, Caitlin Vincent, and Ben, Paul, Michael, and Gloria Bauermeister all helped Emmeline find her voice. Sasha Kay was my go-to source for all things Canadian. The amazing team at Writers House—Amy Berkower, Genevieve Gagne-Hawes, and Alice Martin—stuck with me through five different versions. Leslie Gelbman at St. Martin's Press believed in this book and offered it a true home. And then there is Rylan Bauermeister, my book whisperer, who gave me an editorial path through a very deep forest. I owe you all cookies for life.

While I was writing, I was lucky enough to have a residency at Hedge-brook on Whidbey Island. There, Emmeline tackled some of her most difficult moments and came through strong. Thank you, Amy, Vito, Kathy, Denise, and Julie—for all you do to bring women's words into the world.

The islands in *The Scent Keeper* had their origin in the remote Brough-ton Archipelago in British Columbia. Many thanks to Bruce and Josée McMorran of the Paddler's Inn for their introduction to this extraordinary place, and to Nikki von Schyndel, who opened my eyes and taught me how to forage for food. The dolphins are for you. And while Henry and Colette are fictional characters, the brightly colored cottages at Gordie and Mari-lyn Graham's Telegraph Cove Resort provided inspiration for Secret Cove.

I think all books owe debts of gratitude to the imaginations of others, and that is truly the case for this one. The story of the Nightingale can be found in the works of Hans Christian Andersen. Sissel Tolaas expanded the way I perceive scent. The work of Roman Kaiser provided inspiration for the character of John Hartfell. Amy Radcliffe invented the Madeleine, an "analogue odor camera," just as I was wondering if anyone would ever believe something like the Nightingale could exist. Anjani Millet taught me about the smell games she once played with her own father. Caitlin Vincent was an invaluable resource when it came to questions about trauma and young minds. Ayala Moriel's fragrances took me deep into the scents of the Pacific Northwest, while Richard Weening, Vicki Leslie, and Chris-tophe Laudamiel of Prolitec are proof that scent technology can do wonders in the right hands.

I spent many hundreds of hours deep in books, learning about every-thing from scent branding to fairy tales, microexpressions, and survival techniques. So, here's a tip of the hat to the authors whose works taught me so much—Mandy Aftel, Diane Ackerman, Patrick Süskind, Jean-Claude Ellena, Luca Turin and Tania Sanchez, Chandler Burr, Barbara Herman, Piet Vroon, C. Russell Brumfield, Martin Lindstrom, Annick Le Guérer, Molly Birnbaum, Alyssa Harad, Denyse Beaulieu, Lawrence D. Rosenblum, Rachel Herz, Avery Gilbert, Constance Classen, Laurence

Gonzales, Bill Proctor, Paul Ekman, Helen Keller, M. J. Rose, and Bruno Bettelheim.

My husband and kids come along for the ride, with every book. They live with my imaginary friends as if they are real people and make the rest of my life full. These words are yours.

And finally, a deep bow to Greg Critser, whose books and friendship showed me what being a writer was all about. We miss you, honey.

1. What is the smell of childhood for you?

2. If you could preserve one scent, what would it be?

3. If technology was not an issue, what invention would you create?

4. In the course of the book, Emmeline lives on the island, in Secret Cove, and in the city. Each location affected her profoundly and differently. How have the places you've lived affected you?

5. What do you think the story of the nightingale means to John? To Emmeline? Why do you think John cut it from the book?

6. The Nightingale machine is a fictional invention. Discuss its role in the book.

7. Both John and Victoria have a wall of scents. What do you think they mean to each of the characters?

8. Emmeline's father strives to preserve memories through scent. Emmeline's mother uses scent to influence others. Rene is trying to re-create scents that are disappearing in the modern world. What are the up- and downsides to their actions?

9. What do you think about Emmeline's relationship with scent? How does it change as she grows older?

10. Secrets are an important element in *The Scent Keeper*. Which secrets do you think the characters were right to keep? Which should they have told and when?

11. What do you think about John's decision to take Emmeline to the island? How do you feel about their relationship?

12. What do you think was the most important lesson that Emmeline learned on the island?

13. At one point, Emmeline comes to understand her father has been revealing his past through stories. What do you think he'd been trying to tell her?

14. Emmeline experiences the deaths of Cleo, her father, and Dodge. How does her reaction to each differ? What does each one tell us about her?

15. How do you see Emmeline's relationship with her parents change throughout the book?

16. What role does Fisher play in Emmeline's life? How does that change?

17. What do you think about Emmeline's decision to take Fisher to the island? How does it compare to her father's decision to take her there as a baby?

18. Emmeline blames herself for her father's death, and for the confrontation between Fisher and his father. Do you think she was right to do so?

19. Fisher chose to leave his abusive father (and Emmeline). His mother chose to stay. What do you think about each of their decisions?

20. At one point in the book, Fisher's mother says: "Martin used to tell me how salmon always return to the same river to spawn. He said it's the smell that draws them upstream. Maybe we're more like fish than we think." How does this apply to the characters in the book? Do you agree with the statement?

21. Several chapter titles are repeated in the book. Why do you think that is?

ST.
MARTIN'S
GRIFFIN

22. *The Scent Keeper* is told through Emmeline's perspective. Imagine if it had been told through the varying perspectives of the major characters—Emmeline, Fisher, John, and Victoria. How would that change the book?

23. How do the prologue and epilogue affect your reading of the rest of the novel?

24. Fairy tales and stories are present throughout the book. What is their role in the book? In our lives?